The Van Alen Legacy

a Blue Bloods novel

Also by Melissa de la Cruz

The Van Alen Legacy

a Blue Bloods novel

MELISSA DE LA CRUZ

HYPERION • DBG
New York

First Edition
3 5 7 9 10 8 6 4
V567-9638-5-09305
Printed in the United States of America
This book is set in 12-point Baskerville.
Designed by Elizabeth H. Clark

Library of Congress Cataloging-in-Publication Data on file.
ISBN 978-1-4231-0226-7
Reinforced binding

Visit www.hyperionteens.com

For my mom, Ching de la Cruz,
who always said Blue Bloods would be "the one"

And for Mike and Mattie, always

The murdered do haunt their murderers.

—Emily Bronte, *Wuthering Heights*

I've been sleeping a thousand years it seems, got to open my eyes to everything. . . .

—Evanescence, "Bring Me to Life"

A Conversation

"It is said that Allegra's daughter will defeat the Silver Bloods. I believe Schuyler will bring us the salvation we seek. She is almost as powerful as her mother. And one day she will be even more powerful."

"Schuyler Van Alen . . . the half-blood? Are you certain she is the one?" Charles asked.

Lawrence nodded.

"Because Allegra had two daughters," Charles said, in a light, almost playful tone. "Surely you have not forgotten that."

The Elder Van Alen's voice turned cold. "Of course not. But it is beneath you to make sport of such a serious matter as Allegra's firstborn."

Charles dismissed Lawrence's rebuke with a wave. "My apologies. I meant no offense to the dead."

"Her blood is on our hands," Lawrence sighed. The events of

the day were tiring him, as were the memories of the past. "Only, I wonder . . ."

"Yes?"

"As I've wondered all these years, Charles, if such a one could ever be truly destroyed."

LAWRENCE VAN ALEN,

105, Philanthropist and Philosopher, Dies

Lawrence Winslow Van Alen, a professor of history and linguistics at the University of Venice, died last night in his home on Riverside Drive in Manhattan. He was 105. His death was confirmed by Dr. Patricia Hazard, his attending physician. The cause of death was listed as advanced age.

Professor Van Alen was a descendant of William Henry Van Alen, known as the Commodore, an American icon and one of the richest men of the Gilded Age, whose wealth came from steamships, railroads and private investment and brokerage businesses. The Van Alens founded the New York Central Railroad Line and what is now Grand Central Terminal. The family's charitable trust, the Van Alen Foundation, was a cornerstone in the development of the Metropolitan Museum of Art, the Metropolitan Opera, the New York City Ballet and the New York Blood Bank.

Lawrence Van Alen is survived by his daughter, Allegra Van Alen Chase, who has been in a coma since 1992; and his granddaughter, Schuyler Van Alen.

ONE

Schuyler

here had been little time to mourn. Upon returning to New York after Lawrence's murder in Rio
(covered up by the Committee with a proper obituary in the
Times), Schuyler Van Alen had been on the run. No rest. No
respite. A year of constant motion, barely one step ahead
of the Venators hunting her. A flight to Buenos Aires followed by one to Dubai. A sleepless night in a youth hostel
in Amsterdam followed by another in a bunk bed in an auditorium in Bruges.

She had marked her sixteenth birthday aboard the
Trans-Siberian Railway—celebrating with a cup of wa-
tery Nescafé coffee and several crumbly Russian tea cookies.
Somehow, her best friend, Oliver Hazard-Perry, had found
a candle to light in one of the *suharkies*. He took his job as
human Conduit pretty seriously. It was thanks to Oliver's
careful accounting that they had been able to stretch their

money so far. The Conclave had frozen his access to the well-funded Hazard-Perry accounts as soon as they had left New York.

Now it was August in Paris, and hot. They had arrived to find most of the city a ghost town: bakeries, boutiques, and bistros shuttered while their proprietors absconded to three-week vacations in the beaches up north. The only people around were American and Japanese tourists, who mobbed every museum gallery, every garden in every public square, inescapable and ubiquitous in their white sneakers and base-ball caps. But Schuyler welcomed their presence. She hoped the slow-moving crowds would make it easier for her and Oliver to spot their Venator pursuers.

Schuyler had been able to disguise herself by changing her physical features, but performing the *mutatio* was taking a toll on her. She didn't say anything to Oliver, but lately she couldn't even do so much as change the color of her eyes.

And now, after almost a year of hiding, they were coming out into the open. It was a gamble, but they were desperate. Living without the protection and wisdom of the secret society of vampires and their select group of trusted humans had taken its toll. And while neither of them would ever admit it, they were both tired of running.

So for now Schuyler was seated in the back of a bus, wearing a pressed white shirt buttoned to the neck over slim black pants and flat black shoes with rubber soles. Her dark hair was pulled back in a ponytail, and except for a hint of lip gloss, she wore no makeup. She meant to blend in with the rest of the catering staff who had been hired for the evening.

But surely someone would notice. Surely someone would hear how hard her heart was beating, would remark on how her breathing was shallow and quick. She had to calm down. She had to clear her mind and become the blasé contract caterer she was pretending to be. For so many years Schuyler had excelled at being invisible. This time, her life depended on it.

The bus was taking them over a bridge to the Hôtel Lambert on the Île Saint-Louis, a small island on the Seine River. The Lambert was the most beautiful house in the most beautiful city in the world. At least, she had always thought so. Although "house" was putting it mildly. "Castle" was more like it, something out of a fairy tale, its massive river walls and gray mansard roofs rising from the surrounding mist. As a child she had played hide-and-seek in the formal gardens, where the conical sculpted trees reminded her of figures on a chessboard. She remembered staging imaginary productions inside the grand courtyard and throwing bread crumbs to the geese from the terrace overlooking the Seine.

How she had taken that life for granted! Tonight she would not enter the hotel's exclusive, exalted domain as an invited guest, but rather as a humble servant. Like a mouse creeping into a hole. Schuyler was anxious by nature, and she needed almost all her self-control to keep it together. At any moment she feared she might scream—she was already so nervous she couldn't stop her hands from trembling. They vibrated, fluttering in her lap like trapped birds.

Next to her, Oliver was handsome in a bartender's uniform, a tuxedo with a black silk bow tie and silver shirt studs. But he was pale beneath his butterfly collar, his shoulders tense under a jacket that was a little too big. His clear hazel eyes were clouded, looking more gray than green. Oliver's face did not display the same blank, bored look as the others'. He was alert, ready for a fight or flight. Anyone who looked at him long enough could see it.

We shouldn't be here, Schuyler thought. What were we thinking? The risk is too great. They're going to find us and separate us . . . and then . . . well, the rest was too horrible to contemplate.

She was sweating under her starched shirt. The air-conditioning wasn't working, and the bus was packed. She leaned her head against the windowpane. Lawrence had been dead for over a year now. Four hundred forty-five days. Schuyler kept count, thinking that maybe once she hit a magical number, it would stop hurting.

This was no game, although sometimes it felt like a horrid, surreal version of cat and mouse. Oliver put a hand on top of hers to try and stop her hands from shaking. The tremors had begun a few months ago, just a slight twitching, but soon she realized she had to concentrate whenever she did something as simple as pick up a fork or open an envelope.

She knew what it was, and there was nothing she could do about it. Dr. Pat had told her the first time she visited her office: she was the only one of her kind, *Dimidium Cognato*, the first half-blood, and there was no telling how her human body would react to the transformation into immortal; there would be side effects, obstacles particular to her case.

Still, she felt better once Oliver held her hand in his. He always knew what to do. She depended on him for so much, and her love for him had only deepened in the year they had spent together. She squeezed his hand, intertwined her fingers around his. It was his blood that ran through her veins, his quick thinking that had secured her freedom.

As for everyone and everything they had left behind in New York, Schuyler did not dwell on it anymore. All of that was in the past. She had made her choice and was at peace with it. She had accepted her life for what it was. Once in a while she missed her friend Bliss very keenly, and more than once wanted to get in touch with her, but that was out of the question. No one could know where they were. No one. Not even Bliss.

Maybe they would be lucky tonight. Their luck had held so far. Oh, there had been a few close calls here and there— that one evening in Cologne when she'd abruptly run from a woman who had asked for directions to the cathedral. *Illuminata* had given the agent away. Schuyler had caught that soft imperceptible glow in the twilight before booking as fast as she could. Disguises only went so far. At some point, your true nature revealed itself.

Wasn't that what the Inquisitor had argued during the official investigation into the events in Rio? That maybe Schuyler wasn't who she was supposed to be?

Outlaw. Fugitive. That's what she was now. Certainly not Lawrence Van Alen's grieving granddaughter.

No.

According to the Conclave, she was his killer.

O h, gross! She'd stepped in something icky. Beyond icky. It squished beneath her foot—a wet, gasping sound. Whatever it was, it was sure to ruin her pony-hair boots. What was she doing wearing pony-hair boots to a reconnaissance mission anyway? Mimi Force lifted her heel and assessed the damage. The zebra pattern was stained with something brown and leaky.

Beer? Whiskey? A combination of all the bottom-shelf alcohol they served in this place? Who knew? For the umpteenth time this year, she wondered why on earth she'd ever signed up for this assignment. It was the last week of August. By all rights she should be on a beach in Capri, working on her tan and her fifth limoncello. Not creeping around some honky-tonk bar in the middle of the country. Somewhere between the dust bowl and the rust belt—or was it the rust bowl and the dust belt? Wherever they were, it was a sleepy, sad little place, and Mimi couldn't wait to leave it.

"What's wrong?" Kingsley Martin nudged her. "Shoes too tight again?"

"Will you leave me alone?" she sighed, moving away from him, making it clear she found the alcove they were hiding in too close quarters. She was tired of his teasing. Especially since, to her complete and utter horror, she discovered she was starting to like it. That was simply unacceptable. She *hated* Kingsley Martin. After everything that he'd done to her, she couldn't see how she could feel otherwise.

"But where's the fun in that?" He winked. The most infuriating thing about Kingsley—other than the fact that he had once tried to bring about her demise—was that somewhere between chasing down leads on the beaches of Punta del Este or through the skyscrapers of Hong Kong, Mimi had started to find him . . . attractive. It was enough to make her stomach turn. "C'mon, Force, lighten up. You know you want me," he said with a smug smile.

"Oh my god!" she huffed, turning around so that her long blond hair whipped over her shoulder and hit him square in the face. *"As if!"* He might be faster and stronger than she was—the big man on the Venator team, and for all intents and purposes her boss—but really *she* should be the one leading them, as she outranked him in the Conclave hierarchy. If you could call that sorry group of cowards a Conclave.

Kingsley Martin had another think coming if he thought he had any chance with her. He might be too cute for words (damn those rock-star looks), but it didn't matter one iota. She was not interested, no matter how much her pulse quickened whenever he was near. She was bound to another.

"Mmm. Nice. You don't use the hotel shampoo from the airport Hilton, do you? This is the good stuff," he purred. "But is it the conditioner that makes it so soft and silky?"

"Shut up . . . just—"

"Hold on. Save your speech for the after-party. I see our guy. You ready?" Kingsley interrupted, his voice serious now, controlled.

"Like a shot." Mimi nodded, all business as well. She saw their witness, the reason they were a few miles outside of Lincoln, Nebraska (that was it! She remembered now) in the first place. A former frat boy, probably just shy of thirty, with a baby beer gut and the beginnings of middle-age "carb face." He was the type of guy who looked like he'd played cornerback in high school, but whose pounds of muscle had turned to fat after a few years behind a desk.

"Good, because this is not going to be easy," Kingsley warned. "Okay, the boys will bring him to that corner booth and we'll follow. Square him off and then go. No one will notice as long as we don't get up. Waitress won't even bother to come around."

It was easier and more painless to enter the mind of another during REM sleep, but they didn't have the luxury of waiting until their suspect had drifted off to la-la land.

Instead they planned to barge into his subconscious with no warning and no consideration. Better that way: there would be no place for him to hide. No time to prepare. They wanted the unadulterated truth, and this time they were going to get it.

The Venators were truth-tellers, skilled in the ability to decipher dreams and access memories. While only a blood-letting would allow them to tell true memory from false, there were other, quicker ways to discriminate fact from fiction without having to resort to the Sacred Kiss. Mimi learned that the Committee only consented to the blood trial when a most grievous charge had been levied, as in her case. Otherwise, the practice of memory hunting, *venatio*, while not infallible, was acceptable for their purposes. Mimi had been given a crash course in Venator training before joining up. It helped that she had been one in previous lifetimes. Once she had relearned the basics, it was just like riding a bike— her core memories kicked in and the whole exercise became second nature.

Mimi watched as Sam and Ted Lennox, the twin brothers who rounded out their Venator team, led their witness to a dark corner booth. They had been plying him with pitcher after pitcher of beer at the bar. Mr. Glory Days probably thought he'd just made a couple of new friends.

As soon as they sat down, Kingsley slipped into the opposite bench, Mimi right next to him. "Hey, buddy, remember us?" he asked.

"Huh?" The guy was awake, but drunk and drowsy. Mimi felt a twinge of pity. He had no idea what was about to happen.

"I'm sure you remember *her*," Kingsley said, guiding the witness to lock eyes with Mimi.

Mimi held Frat Boy with her smolder, and for all anyone in the real world knew, the dude was just entranced with the pretty blonde, staring deep into her green eyes.

"Now," Kingsley ordered.

Without a moment to spare, the four Venators stepped into the glom, taking the witness with them. It was as easy as slipping down the rabbit hole.

THREE

Bliss

When she woke up that morning, the first thing that came to mind was that the bright white shutters looked familiar. Why did they look familiar? No. That wasn't right. That wasn't the right question to ask. She was getting ahead of herself again. It happened. But now she had to concentrate. Every day she had to ask herself three very important questions, and that wasn't one of them.

The first question she had to ask herself was, *What is my name?*

She couldn't remember.

It was like trying to decipher a scribble on a sheet of paper. She knew what it was supposed to say, but she couldn't make out the handwriting. Like having something just out of reach, behind a closed door, and she had lost the key. Or like waking up blind. She groped wildly in the dark and tried not to panic.

What is my name??

Her name. She had to remember her name. Otherwise . . . otherwise . . . she didn't want to think about it.

Once upon a time there was a girl named . . . ?

Once upon a time there was a girl named . . .

She had an unusual name. She knew that much. It wasn't the kind of name that you found on ceramic coffee mugs at airport gift shops or emblazoned on mini–license plate souvenirs you could hang on your bedroom door after you returned from Disneyland. Her name was pretty and unusual and had meaning. Something that meant snow or breath or joy or happiness or . . .

Bliss. Yes. That was it. Bliss Llewellyn. That was her name! She'd remembered! She hugged it to herself as tight as she could. Her name. Her self. As long as she could remember who she was, she was okay. She wouldn't go crazy. At least not today.

But it was hard. It was so, so hard because now there was the Visitor to consider. The Visitor who was in her, who *was* her, for all intents and purposes. The Visitor who answered to *her* name. She called him the Visitor because it made it easier for her to believe that her situation would be temporary. What did visitors do, after all? They *left.*

Bliss wondered, were you still you if someone else made the decisions? Spoke in your voice? Walked with your legs? Used your hands to bring death to the person you loved the most?

She shuddered. A sudden unbidden memory came to her. A black-haired boy lying limp in her arms. Who was that? The answer was somewhere, but she would have to dig for it. The image faded. Hopefully she would remember later. Right now she had to move on to the second question.

Where am I?

The shutters. The shutters were a clue. It was enough that she was able to *see* something. It happened so rarely now. Most of the time she woke up in darkness. She concentrated on the shutters. They were wooden and painted white. Charming in a way, something that recalled a farmhouse or an English cottage—except they were too bright, too shiny and perfect. More like Martha Stewart's idea of an English cottage than a real one. Ah. No wonder they looked familiar.

Bliss knew where she was now. If she could still smile, she would have.

The Hamptons. She was in her Hamptons house. They were in Cotswold. BobiAnne had named the house. BobiAnne? Bliss saw an image of a tall, lanky woman wearing too much makeup and gargantuan jewelry. She could even smell her stepmother's noxious perfume. Everything was coming back now, and coming back fast.

One summer during a dinner party at a famous designer's house, BobiAnne had learned that all the great houses in the area had names. Owners dubbed their homes "Mandalay" or "Oak Valley" according to how pretentious they were. Bliss had suggested they name theirs Dune House for the large sand dune at the beachfront edge of the property. But BobiAnne had other ideas. "Cotswold." The woman had never even been to England.

Okay. Bliss was relieved. She'd figured out where she was, but it didn't make sense.

What was she doing in the Hamptons?

She was a stranger in her own life, a tourist in her own body. If someone had asked her what it was like, Bliss would have explained it this way: it's like you're driving a car, but you're sitting in the backseat. The car is driving itself, and you're not in control. But it's your car, at least you think it is. It used to be yours, anyway.

Or like being in a movie. The movie is your life, but you don't star in it anymore. Someone else is kissing the handsome lead and making the dramatic monologues. You're just watching. Bliss was an observer of her own life. She was not Bliss anymore, but simply the memory of the Bliss that had been.

Sometimes she wasn't even sure that she had ever really existed.

FOUR

Schuyler

*T*he bus pulled to a stop up past the gates, and the group silently filed out. Schuyler noticed that even the most jaded of her coworkers, a rather haughty collection of moonlighting actors and actresses along with a smug culinary student or two, were looking around in amazement. The building and its immaculate grounds were as opulent and intimidating as the Louvre, except someone still *lived* here. It was a home, not a national monument. The Hôtel Lambert had been closed to the public for much of its history. Only a vaunted few had been welcomed inside its massive doors. The rest of the world could leaf through pictures of it in books. Or enter as catering staff.

As they walked past the burbling fountains, Oliver nudged her. "All right?" he asked in French. One more reason to be thankful for the Duchesne School. Years of mandatory foreign language requirements meant they had been able to pass for two restaurant workers from Marseille at the job interview—although their textbook accents were in danger of giving them away at any time. "You look worried. What's wrong?"

"Nothing. I was just thinking about the investigation again," Schuyler said as they made their way toward the service entrance located at the back of the house. She remembered that terrible day at the Repository, when she'd been accused so unjustly. "How could they have believed that of me?"

"Don't waste any more time on it. It's not going to change anything," Oliver said firmly. "What happened on Corcovado was terrible, and it wasn't your fault."

Schuyler nodded, blinking back the tears that came whenever she thought of that day. Oliver was right as always. She was wasting energy wishing for another outcome. What was past was past. They had to focus on the present.

"Isn't this place beautiful?" she said. Then, whispering so no one would hear, "Cordelia brought me here a couple of times, when she came for meetings with Prince Henri. We stayed in the guest apartments in the east wing. Remind me to show you the Hercules galleries and the Polish library. They have Chopin's piano."

She felt a mixture of awe and sadness as she followed the hushed crowd through the gleaming marble halls. Awe at the beauty of the place, which had been built by the same architect who had designed the Palace of Versailles, and displayed the same gilded moldings and baroque flourishes, and sadness because the building reminded her of Cordelia. She could sure use some of her grandmother's brusque tenacity right then. Cordelia Van Alen wouldn't think twice about crashing a party to get what she wanted, whereas Schuyler had too many doubts.

The party that evening was called A Thousand and One Nights, in homage to the extravagant Oriental Ball thrown at the residence in 1969. Like that party, tonight's would feature dancing slave girls, half-naked torchbearers, zither players, and Hindu musicians. Of course, there would also be a few modern additions: the entire cast from a Bollywood musical would perform at midnight, and instead of having papier-mâché elephants at the entrance, a pair of real Indian elephants had been borrowed from a traveling Thai circus. The pachyderms would be carrying riders under golden canopies.

The newspapers had already nicknamed it The Last Party. The party to end all parties. The party that would mark the end of an era. The last night that the fabled building would house royalty.

Because the Hôtel Lambert had been sold. Tomorrow it would no longer be home to the surviving family of Louis-Philippe, the last king of France. Tomorrow the property would belong to a foreign conglomerate. Tomorrow the chateau would fall into the hands of developers who were rich enough to have met its steep asking price. Tomorrow it would be divided up, or renovated, or made into a museum, or whatever the conglomerate had planned for it.

But tonight it was the scene of one last grand *Bal des Vampires*: Parisian Blue Blood society gathering together one final time in a celebration worthy of Scheherazade.

"Cordelia told me Balzac made a pass at her once, during a ball here. She was a deb then, in an earlier cycle, before she became my grandmother," she told Oliver as they made their way down into the vast basement kitchens, where modern stainless-steel appliances were installed next to medieval hearths. "She said he was pretty drunk. Can you imagine?"

"One of France's leading lights hitting on an eighteen-year-old girl?" He smirked, pushing open a swinging door. "Totally."

The party was in two hours, and they found the cooks angrily yelling at each other, the whole kitchen in a flurry of hurried preparation. Steam was billowing from giant industrial-size vats, and the place smelled of sizzling butter—smoky and delicious.

"What are you doing here?" the head chef demanded when the waitstaff arrived. "*Allez, allez,* upstairs with you!"

The chef had a brief argument with the staff director, but in the end they agreed that the servers could help the grounds crew, and Schuyler and Oliver were separated.

Schuyler was sent outside, where she found the elephant trainers explaining to the actor and actress playing the King and Queen of Siam how to manage the beasts. Looking to be useful, she set about lighting candles, smoothing down tablecloths, and arranging the floral centerpieces just so. All around her, the courtyard was a cacophony of noise, with performers and acrobats jumping off the roofs, musicians tuning up, and dancing slave girls giggling at the half-naked male models.

Finally all the candles were lit. The tables were set. Everything was ready. One thing was for sure. This was going to be some party.

She found Oliver polishing glassware at his station. "Remember—meet me at the bottom of the staircase after your first round," Oliver whispered, trying not to attract too much attention from the other servers. "I'll look out for you." They had been ordered by their superiors to turn off their cell phones, not that it mattered since neither of them was able to get a signal. No cell phone towers were allowed on the exclusive part of the island.

Schuyler nodded. They had their assignments: she would be part of the team responsible for welcoming guests with trays of champagne the minute they alighted from the boats. Oliver would be upstairs, working the back bar.

"And, Sky? It'll be all right. She'll have to see you." He smiled. "I'll make sure of it." His bravado endeared him to her even more. Dear, sweet, kind Oliver, who had left everything he loved in New York to save and protect her. She knew he was just as afraid as she was, but he wasn't going to show it.

Tonight's plan was a long shot at best. She didn't even know if the Countess of Paris, the evening's hostess and the soon-to-be-former owner of the Hôtel Lambert, would remember her. Much less offer them the refuge they so desperately sought. But she had to ask, for her sake and for Oliver's. And if she ever wanted vengeance on the demon who had killed her grandfather, she had to try.

The European Conclave was her last and only hope.

FIVE

Mimi

*S*tepping into someone's subconscious is like discovering a new planet. Everyone's internal world is different and unique. Some are cluttered, stuffed with dark and kinky secrets pushed to the edge of their minds, like racy underwear and handcuffs shoved in the back of a closet. Some are as pristine and clear as a spring meadow: all hopping bunnies and falling snowflakes. Those are rare. This guy's psyche looked pretty standard, and Mimi chose a neutral environment in which to interrogate him—his childhood home. A suburban kitchen: white tiles, Formica table—clean, orderly, ordinary.

Kingsley pulled up a stool across from Frat Boy. "Why did you lie to us?" he asked. In the glom the Venator looked fiercely handsome. The glom did that to vampires: made them look even more beautiful than they already were.

"What are you talking about?" the guy asked, a confused look on his face.

"Show him."

Mimi found the memory and played it on the television set on the kitchen counter.

"You remember this night?" Kingsley asked as they observed Frat Boy step out onto a hotel balcony and watch a tall man carrying a child-size bundle out of the resort gates. "You remember this man?"

Jordan Llewellyn had been missing for over a year. The eleven-year-old girl had been kidnapped from her hotel room at the same time the Conclave was being slaughtered at a party by Silver Bloods.

The Venators had scanned the mind-memories of everyone at the hotel who was there the night the little girl had disappeared—every guest, every staff member, from security guards to the chambermaids—with no luck. The Llewellyns had been too traumatized to be of much help. Which was understandable, but still useless. No one knew anything, no one remembered anything. Except for the guy sitting in front of them now.

"You told us you saw something. That you saw this man when you stepped outside for a cigarette that night," Kingsley said. "This man does not exist. You lied to us."

"But I don't smoke," Frat Boy protested. "I don't remember this at all. What is this? Who are you?" In the bar,

Mimi could see that he was starting to stir. They didn't have much time.

"Why did you lie to us? Answer the question!" Kingsley barked.

For months they had tracked down every man who had stayed in the hotel who fit the description Frat Boy had given them. They had chased down marketing executives, businessmen on holiday, tourists and locals. But nothing of significance had turned up. After the better part of a year, they began to wonder if they were chasing a ghost, a phantom, a mirage. The whole team was frustrated and on edge. Just yesterday the Conclave had ordered them to give up the mission and return to New York. Jordan was gone, case closed. But Kingsley decided they needed to pay their witness another visit.

"Let me rephrase this: who told you to lie to us?" Kingsley asked.

"Nobody . . . I don't know what you want me to say . . . I don't remember that night. I don't even remember you guys. Who are you? What are you doing in my mom's kitchen?"

"Why were you in Rio?" Ted Lennox asked mildly, playing good cop.

"A buddy of mine was getting married. . . ." he slurred. "We were there for the bachelor party."

"You went all the way to Rio for a bachelor party? You?" Mimi scoffed, peering through to the real world, looking down at his prone form sprawled on the table. The guy looked like the farthest he ever traveled was the corner 7-Eleven.

"Hey, I lived in New York not too long ago. I was a banker. We always went away whenever anyone got married. Thailand. Vegas. Punta Cana. But then I lost my job and had to move back in with my parents. Don't be a hater now."

"Laid off?" Sam Lennox asked.

"No . . . just . . . I don't remember things that well anymore. I took a leave of absence and haven't gone back. Something wrong up here," he said, knocking on the side of his skull with a worried look on his face.

Come to think of it, something about the witness did seem odd. Mimi remembered Frat Boy differently. The guy they had questioned a year ago had been much more articulate and alert, much cockier. She had found it strange that they had tracked him down in the boondocks. She had assumed anyone who stayed at such a fancy hotel also came from a fancy place.

"He's not lying," Sam said. "Look at his prefrontal cortex. It's clear."

"He doesn't remember that night," Ted agreed.

"Bring it up again," Kingsley said. "This doesn't make sense."

Mimi pulled up the memory for a second time. The four of them watched it intently. It was the same: the tall man,

29

the bundle, the cigarette. But Sam was right—his prefrontal cortex showed the guy wasn't lying when he said he didn't remember it.

"Oh, dear lord. How could we have missed this? Look at this. Force! Lennox! Look!" Kingsley said, magnifying the edge of the picture.

Then she saw what Kingsley saw: a slight tear on the border of the guy's memory. It was like a seam that had been repaired. It was so fine, and so well done, you would never even notice it. Whoever had done this was *good*. You needed to be majorly advanced in the glom to pull this off. A false memory expertly weaved into a real one. Enough to have fooled a team of Venators for the better part of a year. Imprinting false memories on Red Bloods was very dangerous. It could mess people up: turn them into raving lunatics, unable to distinguish fact from fiction. Or turn a big-city banker into a slacker who lived with his parents.

"Let him go," Kingsley said wearily.

Mimi nodded. She released her hold on his mind, and the four of them stepped back into the real world. Their witness was slumped over the table, snoring.

This was no suspect.

This was a victim.

SIX

Bliss

*E*very day since that morning on the mountaintop in the middle of Corcovado—the hunchbacked mountain—Bliss had to ask herself three important questions. *Who am I? Where am I? What happened to me?*

She'd started the practice one day not too long ago when she'd woken up to find she couldn't remember why she was so sad. Then the next day, she couldn't remember whether or not she was an only child. But what really scared her was the day she'd looked in the mirror and thought she saw a stranger. She had no clue who the girl with the red hair was.

And that's when she got the idea to ask herself the three questions every morning.

If she didn't take the time to remember who she had been, then the Visitor would take over completely. And the real Bliss Llewellyn, the girl who had once failed her driving test in an old 1950s Cadillac convertible, would be no longer. Not even this half-faded memory of her that lingered in a small corner of her brain.

So. They were in the Hamptons. It was morning. She was getting up for breakfast; her servant was calling for her. No; not her servant—her father. "Servant" was the Visitor's word for Forsyth, not hers. Sometimes that happened. Sometimes she would find she could hear the Visitor so clearly. But then a door would slam, and she would be on the other side, in the dark again. The Visitor had access to her past, to her entire life, but she had no entree to his. His conversations with Forsyth were behind a closed door, his thoughts hidden in shadow.

A part of her was relieved that the Visitor did not talk to her anymore. She dimly remembered that there had been little conversations between them once, but those had ceased. Now there was just silence. She understood it was because he didn't need to communicate with her any longer to assume control. He used to take over during her blackouts, but now he did not need them to do what he pleased. He was in the driver's seat.

Still, she wasn't exactly abandoned on the side of the road, either. She had answered the first question successfully, hadn't she?

She was Bliss Llewellyn. The daughter of Senator Forsyth Llewellyn and stepdaughter of the late BobiAnne Shepherd. She had grown up in Houston until her family moved to Manhattan soon after her fifteenth birthday. She was a student at the Duchesne School on E. 96th Street, and her favorite hobbies were, in no particular order: cheerleading, shopping, and modeling. Oh my god, I'm a bimbo, Bliss thought. There had to be more to her than that.

Start again. Okay. Her name was Bliss Llewellyn, and she'd grown up in a big, grand house in Houston's River Oaks neighborhood, but her favorite part of Texas was her Pop-Pop's ranch, where she would ride horses over lush prairies blanketed with wildflowers. Her favorite subject in school was Art Humanities, and one day she had hoped to own her own art gallery or, barring that, become a curator at the Met.

She was Bliss Llewellyn, and right now she was in the Hamptons. An upscale beach community two hours away from Manhattan (depending on traffic) where people from the city went to "get away from it all" only to find themselves smack-dab in the middle of everything. August in the Hamptons was as frantic as September in New York. Back when she was still just Bliss and not a vessel for evil (or V.F.E., as she had come to think of her situation when she wanted to laugh instead of cry), her stepmother had dragged them out here because it was "the thing to do."

BobiAnne had been big on "the thing to do" and had compiled a huge list of dos and don'ts—you'd think she had been a magazine editor in a former life. The sad thing about BobiAnne was that she always tried so hard to be fashionable and always ended up the complete and total opposite.

Images from Bliss's last real summer in the Hamptons began to flood her brain. She was an athletic girl, and had spent the three months horseback riding, sailing, playing tennis, learning to surf. She had broken her right wrist again that year. The first three times had been because of sports— skiing, sailing, and tennis. This time she'd fractured it for a stupid Hamptons-style reason. She'd tripped on her new Louboutin platforms and landed on her wrist.

Now that she had answered the first and second questions in detail, she had no choice but to move on to the third. And it was always the third question that was the most difficult to answer.

What happened to me?

Bad things. Terrible things. Bliss felt herself grow cold. It was funny how she could still feel things, how the ghost-memory of being alive and fully aware through each of her senses lingered. She could feel her phantom limbs, and when she slept, she dreamed she was still living an ordinary life: eating chocolates, walking the dog, listening to the sound of the rain as it drummed on the roof, feeling the softness of a cotton pillowcase against her cheek.

But she couldn't dwell on that. Right now there were things she did not want to remember, but she had to force herself to try.

She remembered their apartment in the city, how the white-gloved doormen called her "Miss" and always made sure her packages were sent up quickly. She remembered making friends at school: Mimi Force, who had taken her under her wing and had laughed at her white leather handbag. Mimi was patronizing and intimidating at the same time. But she'd had other friends, hadn't she? Yes, of course she had. There was Schuyler Van Alen, who had become her best friend, a sweet girl who had no idea how strong she was—or how beautiful—and Oliver Hazard-Perry, the human boy with the wry sense of humor and the impeccable wardrobe.

She remembered a night at a club, shared cigarettes in an alley—and a boy. She had met a boy. The black-haired boy, lying limp in her arms. Dylan Ward. She felt numb. Dylan was dead. She remembered everything now. What had happened in Rio. Everything. The killing. Lawrence. Running down the hill, away from Sky and Oliver because she did not want them to see her face—to see her for who she really was.

Silver Blood spawn.

With Forsyth, she had returned to New York for BobiAnne's funeral. A memorial, really, because like the other dearly departed members of the Conclave, there was nothing to bury. There was nothing left of BobiAnne—not even a singed lock of her highlighted hair. A giant blown-up glamour shot on an easel took the place of a coffin at the front of the altar. The photograph showed her stepmother at her finest moment, when she had been profiled in a society magazine.

The funeral had been packed. The entire Blue Blood community had come out for it, to show support for those who had stood against the Silver Bloods. Mimi had been there with her twin brother, Jack. They had offered her words of solace and comfort.

If they only knew.

At the funeral Bliss was still aware enough of what was around her. She had heard Forsyth tell her (but not her; he was talking to the Visitor even then, she understood now) not to worry—Jordan was no longer a problem.

Worry about what? What problem? Oh. Right. She'd almost forgotten. Her little sister. Jordan had known that Bliss carried the Visitor inside her. Jordan had tried to kill her.

The exercise was over. She knew who she was, where she was, and what had happened to her. She was Bliss Llewellyn, she was in the Hamptons, and she was carrying the soul of Lucifer inside her body.

That was her story.

The next day she would have to remember it all over again.

The Investigation

awrence's killer. Her grandfather's killer. Okay, so the Inquisitor didn't come out and say it—no, nothing so coarse as that. But he'd hinted enough. Cast enough doubt on her story that he might as well have branded the word across her forehead.

She hadn't seen it coming. She was still in shock from losing Lawrence so violently—forget about having to defend herself to the Conclave afterward. She had told them what happened as well as she could, never even considering the possibility that they might not believe her.

"Miss Van Alen, allow me to walk you through your testimony. According to your recollection of the events at Corcovado, a boy had been transformed into the image of Lucifer himself. Your grandfather ordered you to kill him, but you missed. Lawrence then struck the fatal blow, mistakenly killing an innocent and unlocking Leviathan's prison, setting the demon free. The demon then murdered him. Is this all correct so far?"

"Yes," she said quietly.

The Inquisitor consulted his notes for a moment. Schuyler had met him once before, when her grandfather had hosted a few members of the Conclave at the house. His name was Josiah Archibald, and he had retired from the Conclave years ago. His granddaughters were her classmates at Duchesne. But if he felt at all sympathetic to her plight, he masked it well. "He was right in front of you, was he not? The boy?" the Inquisitor asked, looking up.

"Yes."

"And you say you were holding your mother's sword?"

"Yes."

He snorted, looking pointedly at the assembled Elders, who then leaned forward or shuffled in their seats. The only active surviving member of the Conclave present was Forsyth Llewellyn, who sat in the back, his head covered in bandages and his left eye swollen shut. The others were emeritus members like the Inquisitor. They sat clustered in a semicircle, looking like a group of shrunken elves. There were so few of them left: old Abe Tompkins had been fetched from his summer home on Block Island; Minerva Morgan, one of Cordelia's oldest friends and the former chairwoman of the New York Garden Society, sat gargoyle-still in her knit boucle suit; Ambrose Barlow, who looked like he was fast asleep.

"Gabrielle's sword has been lost for many, many years," the Inquisitor said. "And you say your mother appeared to you—poof! Out of nowhere, and handed it to you. Just like that. And then disappeared. To go back to her bed at the hospital, presumably." His voice dripped with sarcasm.

Schuyler shifted uncomfortably in her seat. It did seem fantastic and

amazing—and unreal. But it had happened. Just as she had described.
"Yes . . . I don't know how, but yes."

The Inquisitor's tone was condescending. "Pray tell us, where is this sword now?"

"I don't know." She didn't. In the chaos afterward, the sword seemed to have disappeared along with Leviathan, and she told them so.

"What do you know about Gabrielle's sword?" the Inquisitor asked.

"Nothing. I didn't even know she owned a sword."

"It is a true sword. It holds a special kind of power. It was forged so that it always meets its target," he grumbled, as if her ignorance were a sign of guilt.

"I don't know what you're getting at."

The Inquisitor spoke very slowly and carefully. "You say you were carrying your mother's sword. A sword that has been lost for centuries and that has never failed to strike its enemies in all its history. And yet . . . you did. You failed. If you were indeed holding Gabrielle's sword, how could you miss?"

"Are you saying that I wanted to miss?" she asked, incredulous.

"I'm not saying that: you are."

Schuyler was shocked. What was happening? What was this?

The Inquisitor turned to his audience. "Ladies and gentlemen of the Conclave, this is an interesting situation. Here are the facts of the matter. Lawrence Van Alen is dead. His granddaughter would like us to believe a rather outrageous story, that Leviathan, a demon that Lawrence himself buried in stone a millennium ago, has been released, and that that same demon killed him."

"It's true," Schuyler whispered.

"Miss Van Alen, you had never met your grandfather until a few months ago, is that correct?"

"Yes."

"You barely knew him from a stranger on the street."

"I wouldn't say that. We became very close in a short amount of time."

"Yet you harbored bitterness against him, did you not? After all, you chose to live with your mother's estranged brother rather than with Lawrence."

"I didn't choose anything! We were fighting the adoption. I did not want to live with Charles Force and his family!"

"So you say."

"Why on earth would I want to kill my grandfather?" she practically shouted. This was insane. A kangaroo court, a charade, a travesty. There was no justice to be served here.

"Perhaps you did not mean to kill him. Perhaps, as you told us earlier, it was an accident." The Inquisitor smiled, looking like a shark.

Schuyler slumped in her seat, defeated. For whatever reasons, the Inquisitor did not believe her story, and it was clear the remaining members of the Conclave would not either. The hidden Silver Blood among their ranks had been discovered—Nan Cutler had perished in the Almeida fire. The Conclave believed that, at least. They had accepted it. Forsyth Llewellyn had been the victim of Warden Cutler's betrayal and had borne witness.

But the ruling body did not want to accept the reality of Leviathan's return. It was one thing to accept the testimony of a fellow Elder, and *another thing to take the word of a half-blood. They would rather believe Schuyler had deliberately killed Lawrence than that a demon stalked the earth once more.*

There were no other witnesses to back her up except for Oliver, and the testimony of human Conduits was inadmissible in a Committee investigation. Humans simply didn't count, when it came down to it.

So the night before the Conclave cast judgment and decided what to do with her, she and Oliver fled the country.

SEVEN

Schuyler

*I*t was ten o'clock in the evening, and the first guests were arriving at the landing. As befitting the Oriental theme, a platoon of authentic Chinese junks rented for the party made a stately procession up the river, banners flying the crests of the Great Houses of Europe. Hapsburg. Bourbon. Savoy. Liechtenstein. Saxe-Coburg. Blue Bloods that had remained in the Old Country in favor of seeking a new home across the ocean.

Schuyler stood sentry with the army of servers lined up against the stone wall, just another faceless drone, or so she hoped. Each of them carried a different libation: there were pink cosmopolitans in martini glasses, goblets of the finest Burgundy and Bordeaux from the hostess's vineyards in Montrachet, sparkling water with lemon slices for teetotalers. She carried a heavy tray of champagne flutes, bubbles clustered at the lip, golden and bright.

She could hear the crack-thump of the wind whipping against the multiple sails. Some were decorated as dragon boats, complete with gold-plated scales and luminescent emerald eyes at the bow. Some were kitted out as warships with brightly colored "cannons" poking out of the stern. A grand imperial parade, at once indulgent and beautiful. She noticed something else as well—the crests on the banners were *moving*, changing with the light, transforming in a fluid dance of form and color. "Do you see that?" She turned to the girl standing next to her.

"See what? A bunch of rich people in some stupid boats?" the waitress cracked, looking at her dubiously. Only then did Schuyler realize that the flashing symbols were visible only to those with the vampire sight. They were Blue Blood *siguls*, from the Sacred Language.

She had almost given herself away, but thankfully no one had noticed. Her lip quivered, and she could feel her body tense as the guests walked down the dock and approached the waiters. What if someone recognized her? What if someone from the New York Coven were at the party? What then? It was madness to think she and Oliver could get away with this. There were sure to be Venators here, weren't there? If any of the Blue Bloods recognized her before she was able to make her case to the countess, she wouldn't have a chance in the world, and what would become of them then? She wasn't afraid so much for herself as for Oliver. She feared what the vampires would do to a human Conduit of whom they disapproved.

Hopefully the crowd would remain as oblivious as they looked—another bunch of pleasure-seeking socialites, as her coworker had dismissed them. Just because they were immortal didn't mean they didn't enjoy the trivial. Schuyler tried not to stare at the women, most of whom looked even more fantastic than the boats. The female guests were dressed variously as Japanese geishas, in full white powder makeup and gaily printed kimonos, or Chinese empresses with tasseled pointy red-and-gold headdresses, or Persian princesses with real jewels pasted on their foreheads. One famous German socialite known for her outrageous wardrobe came dressed as a pagoda, a heavy metal costume that wouldn't allow her to walk or sit for the entire evening. Instead, she rolled out of the boat on a Segway. For a moment Schuyler forgot her nerves and tried not to laugh as the archduchess almost mowed down a group of waiters carrying caviar and blinis.

The men wore Russian officers' uniforms, Fu Manchu mustaches, and turbans. It was all so politically incorrect and yet stupendously fabulous and anachronistic. One guest, the head of Europe's largest bank, was decked out in a large sable hat and a plush wolf-fur-trimmed cape. It was August! He had to be suffocating in the heat, and yet—like the lady in the pagoda who could not sit down—he was suffering to make a statement. Schuyler hoped it was worth it.

Human familiars were in attendance as well, only the small, discreet scars at the base of the neck giving them away. Otherwise they were just as festively attired and barely distinguishable from their vampire masters.

The night was balmy and clear. Sitar music wafted down from the rotunda—a distinctive high-pitched wailing—and the line of junks waiting to disembark their fancifully dressed passengers was growing. Several speedboats carrying young European Blue Bloods cut the line. They were much more daring in costume than their elders. One of the girls, the daughter of the Russian finance minister, was wearing nothing but draped metal ropes and a wisp of black chiffon. Another svelte nymph was dressed in see-through chain mail. Of course, the boys were dressed as ninja assassins in black silk jumpsuits or as samurai warriors, and carried decorative swords.

When her tray was empty, Schuyler headed back, walking past Oliver's sight line from the second level. She glanced up and saw him making a turquoise-colored cocktail adorned with sizzling firecrackers.

She saw him nod, and she knew he had seen her. She ditched her tray in a dark corner and walked swiftly into the main hall, past cordoned-off areas of the residential wing. This is where she and Cordelia had stayed on their visits. There was a bathroom to the right, behind the Sabine murals.

It was empty. She locked the door and took a deep breath. Phase one of the plan was complete. They had succeeded in worming their way into the party. Now it was time for phase two.

She shook out her ponytail and slipped out of her catering uniform, peeling off the layers. She found the small rucksack she had hidden underneath the sink earlier. She removed its contents and began to dress, putting on a bejeweled sari, luscious pink silk encrusted with diamonds. Oliver had helped her pick it out at the shop in Little Jaffna in the 10th *arrondissement*. He'd insisted on getting it even though it had been prohibitively expensive.

The silk draped elegantly over her bare shoulders, and the dazzling pink made a nice contrast to her long blue-black hair. She looked at herself in the mirror. She was thinner than she had ever been: lack of sleep and security would do that to anyone. Her cheekbones, already sharp, were thrown into sharper relief, cut like the edge of a blade. The bright sari brought color to her cheeks, and the dazzling gemstones glittered in the light. She sucked in her stomach even though her hip bones were prominent above the dress's low-waisted harem pants.

She removed a tiny cosmetic bag from the same backpack and began to apply some makeup. She dropped her powdered compact to the floor, and only then realized her hands were shaking again.

She wasn't ready for this. Whenever she contemplated what she was about to do, what she was about to ask, she couldn't breathe. What if the countess turned her away? She couldn't run forever, could she?

If the countess refused them an audience, they had nowhere else to go.

More than anything, Schuyler wanted to go home. She wanted to be in the same place her grandparents had lived. Back in her small bedroom with the peeling paint and the clanging heater. She had already missed an entire year of school. In a month, Duchesne would be back in session. She wanted to go back to that life, even though she knew it was lost to her. Even if the European Conclave gave her shelter, it did not mean she would be able to return to New York.

Outside the band was playing "Thriller," Michael Jackson to a bhangra beat, cymbals crashing. She bundled her waiter's uniform into the bag and stuffed it in a trash can, then left the powder room, slipping past the velvet rope.

"Champagne?" a server offered. Thankfully, the waitress didn't recognize Schuyler as a fellow serf on the bus.

"No, thank you," Schuyler demurred.

She walked to bottom of the staircase, elaborately costumed as an Indian princess. She held her head high even as her throat constricted with fear. She was ready for whatever the night would bring, and she hoped she wouldn't have to wait too long.

EIGHT

Mimi

"The Silver Bloods are much more clever than we give them credit for," Kingsley said, when they arrived at yet another airport. They had left the U.S. the night before. Now they were back where it had all started, before that wild-goose chase had sent them halfway around the world. Back in Rio.

"You think?" Mimi replied, not even trying to hide the sarcasm in her voice. "You should know. You are one." She put on her oversize sunglasses and rescued her battered Valextra roller from the luggage carousel. She was irritated that Kingsley made them fly economy everywhere. She was used to having her bags wrapped and secured in plastic whenever she traveled internationally. Her poor little valise was not surviving the rough treatment from the baggage handlers. She spotted yet another muddy footprint on its smooth leather surface.

"It's not funny," Kingsley said as he took her bag and tossed it into the baggage cart, almost as if he were dunking a basketball and not lifting a seventy-pound weight. (Mimi never traveled light. A girl needed choices.)

"I'm not laughing," Mimi snapped. "I just don't know how we could've missed it the first time."

"Just because we're Venators doesn't mean we don't make mistakes. And it's one thing to be incompetent, but it's another thing to be deceived. We weren't looking for it, that's why we missed it." They walked out of the terminal and into the mild, tropical afternoon. Thank goodness for the upside-down weather here. Mimi had braced herself for blistering heat, and discovering it was winter in South America was a pleasant surprise.

The Lennox boys had hailed their own cab to the hotel, which meant she and Kingsley were stuck with each other again. The two brothers had been under Kingsley's command for centuries, but kept to themselves. They preferred their own company and often only spoke when they were spoken to, in monosyllabic grunts. She and Kingsley had had no choice but to talk to each other or die of boredom.

Kingsley whistled for a cab, and they piled in the back and drove slowly into town. The city looked the same, as gorgeous and exotic as ever, but somehow seeing the Redeemer statue above Corcovado mountain did not give Mimi the same thrill it once had. She didn't know what to think—she sure knew what the Conclave thought—even Kingsley had wanted to go after Leviathan as soon as he'd read the report, but he had been sent on this little adventure instead. Forsyth Llewellyn had pressed upon the surviving Elders to make finding the Watcher a top priority. Mimi wasn't wholly convinced, as the senator was, that the Silver Blood traitors had been fully unmasked by the Almeida fire—sure Nan Cutler, their leader, had perished—but there had to be others among the Coven. Warden Cutler had to have had help. But that wasn't really Mimi's problem right now.

All Mimi knew was that when Kingsley began assembling his team, she had volunteered. She'd wanted to get out of New York, away from the shocked, mournful faces of the surviving members of the Conclave. They were all so weak and frightened! It annoyed her to see them cowed and terrified. They were vampires; where was their pride? They were acting like cornered sheep, bleating to Forsyth about how they should hide.

Well, she wasn't going to hide. She wanted to find whoever was responsible for that terrible night, hunt them down and kill them one by one. Sacrilege is what it was, disrespect. The Silver Bloods' attack was vicious in its scope and intensity. They had attempted to wipe out the clan's Elders and Wardens, leaving the community with the irrelevant and the feeble. They had shown them no mercy. Mimi planned to show them the same.

But first they had to find Jordan. Jordan would tell them

what had happened; Jordan would know who the Silver Bloods were and where they were hiding.

Because Jordan Llewellyn was only pretending to be a child. Jordan was the Watcher, Pistis Sophia, Elder of Elders, a soul born with its eyes open—that is, with the full command and understanding of all its memories. Sophia had slumbered for thousands of years until Cordelia Van Alen had asked the Llewellyns, one of the oldest and most trusted families in the Conclave, to take her spirit as their newborn. The Watcher was supposed to keep vigilance against their enemies and to sound the alarm should the Dark Prince ever return to Earth. During the time of the Roman crisis it had been Sophia who had first discovered the Croatan betrayal. Or something like that, anyway.

It was all so long ago, and Mimi couldn't be bothered to remember. When you had lived for thousands of years, going through your memories was like trying to find a contact lens in a pile of broken glass. The past wasn't filed away in a neat tree of folders on a computer screen, marked accordingly with dates and labels for easy access. Instead, the past was a jumble of images and emotions, of knowledge that you did not understand and information you did not remember possessing.

Sometimes, when she had a moment to herself, Mimi wondered why she had volunteered so gladly. She had missed her senior year of high school, and wouldn't be able to graduate with her class. And it wasn't as if she cared about Jordan Llewellyn. She'd only met her a couple of times, and each time, Jordan had made either a face or a rude remark. But something told her she had to go, and Jack hadn't stopped her either.

It was strange how things never turned out the way one expected. Mimi had thought she and Jack would become closer after everything that had happened, especially with that stupid Van Alen brat finally out of the way. Maybe they just took each other for granted now that there was no one between them. But why was it she was here, and he was somewhere else?

"Penny for your thoughts?" Kingsley asked, as if he'd just noticed the silence in the taxicab.

"It's going to cost much more than that," Mimi said. "Let's just say however much it is, you'll never be able to afford it."

"Oh really?" Kingsley cocked an eyebrow. His signature move. Guaranteed to pull in the ladies. She could read it all over his arrogant face. "Never say never."

The hotel they'd booked was a modest one: three stars, and that was stretching it. It was miles from the beach, and the elevator was broken when they arrived. Mimi spent a listless night on itchy sheets and was surprised to find the team in extraordinarily good spirits the next morning. Well. Someone had to like percale.

Kingsley sat at the breakfast table looking newly

energized, and not just from the four shots of espresso in his café con leche. He drank coffee like some vampires drank blood. "We've been thinking like humans," he sighed. "Looking for suspects, interrogating witnesses. These are Croatan we are up against. And they took the time to manipulate a memory that led us everywhere but here."

"It means she's here. In Rio. I get it." Mimi nodded. "They sent us as far away as possible."

"She's probably right under our nose," Kingsley said. "In one of the most populous cities in the world."

"Ten million people," Mimi said. "That's a lot." Her heart began to sink just thinking about how many more dreams they would have to read, how many endless nights they would have to spend chasing shadows in the dark.

She watched Kingsley walk away from the table and over to the buffet, where the hotel had laid out a full breakfast: platters of cheese buns and salted biscuits; freshly cut papayas, mangoes, and watermelons. Bowls of avocado cream. Chafing dishes filled with slices of honey ham and crispy bacon. He picked up a watermelon wedge and took a bite, standing in front of the full-length windows that had a panoramic view of the city.

Mimi followed his gaze out to the clustered hillsides. The favelas were as crowded and structurally ingenious as ant farms, precariously towering over the cliffs, a Byzantine maze of ghettos housing Rio's urban poor.

"Amazing, aren't they? A city within a city, really," Mimi

said. "It's a wonder they all don't come crashing down during flood season."

Kingsley put down the melon rind. "The shanty towns . . . of course. The Silver Bloods have always been drawn to chaos and disorder. That's where we'll start."

"Are you serious?" Mimi groaned. "No one goes there unless they have to."

NINE

Bliss

*T*he Visitor was annoyed. Bliss felt his irritation like a blister. It was afternoon, as far as she could tell. The days slipped by one after the other so easily that it was hard to figure out what time it was, but Bliss tried to keep track as best she could. When he was quiet, it was night, and when she could sense his awareness, it was day.

Usually she would get a glimpse of the outside world when he woke up. Like yesterday morning, with the white shutters. Then the blinds would shut again. Only when he let his guard down was Bliss able to get a quick image of the outside world.

Like now, for the Visitor had been taken by surprise.

One minute they were striding through the house, and the next they were smack in the middle of a bunch of animals: grotesque and pitiful. Ugly. What was this? What was she looking at? Then she realized she was seeing the world through his eyes. Only when she pushed herself a little harder did she see that they were just among an ordinary group of people. A lady wearing a beige suit and sunglasses was ushering a family through the foyer. They looked like the typical Hamptons crowd, Dad in a pastel alligator shirt with a white tennis sweater over his shoulders, Mom in lavender seersucker, the kids—two boys—in miniature versions of Dad's outfit.

"Oh, hello . . . I'm sorry. We were told the owners wouldn't be here for the showing," the lady in the business suit said with a fake smile. "But since you're here, do you know if your father's contractor is still available to complete the renovation?"

Then it all went black and the image disappeared again, even though Bliss had been able to hear the question. Bobi-Anne had been in the midst of renovating before she died. The Hamptons house was supposed to be completed by now, but when they returned from South America, Forsyth had ordered the construction ceased. The entire back half of the house was missing. In its place was a big hole in the ground covered in plaster dust, sawdust, and plastic.

The senator had returned to New York only to discover that he had been cleaned out in the latest financial upheaval. Some kind of Ponzi scheme, Bliss understood; a total scam. She wasn't sure, except that whatever it was, it had been enough to get Forsyth out of Conclave duties for a while. She couldn't quite tell what had happened, since it was around this time that the Visitor began to take over completely; but she had a feeling they were bankrupt. Forsyth was trying to get a loan from the Committee to tide them over, but it would not be enough. His salary as a U.S. senator was trifling. The Llewellyns, like many Blue Blood families, lived on investment returns.

And apparently those investments were gone.

Which was probably the reason why there was a real estate agent at the house with her clients. Forsyth was selling the house. The thought didn't make Bliss very sad. They didn't spend so much time in the Hamptons that she would miss it. She had been much more despondent when they had left their home in Texas. She still missed that house sometimes: the way her two-level attic bedroom rested under the leaves of an old willow tree, afternoons spent reading on the porch swing, the old antique mirrors in the bathrooms that made everyone look a little bit mysterious and faerie.

The Visitor's been gone awhile, she thought, alone in the darkness. How long, she wasn't certain. It was hard to judge time when you weren't in the physical world anymore.

Bliss wasn't sure, but she thought that there was something different about the solitude. That she might be truly alone this time, and not just cast out of her body while the Visitor did god knows what. Usually she sensed his presence, but there had been times in the past when she was quite convinced she was completely alone. That it was only *her* inside her body, and the other had gone.

Could it be? Was she truly alone? Bliss felt an excitement rising in her chest.

There was nothing. The Visitor was gone, she could feel it. She was sure. She knew what she had to do. But she didn't know if she still *could.*

Open the blinds. Open your eyes.

Open them!

Open!

But where were they? *Disembodied.* She truly understood the meaning of the word. It was like floating without an anchor. She had to get grounded again, to feel her way around until—yes—there it is, a crack of light—maybe she just imagined it—but if she could just force it open—there— just a little more . . .

Bliss opened her eyes slowly. She'd done it! She looked around. It was amazing to be able to see the world on her terms, and not how the Visitor saw it, through his hate-colored glasses. She was in the library. A small cozy nook surrounded by walls of books. Her stepmother's decorator had insisted that all the "good homes" had one. BobiAnne read magazines. Forsyth liked to stay in his den with his large-screen television. The library had become the sisters' territory. Bliss remembered how she and Jordan would sit at the window seat, looking out at the pool and the ocean while they read. Bliss saw an old summer reading stack on a shelf next to the Victorian rolltop desk. *The Brothers Karamazov. The Grapes of Wrath. Persuasion.*

She thought she heard a noise. Whether it was from inside or out, she did not know. *Close the blinds. Close your eyes,* she thought frantically. *Close them before he comes back.*

She closed them.

Nothing. She was still alone.

She waited for a long time. Then she opened her eyes again. Nothing. She really was alone. She had to take advantage of this. Bliss had had a plan ever since she'd noticed his prolonged absences.

She had to do something more than just look around. Dare she? Her body felt sluggish and heavy. So heavy. This was going to be impossible. What if he came back? What then? She had to try, she told herself. She had to do something. She couldn't just live like an invalid, in limbo, in paralysis.

If I can open my eyes, I can do something else. I'm still Bliss Llewellyn, aren't I? I've won tennis tournaments and run marathons. I can do this.

Move your hand. Move your hand.

Can't. Too heavy. Where is my hand? I have a hand? What is a hand? There. I can feel my five fingers, but they feel so far away, as if behind glass, or submerged underwater. She remembered seeing a magician on the *Today* show who had attempted to live underwater for several days. How immobilized and swollen he had looked. She was no magician, but there was no reason to remain trapped underneath her own fear either. *Move it. Move. Your. Hand. Oh God. It weighs three thousand pounds. I can't do it. I can't, I can't. But I have to.*

Do it!

She remembered how hard it had been to learn the four-base pyramid scorpion, one of the most difficult moves in cheerleading. It required acute coordination and the skill of a trapeze artist. Bliss was the only cheerleader on the team who could do it. She remembered how scared she had been the first time. If she didn't connect with the base's hands on the way up, she would fall; if she missed the back spotter on the extension, she would fall; if she didn't balance correctly on her left foot, she would fall.

But she would connect with the base, hit her mark, stand with her right leg bent back above her head, and hold the pose until she was thrown upward in a triple-somersault pop-flick to land on her feet.

Too bad Duchesne didn't have a squad. Bliss had tried to start one, but no one was interested. Snobs! They didn't know what they were missing. The feeling of the night of a big game. The anticipation of the crowd. The thrill of running out on the field, pom-poms bouncing, the roar from the stands, the jealousy and the admiration. On Fridays, cheerleaders were allowed to wear their uniforms to class. It was akin to wearing a crown.

The scorpion.

She'd nailed it.

If I could do that, I can do this, she told herself.

Move. Your. Hand!

She could feel her bangs in her face. The Visitor had not bothered with haircuts, or manicures either. Bliss was annoyed. All that work to look cute gone down the drain. Her hair was wild and untamed, rough to the touch. She had to do something about it.

There. *Urrrgh!* Her hand jerked away, moving like a marionette, like a puppet on strings. But she'd done it. Her hand awkwardly brushed her hair, moved it away from her eyes.

So.

I can do it.

I can take control of my body. It's going to be difficult and painful and slow, but I can do it. I'm not out of the game yet.

Now all she had to do was learn how to walk again.

The Conduit

or almost seventy years, Christopher Anderson had served as faithful human Conduit to Lawrence Van Alen. He was the one who had brought Schuyler to the hospital to have her arm properly looked at after they'd returned from Corcovado with the news of his master's passing. The spry, gracious gentleman had never struck Schuyler as being particularly elderly, but since Lawrence's death it looked as if age had finally caught up with him. He was frail now and walked with a cane.

Anderson visited her that last night at Oliver's, where she had been staying since returning from South America. She hadn't the courage to go back to the brownstone on 101st Street. It hurt too much to know that there would be no Lawrence puffing on his cigar in his study.

Her grandfather's Conduit advised her to leave the country as soon as possible. He had read the transcript of the investigation. "You cannot take chances. No one knows what will happen tomorrow. It is better that you go now and disappear before they can renounce you as a traitor."

"*I told you,*" *Oliver said, looking meaningfully at Schuyler.*

"*But where would we go?*" *she asked.*

"*Everywhere. Do not stay anywhere for longer than seventy-two hours. The Venators are fast, but they will be using the glom to find you, and it will slow them down a little. Wherever you go, make sure you end up in Paris next August.*"

"*Why Paris?*" *Schuyler asked.*

"*The full European Coven converges every other year for a grand party and a congress,*" *Anderson said.* "*Lawrence had been planning to attend the biannual meeting. You shall take his place instead. The countess will see you. The Conclaves have been estranged ever since the Blue Bloods left the Old Country. She never had any faith in Michael and the New York Coven. She will have even less faith now, when she hears of Lawrence's demise. She was one of his oldest friends.*"

The countess had been a friend to Cordelia as well, Schuyler realized later. She vaguely remembered the royal couple: their stately home had made more of an impression. She hadn't thought anything in particular of them except that they had seemed gracious and extremely wealthy, just like everyone in Cordelia's circle. Now Schuyler understood they were special. The countess had been married to the late Prince Henri, who would have been the King of France save the Revolution. Henri had been Regis of the European Conclave. Upon the end of his cycle, his queen had assumed the title.

Anderson was leaving the city too. Upon a vampire's death, human Conduits were released from service and allowed a choice: the Repository or freedom. They could work for the Coven at large, or they could have a normal life.

Anderson told them he had no desire to live out the rest of his life in a basement. He was going back to Venice, back to the University. Of course, his memory would be erased by the Conclave. That was a prerequisite to his leaving them. The Blue Bloods kept their secrets.

Schuyler understood Anderson's choice, but it saddened her all the same. Anderson was the last remaining link to her grandfather. Once he left the Coven, he would be a stranger to her. But she would not deny him his desire for an ordinary existence. He had spent a lifetime in service to the Van Alens.

"Go and find the countess," Anderson continued. "Tell her everything that has happened. There has been distrust between the covens, so she might not know the truth about the massacre in Rio. And, Schuyler?"

"Yes?"

"I know what they've planned for me tomorrow at my exit interview. The forced amnesia. But don't worry, I will never forget you." He shook her hand, and she clasped his in hers.

"Nor shall I forget your great kindness," Schuyler replied. Oliver was right as usual. They had to leave immediately. The Venators would come for her that evening. They would come to take her away.

"The countess will help you."

Schuyler hoped her grandfather's old friend was right.

TEN

Schuyler

"Look at you," Oliver murmured, coming up from behind to rest a warm hand on Schuyler's exposed hip. She turned to him with a soft smile and placed her hand firmly on top of his so that they were practically embracing. Whatever happened tonight, at least they had each other. It was a source of great consolation to both of them. "You don't look too bad yourself," she said. He was dressed as a Mogul prince, in a fine gold brocade riding jacket and a white turban atop his caramel-colored hair.

In answer, Oliver took her bejeweled hand and pressed it to his lips, sending a delicious shiver up her spine. Her friend and her familiar. They were a team. Like the Los Angeles Lakers, unbeatable, Schuyler couldn't help thinking. She always made corny jokes when she was nervous.

"What's this?" she asked, as Oliver pressed something into her palm.

"I found it in the garden earlier," he said, showing her the crushed four-leaf clover. "For luck."

I don't need luck, I have you, she wanted to say, but she knew Oliver would think it was cheesy. Instead, she accepted the flower and tucked it into her sari with a smile.

"Shall we?" he asked, when the bhangra pop ended and the orchestra switched to a waltzy version of the Beatles' "Norwegian Wood."

He led her out to the middle of the dance floor located in the grand ballroom just off the courtyard. The room was festooned with floating Chinese lanterns, delicate orbs of light that looked incongruous against the French classical architecture. There were only a few people dancing, and Schuyler worried they would look conspicuous as the youngest people on the dance floor by several decades.

But she had always loved this song, which wasn't so much a love song as the opposite of one. *"I once had a girl, or should I say, she once had me."* And she loved that Oliver wanted to dance. He held out his arms and she stepped into them, resting her head on his shoulder as he circled her waist. She wished dancing was all they had to do. It was so nice just to live in the moment, to enjoy holding him so closely, to pretend for a little while that they were merely two young people in love and nothing else.

Oliver led her smoothly through every dance, a product of mandatory ballroom lessons from his etiquette-obsessed mother. Schuyler felt as graceful as a ballerina in his confident direction. "I never knew you could dance," she teased.

"You never asked," he said, twirling her around so that her silk pants floated prettily around her ankles.

They danced through two more songs, a catchy polonaise and a popular rap song—the music a schizophrenic mix of high and low, Mozart to M.I.A., Bach to Beyoncé. Schuyler found she was actually enjoying herself. Then the music stopped abruptly, and they turned to see what had caused the sudden silence.

"The Countess of Paris, Isabelle of Orleans," the orchestra conductor announced, as an imposing woman, very beautiful for her age, with coal black hair and a regal bearing entered the room. She was dressed as the Queen of Sheba, in a headdress made of gold and blue lapis. Her right hand held an immense gold chain, and standing at the end of it was a black panther wearing a diamond collar.

Schuyler held her breath. So that was the countess. The prospect of asking that woman for shelter suddenly seemed more daunting than ever. She had expected the countess to be plump and elderly, frumpy even—a little old lady in a pastel suit with a bunch of corgis. But this woman was sophisticated and chic; she came across as remote and distant as a deity. Why would she care what happened to Schuyler?

Still, maybe the countess only looked imperious and inaccessible. After all, this party could not have been easy for her. Schuyler wondered if the countess was sad to have lost her home. The Hôtel Lambert had been in her family for generations upon generations. Schuyler knew the recent global financial crisis had humbled even the grandest houses and the richest families. The Hazard-Perrys had invested well: Oliver told her they had gotten out of the market years before it crashed. But all over the Upper East Side, Schuyler heard, jewelry was being auctioned, art appraised, portfolios liquidated. It was the same in Europe. None of the other Blue Blood families could even afford to buy the Lambert. It had to go to a corporation, and it did.

The countess waved to her guests as the ballroom exploded in applause, Schuyler and Oliver clapping as heartily as the rest. Then Isabelle took her exit, the music started up again, and the tension in the room abated. A collective exhale.

"So what did the baron say?" Schuyler asked, as Oliver twirled her away from the center of the room.

The Baron de Coubertin was in the countess's employ and served his lady as human Conduit, as Oliver was to Schuyler. Anderson had told them a meeting with the countess could only be facilitated by the baron. He was the key to an appeal. Without his permission, they would never be able to even get within a hairsbreadth of the countess. The plan was for Oliver to introduce himself the minute the baron arrived at the party, waylaying him as he stepped off the boat.

"We'll find out soon enough," Oliver said, looking apprehensive. "Don't look up. He's coming our way."

ELEVEN

Mimi

*T*he four Venators made very little sound as they landed on the roof of the building. Their footsteps could be mistaken for the rustle of bird's wings, or a few pebbles dislodged from the hillside. It was their fourth night in Rio, and they were in the favela de Rocinha, systematically going through the population, block by block, street by street, dilapidated shack by dilapidated shack. They were looking for anything—a scrap of memory, a word, an image—that could maybe shed some light on what had happened to Jordan and where she might be.

Mimi knew the drill so well she could do it in her sleep. Or actually, *their* sleep. Look at these Red Bloods, so cozy and secure in their slumber, she thought. They had no idea that vampires tiptoed through their dreams.

Memories were tricky things, Mimi thought as she entered the twilight world of the glom. They weren't stable.

They changed with perception over time. She saw how they shifted, understood how the passage of time affected them. A hardworking striver might recall his childhood as one filled with misery and hardship, marred by the catcalls and name-calling of playground bullies, but later have a much more forgiving understanding of past injustices. The handmade clothes he had been forced to wear became a testament to his mother's love, each patch and stitch a sign of her diligence instead of a brand of poverty. He would remember Father staying up late to help with the homework, the old man's patience and dedication, instead of the sharpness of his temper when he returned home, late, from the factory.

It went the other way as well. Mimi had scanned thousands of memories of spurned women whose handsome lovers turned ugly and rude, Roman noses perhaps too pointed, eyes growing small and mean, while the ordinary-looking boys who had become their husbands grew in attractiveness as the years passed, so that when asked if it was love at first sight, the women cheerfully answered yes.

Memories were moving pictures in which meaning was constantly in flux. They were stories people told themselves. Using the glom—the netherworld of memory and shadow, a space the vampires could access at will in order to read and control minds—was like stepping into a darkroom, into a lab where photographers developed their prints, submerging them in shallow pans of chemicals, drying them on nylon racks. Mimi remembered the darkroom at Duchesne, how she used to hide there with her familiars. Spinning through the revolving door, leaving the Technicolor world of school behind to enter a small, cramped space that was so dark she'd wonder for a second if she had gone blind. But vampires could see in the dark, of course.

Did they even have darkrooms anymore, other than in movies where they had to track down the serial killer? Mimi wondered. Everyone had digital cameras now. Darkrooms were prehistoric. Like handwritten letters and proper first dates.

Darkrooms, Force? You don't strike me as a photographer.

But I will strike you, Mimi sent back.

Har-har.

Go back to your patient. You're going to wake mine.

It was against protocol for Kingsley to pop into her head space. The four Venators could sense each other, but they were supposed to be on separate channels, watching different dreams. They had entered a women's dormitory, a place in the city where girls from the outlying provinces paid a pittance for a bed.

Mimi was in a girl's mind. The girl was the same age as her, roughly, for this cycle: seventeen.

The girl worked as a chambermaid in one of the hotels. Mimi scanned the last three months of her life. Saw her making the beds and clearing out the trash, vacuuming rugs and pocketing the small tips the guests left on the bedside tables. Saw her waiting for her boyfriend, a bike messenger, after work at a small café. Work, boyfriend, work, boyfriend. *What's this?* The hotel manager was forcing the girl into his office and making her take off her clothes. Interesting. But was it real?

Venator training meant Mimi had learned how to distinguish fiction from reality, expectation from realization. Was the girl really being abused by her boss or was she just fearful that it would happen? It looked like a fear-dream. Mimi placed a compulsion: she imagined the girl pushing her boss away, kicking him right where it hurt. There. If it ever happened, the girl would know what to do now.

"Call it. Lennox One?" Kingsley's voice echoed through the darkness.

"Clear."

"Two?"

"Clear."

"Force?"

Mimi sighed. There was no sign of the Watcher in any of the girl's thoughts. "Clear." She blinked her eyes open. She was standing over the girl, who was sleeping soundly under the covers. Mimi thought she had a small smile on her lips. *There is no need to be afraid,* Mimi sent. *A girl can do anything she wants to do.*

"Right. Move out." Kingsley led them into the night, through the unpaved roads and rickety steps leading farther into the tumbledown, jigsaw row of makeshift houses and apartment buildings cut into the mountains.

She followed the team up the hill, walking by overflowing garbage cans and piles of rotten junk. Not all that different from certain parts of Manhattan, Mimi thought, although it was amazing to see how closely people lived and how twisted their priorities were. She had seen homes—hovels, really—with no running water or toilets, but whose living rooms boasted forty-two-inch flatscreen televisions and satellite dishes. There were shiny German cars in the makeshift garages while the children went without shoes.

Speaking of children: she heard them before she saw them. The merry little band of brats who had been following them around all week. Their dirty faces streaked with tar, their ragged clothes bearing faded American sports team insignias, their hands outstretched, palms facing upward, empty. It reminded her of a public-service announcement that used to run in the evenings: "It's ten p.m. Do you know where your children are?"

"*Senhora Bonita, Senhora Bonita,*" they chanted, their bare feet slapping on the wet path.

"Shoo!" Mimi hissed, batting them away like pesky flies. "I have nothing for you today. *Nada para voce. Deixe-me sozinho!*" Leave me alone.

Their begging gave her a headache. She wasn't responsible for these people, for these children. . . . She was a Venator on official business, not some celebrity on a public relations campaign. Besides, this was Brazil, a developing country. There were places around the globe that were far more desperate. Really, the little urchins didn't know how lucky they were.

"*Senhora, senhora.*" The little one—a cherub in a stained undershirt, dark curls bobbing—had grabbed the back of her shirt. Like the other Venators, Mimi was wearing a black polyver coat and waterproof nylon pants, standard-issue wear. She'd refused to wear the clunky boots (they made her feet look fat), and was wearing the high-heeled pony-hair boots again.

"Oh, all right," Mimi said. It was her fault the kids were around them. For as much as she tried to harden her heart, to remain impassive and stoic and indifferent in the face of truly appalling poverty—Mimi considered her standard room back at the hotel (not even a suite!) deprivation enough—she found that whenever the children crowded around her, she always had something to give them.

A piece of candy. A dollar. (Yesterday ten dollars each.) A chocolate bar. Something. The children called her The Beautiful Lady, *Senhora Bonita*.

"Nothing for you today! Really! I'm out!" she protested.

"They'll never believe you. Not since you caved the first day," Kingsley said, looking amused.

"As if you're any better," Mimi grumbled, reaching into her backpack. The four of them were a soft touch. The silent twins gave out bubble gum while Kingsley could always be counted on to pay for deep-fried *kibe* snacks from the street carts.

The little girl with the curls waited patiently as Mimi brought out a stuffed toy dog she'd bought from the gift shop that morning especially for her. The stuffed animal had a face that reminded her of her own dog. She wished the gentle chow were with her, but need for the canine familiar's protection lessened in the later years of the transformation. "Here. And this is for all of you to share," she said, handing over a huge box of bonbons. "Now go!"

"*Obrigado! Obrigado, senhora!*" they yelled as they ran away with their booty.

"You like them," Kingsley said with a twisted half smile that Mimi found infuriating because it made him even more handsome than he needed to be.

"No way." She shook her head, not meeting his eyes. Maybe she'd been drinking too much of the super-sweet Mexican Coca-Cola they had down here. Or maybe she was just tired, alone, and far from home. Because somewhere in the brittle, concrete center of Azrael's dark heart, something was melting.

Missing

"*Y*ou must ask Charles. You must ask him about the gates . . . about the Van Alen legacy and the Paths of the Dead.*"

Those were her grandfather's last words.

But Charles Force was gone when Schuyler returned to New York. Oliver had found out through his contacts at the Repository that Charles had embarked on his usual amble across the park one afternoon but had never come home. That was a week ago. The former Regis had left no note, no explanation. Apparently, he had left everything a mess. The Force corporation had lost half its value in the stock market crash, and the board was up in arms: their company was sinking and there was no captain steering the ship.

But somebody must know where he was, Schuyler thought, and one morning she waylaid Trinity Force at the salon where she had her hair highlighted. The leading social doyenne of New York was wrapped in a silk robe, sitting under a heat lamp.

"I take it you've heard the news," Trinity said dryly, putting down her magazine as Schuyler took the seat next to her. "Charles must have good reasons for his actions. I only wish he would have shared them with me."

Schuyler told her about Lawrence's last words on the mountaintop, hoping that maybe Trinity could shed a little light on his message.

"The Van Alen legacy," Trinity said, staring at herself in the mirror and patting the plastic cap covering her foils. "Whatever it is, Charles turned his back on everything that had to do with his 'family' a long time ago. Lawrence was living in the past, as he always had."

"But Lawrence insisted that Charles was the key."

"Lawrence is finished." The way Trinity said it, it sounded as if Lawrence were an actor who had merely finished his role in a play. Not passed away. Not dead. Not gone forever.

Finished.

There was another thing—something strange her grandfather had said that Schuyler wanted confirmed. She wasn't sure if Trinity would know anything about it, but she had to ask. "He also said that I have a sister, and that she will be . . . that she will be our death." Schuyler felt silly repeating such a dramatic statement. "I have a sister?"

Trinity did not answer for a long time. The sound of hair dryers and patrons gossiping with their stylists filled the silence. When she finally spoke, her voice was quiet and guarded. "In the sense that your mother had another daughter, yes. But that was long ago, long before you were born, in a different cycle, in a different century. And the girl was taken care of. Lawrence and Charles saw to that. Lawrence . . . One reason he went into exile was that he never gave up on his fantasies. He was dying, Schuyler, and you will have to understand . . . he was grasping at straws, trying to tie up loose ends. He probably wasn't even in his right mind."

So Lawrence had told the truth. She had a sister. Who? When? She was already dead? Taken care of? What did that mean? But Trinity refused to elaborate further. "I have already told you too much," she said with a frown.

"The Conclave has asked me to testify tomorrow about what happened in Rio. Will you be there?" Schuyler asked a little wistfully. It suddenly struck her how much she needed a mother in her life. Trinity had never tried to fill that role, but she had a pragmatic no-nonsense way about her that reminded Schuyler of Cordelia. It was better than nothing.

"I am sorry, Schuyler, but I won't be able to come. As usual, the Red Bloods have let greed take over their financial system. With Charles gone, I am obligated to the board to do what little I can to staunch the bloodbath. I leave for Washington tonight."

"It's all right." Schuyler hadn't expected anything else.

"And, Schuyler?" Trinity looked at her keenly, as a mother would when chastising a wayward daughter. "Since your return, your room has been empty."

"I know," Schuyler said simply. "I'm not going to live with your family anymore."

Trinity sighed. "I will not stop you. But know that when you are out of our house, you are out of our protection. We cannot help you."

"I understand. I'll take that risk." Out of habit, Schuyler and Trinity exchanged double-cheek air kisses and said good-bye. Schuyler *left the soothing warm cocoon of the beauty salon and went out into the streets of New York, alone.*

Charles Force was gone. Charles Force was a dead end. He had disappeared, taking his secrets with him.

She would have to discover the Van Alen Legacy on her own.

TWELVE

Schuyler

he Baron de Coubertin was dressed as Attila the Hun in full battle armor, with a bow and arrow in a quiver slung over one shoulder, along with a shield and a throwing spear. On his head he wore a pointed metal cap over a wig of long black hair. His long beard was also fake. He approached with a terrifying frown on his face and tapped Schuyler on the shoulder. *"La contesse voudrait que vous me suiviez, s'il vous plait."* The countess would like you to follow me, please. Then he turned abruptly on his heel.

Schuyler and Oliver began to walk together behind him, but the baron stopped them. "The countess grants a meeting only to Miss Van Alen," he said in perfect English, looking sternly at Oliver as if he were a nuisance. "You will stay here."

Schuyler nodded over Oliver's protests. "I'll be fine. I'll meet you after," she said. "Don't worry." She felt stares from the other guests turned their way. Who was the baron talking to? *Who are those two?* They were becoming conspicuous. They needed to melt away before anyone noticed them.

"Don't worry? But then I would be out of a job," Oliver said, raising his eyebrows.

"I can handle it," Schuyler insisted.

"That's what I'm worried about," Oliver sighed. He squeezed her bare shoulder. His hands were rough and callused from travel and work. They were not the soft hands of the boy who used to spend his afternoons in museums. The Oliver whom Schuyler had known had never stayed in anything less than a five-star hotel in his life, let alone the fleabag hostels where they now found themselves residing. She had seen him argue the price of instant noodles in Shanghai, haggling over five cents.

"I'll be fine," she promised, then murmured softly so the baron could not hear. "I have a feeling this is the only way I'm going to get to see the countess."

"Let me talk to him again; maybe he'll listen to me," Oliver whispered, looking from the baron to Schuyler. "If anything happens—"

"I won't be able to live with myself," Schuyler said, finishing his sentence. She removed his hand gently. "I'm scared too, Ollie. But we agreed. We have to do this."

Oliver gritted his teeth. "I don't like it," he said, glaring at the baron. But he let her go.

Schuyler followed the baron out of the courtyard and

into the main hall of the palace. He led her through an en-
filade—a series of rooms all in a row, past the library and
the many function rooms. At the end of a long hallway, he
opened a door to an anteroom and led her inside. It was a
small room, tiled with gold mosaics, empty save for a red
velvet bench in the middle.

"*Arrête.*" Wait.

He left, and the door locked behind him.

Schuyler looked around. There was another door in
the back of the room. That one must lead to the countess's office. Schuyler could feel the wards in place, guard-
ing the room. There was no way out except for the two
locked doors. One of Lawrence's lessons had been to sense
the invisible protections in one's surroundings so that you
could figure out how to get out of them. Escape was ninety
percent preparation and ten percent opportunity, he liked
to say.

Schuyler waited for what seemed like hours alone in the
small chamber. The room was completely insulated from
outside noise. She couldn't hear anything from the party. At
last the door opened.

"Baron de Coubertin?" she called.

"Try again." The voice was heartbreakingly familiar.

No. It couldn't be. Schuyler felt paralyzed. It was as if
the past were taunting her. Someone was playing a sick joke.
There was no way *he* was here. The one person in New York
whom she had tried so hard to forget . . .

Jack Force stepped inside. Unlike the other revelers, he was dressed simply, all in black. A Venator's uniform. His platinum hair was cut short, in military fashion, making his sharp aristocratic features look even more striking. He moved with a natural grace, stalking the edge of the room like a dangerous animal circling its prey. How handsome he was—she had forgotten. Or maybe she had only imagined she had forgotten.

They had not seen each other since their last night at the Perry Street apartment. The night she had told him she loved another. How it hurt to see his beautiful face, so grave and serious, as if he had aged a lifetime in a year.

The hurt was like a physical pain, a longing that she had repressed, suddenly flaring up again: bright and red and angry, surprising in its intensity. An impossible wanting: a hole in her heart that yearned to be filled. *No. Stop. Don't go there.* She was furious at herself for feeling this way. It was *wrong*, and incredibly disloyal to the life she had lived for a year. A betrayal to the life she and Oliver had built together.

If only there was something she could do about her heart. Her wildly beating, treacherous heart. Because all she wanted to do was run into Jack's arms.

"Jack," she breathed. Even saying his name was difficult. Was it so terrible that she had wanted so much to see him again? God knows she had tried to stop thinking about him, had banished all thought of him to the darkest corner of her mind.

Yet he was always there: in her dreams, she always went back to the apartment above the city, to that spot by the fire. You couldn't stop yourself from dreaming, could you? It wasn't her fault. That was the annoying part. However much she wanted to—her unconscious always pulled her back to him.

To see him, living, breathing, right here in front of her was like a direct assault on everything she had tried to hold on to during her year-plus in exile. She had convinced herself that her love for him was dead and buried, locked in a treasure chest below the sea, never to be reopened. She had made her choice. She loved Oliver. They were happy, or as happy as two people could be with a bounty over their heads. Jack was not hers to love, and never had been. Whatever they had once meant to each other was no longer. He was a stranger.

Besides, he was bonded now to his vampire twin, to Mimi, his sister. It didn't make a difference how Schuyler still—*regrettably*—felt about him. It just didn't matter. He was already bound to another. She was nothing to him, and he to her.

"What are you doing here?" she asked, because he was just looking at her in silence, even after she had said his name.

"I'm here for you," he said, his mouth set in a grim line.

Then Schuyler knew. Jack was here on behalf of the

Conclave. He was here to take her back to New York. Back into custody. He was here to take her back to face the Inquisitor for sentencing. Innocent or guilty, it did not matter, she knew what the verdict would be—they had turned against her. Jack was one of them now. Part of the Conclave. The enemy.

Schuyler backed into the opposite wall, toward the other door, knowing it was useless. The wards, the protections in place meant there was no way to go but up and out. She would have to try it. Take a running start on the wall and jump high enough so that she would crash through the glass.

Jack noticed her eyes flick toward the ceiling. "You will destroy this room if you attempt it."

"What do I care?"

"I think you do. I think you love the Hôtel Lambert as much as I do. You are not the only one who used to play in its gardens." Of course Jack had been here before. His father had been the former Regis. The Forces had probably stayed in the same guest wing as she and Cordelia. But so what?

"I'll do it if it's the only way. Watch me."

Jack took a step toward her. "I'm not your enemy, Schuyler. No matter what you think. You're wrong. That way is lost. There is a protection you don't feel, one that Lawrence did not teach you about. You will shatter against the glass. And I will not have any harm come to you."

"No?"

"You don't have a choice. Come with me, Schuyler, please." Jack held out his hand. His flashing glass-green eyes were suddenly gentle, pleading. The foreboding look on his face had all but disappeared. He looked vulnerable and lost. It was the same way he had looked at her that night. When he had asked her to stay.

She gave him the same answer she had back then.

"No."

Before she could take a breath she was already running sideways and up, so fast that she was a pink blur against the gold wall, and then she had thrown herself upward so that she broke through the ceiling, sending a rain of crystal shards crashing down on the marble floor. It was all over in an instant.

He was wrong. She knew the spell that held it in place, and she knew the counterspell that had destroyed it. *Contineo* and *Frango*. Lawrence had been thorough in his tutorials. In this at least, she would not fail her grandfather.

I'm sorry, Jack. But I can't go back there.

Never.

Then she disappeared into the night.

THIRTEEN

Bliss

"Listen! I am not going away until I see Bliss! I insist! You will have to call the police if you want me to leave!" The voice was so strong, so aggressive and braying, so full of itself, brimming with the complete and total assumption that it was one hundred percent in the right, filled with the kind of New York arrogance that only a jaded city dweller could muster. It was the kind of voice that yelled at bike messengers and barked orders at scurrying underlings for half-caf no-foam ventis—so loud and insistent that it pierced through the muffled gauze that kept Bliss from seeing and hearing the outside world.

The Visitor stirred. It was like watching a coiled snake get ready to spring. Bliss held her breath.

The voice continued its tirade. "Can you at least tell her who's here?"

What is the meaning of this nonsense?

Bliss jumped. It was the first time the Visitor had spoken directly to her in a year.

With a start, the lights came on, and she found she could see and was looking out the window. There was a short bald man standing at the front door, looking furious and harassing the maid.

It's Henri, she said.

Who is he?

My modeling agent.

Explain.

Bliss sent images and memories to the Visitor: waiting outside the office at the Farnsworth Agency, her portfolio balanced on her knees, breakfast meetings with Henri over cappuccinos at Balthazar before school, walking the runway during New York fashion week, the photo shoots in the Starret-Lehigh lofts, her ad campaigns for Stitched for Civilization, jetting off for shoots in the Caribbean, her photographs on billboards, magazine spreads, plastered on the sides of buses and on top of taxis.

Um, I'm a model? she reminded him.

The cobra relaxed, coils unfurling, forked tongue withdrawn. But a tense wariness remained. The Visitor was not amused.

A model. A living mannequin.

Quickly he reached a decision. *Get rid of him. I have been remiss to let this happen. We shall keep up appearances. No one must suspect you are not you. Do not fail me.*

What do you mean—what do you want me to do?—Bliss asked, but before she could finish, she was *SMACK*, back in her body, completely in control. This was nothing like last week's pathetic attempt to brush her bangs away from her forehead. She had realized how much of herself he was keeping from her, a thought she tried to shelter from him.

It was like coming back to life after being trapped in a coffin. She wobbled like a newborn colt. It was as if the world was coming into focus after years of watching a grainy, fuzzy movie version. She could smell the hollyhocks outside her window, she could taste the salt in the sea air. Her hands—her hands were her own. They felt light and strong, not weighed down and heavy. Her legs were moving; she was walking! She tripped over the rug. Ouch! She pushed herself up and walked more carefully.

But her freedom came at a price, for she sensed him, a presence, in the space just behind (that rear passenger seat), waiting, watching. This is a test, she thought. He wants to see what I'm going to do. I need to pass. . . . Get rid of Henri. But Henri must not suspect anything odd has happened to me.

She opened her bedroom door, savoring the feel of the cold bronze doorknob in her hand, and ran down the stairs.

"Wait! Manuela! Let him in!" she called, running to the foyer. It was a joy to hear her voice out in the world again— her wonderful throaty voice carrying in the air. It sounded different inside her head. She felt like singing.

"Bliss! Bliss!" the bald man cried. Henri looked exactly the same: the same rimless eyeglasses, the same monochromatic wardrobe. He was dressed all in white, in his summer uniform: a linen shirt and matching pants.

"Henri!"

Henri engulfed her in a flutter of air-kisses. "I've been trying to get in touch with you for months! Everyone feels terrible about what happened! Oh My God! I still can't believe it! I'm so glad to see you're okay! Can I come in?"

"Of course." She led him into the sun-drenched sitting room where the family received guests. BobiAnne had gone a little overboard with the nautical theme. Scull oars were hung on the walls, the blue-and-white pillows were trimmed with rope, and there were miniature lighthouses everywhere. Bliss asked the maid to bring refreshments, and settled into the cushions. Playing the grand hostess came easily; it helped that she had been raised to do this all her life. It stopped her from rubbing her bare feet against the throw rug and from bouncing up and down on the cushions.

She was alive! In her own body! Talking to a friend! But she composed her face as carefully as her thoughts. It would not do to look delirious and ecstatic when half her family was dead or missing. That would certainly arouse suspicion.

"First of all, I'm so sorry about BobiAnne," Henri said, taking off his fancy eyeglasses and cleaning the lenses with the edge of his shirt. "You did get our flowers, right? Not that we were expecting a thank-you card or anything. Don't even worry about it."

Flowers? What flowers? Henri looked concerned when Bliss didn't answer, and she immediately covered up for her confusion, reaching for his hand. "Of course! Of course— they were beautiful and so thoughtful." Of course the agency had sent flowers for BobiAnne's memorial.

Through their conversation, Bliss gathered that the papers had explained the deaths of the Conclave by way of a fire at the Almeida villa. Arson was suspected, but with the slow-moving ways of the *polícia*, there was little hope that justice would ever be served.

The maid returned bearing a pitcher of BobiAnne's favorite: Arnold Palmers—half iced tea, half lemonade (made from lemons picked fresh from their orchard).

"I can't believe it's been a year since I've seen you!" Henri said, accepting a frosty glass filled with the amber drink.

A year!

That was a shock. Bliss almost dropped her glass, her hands were shaking so badly. She had had no idea so much time had passed since she was last in control of her body, of her life. No wonder she had so much trouble trying to remember things.

That meant she had missed her last birthday. The year she turned fifteen, her family had celebrated at the Rainbow Room. But there had been no one around to mark her Sweet

Sixteen. Not even herself, she thought dryly. I wasn't even there for my own birthday. A whole year had gone by while she fought to hold on to a semblance of consciousness. She would never get it back, and time was more and more precious now.

A burning anger rose within her—she had been robbed of an entire year!—but again, she suppressed it. She couldn't allow the passenger in the backseat to know how she felt. It was too dangerous. She would have to remain serene.

She turned to her agent, her friend, and tried to pretend she didn't feel like he had just punched her in the stomach.

FOURTEEN

Mimi

awn was breaking over the hillsides. Another fruitless night in the slums. They had scanned every man, woman, and child in the designated area. Tomorrow they would do the same, starting in the northern slums in Jacarezinho. The team's spirits were starting to flag. Mimi didn't think they were ever going to find Jordan. At least not in Rio. Kingsley put on a good show, but Mimi could tell he was frustrated. "My instinct tells me I'm right, that she's here," he said as they walked quickly down through the maze of makeshift stairways cut into the hillside. The narrow streets were empty, save for junkyard dogs and the occasional random rooster.

"The glom says you're wrong, boss," Mimi said. She knew he hated it when she called him that.

He spit out a wad of tobacco, a brown spittle that arched out of his mouth. Impressive, if it weren't so disgusting.

"I wish you wouldn't do that," Mimi said.

"Why not tell me what you wish I would do?" Kingsley smiled.

Mimi did not dignify his teasing with an answer. She wondered what it was like to be a reformed Silver Blood—whatever that meant. Did he still have a soul mate? Did the same rules apply? What did Silver Bloods do, anyway? Did they still need the Red Blood to survive? Or did they just live on caffeine and sugar—which is what Kingsley seemed to subsist on. The guy was skinny, but he could eat a dozen doughnuts in one sitting.

"Cap," Ted Lennox called. "This little girl wants to talk to Force."

It was the same girl who had followed them earlier that evening. The one to whom Mimi had given the stuffed animal, which the little girl was hugging now.

"Sweetheart, what are you doing walking around by yourself?" Mimi asked. "You should be in bed. It's five in the morning."

"*Senhora. Senhora.* You are looking for someone, yes?" she said in halting Portuguese.

Mimi nodded. The Venators had a cover. If anyone asked for the reason they were in the slums, they played policemen on a missing person case.

"Yes. We are," Mimi replied in the girl's native language.

"A little girl like me."

"How did you know?" Mimi asked sharply. That wasn't part of the story. The fiction was that they were looking for a thief, a criminal, an escaped convict, a grown man. No one knew they were looking for a young girl, because then it would cause red herrings in the dreams. If the people knew what they were looking for, they would be sure to dream about it, and it would make the Venators' work that much harder. "How did you know we were looking for a little girl?"

"Because she told me."

"Who told you? Told you what?" Mimi demanded.

The little girl shook her head, looking suddenly afraid.

"Did you scan her?" Kingsley asked with a tilt of his head.

Mimi nodded. That first night they'd arrived, she'd scanned all the kids. There had been nothing. But had she been thorough? Or had she been too gentle? The glom was unpredictable—some humans did not take well to the invasion of their consciousness. If they woke up during a session, there was a chance it could harm them, even drive them insane. Look what had happened to that so-called witness of theirs.

The Venators were skilled and meticulous, and hadn't damaged any Red Bloods so far. But maybe Mimi hadn't wanted to take that chance. Not with this little girl. She had done a cursory examination and had resisted probing the girl's core subconscious.

Sam removed a picture from his pocket. It was Jordan's

school picture. She looked troubled and serious in her plaid uniform. "Have you seen her? Is she the one?"

The little girl nodded, clutching the stuffed puppy to her chest for dear life.

"Well, what do you know? Follow the little children, indeed," Kingsley said.

"Shush!" Mimi chided. Her heart began to pound. Could it be possible that all along, the answer to their quest had been right in front of their noses? Following them every step of the way? When had the kids started following them? They had been there since the beginning, that first night. Could they have missed it because Mimi had been too weak, too much of a soft touch, to have scanned the girl correctly?

"Are you sure? Are you sure you have seen her?" Mimi wanted to shake the girl, although it was really herself she wanted to shake. She had let her feelings for the girl get in the way of her job. And since when did Azrael have feelings?

The little girl nodded. "Yes. That's her. Sophia." She called Jordan by her real name. Mimi felt chills up her spine.

Ted knelt before the girl. "How did you know her?"

"She lived over there," the little girl said. "With her grandma. We were scared of the lady. Sophia too."

"Where is she now?"

"I don't know. They took her."

"Who?"

The girl wouldn't say.

"*Propon familiar,*" Mimi said gently, in the coercive tones of the sacred language. *Tell your friends.* She used compulsion. She didn't want to bring any harm to the girl, but they had to know. "Nothing will happen to you. Tell us what you remember."

"Bad people. A man and a woman. They took her away," the girl said in a flat voice. "On Monday."

The Venators exchanged sharp glances. They had arrived in Rio that day.

"And this grandmother of hers . . . is she still here?" Mimi asked.

"No. She went away a few days later." The little girl looked at them with large, fearful eyes. "Sophia said there would be people coming for her, good people and bad people. We weren't sure what kind you were at first. But she told us the good people would be with a beautiful lady, and you would give me a toy dog," the girl said haltingly.

"She told you we were coming?" Mimi demanded.

"When the good people come, she said to give them this." The little girl removed an envelope from her pocket. It was grubby and streaked with dirt. But the handwriting was beautiful calligraphy script, the kind usually found on ivory envelopes that announced a bonding.

It was addressed to *Araquiel.*

The Angel of Judgment, Mimi knew. Also called the Angel with Two Faces. The angel who carried both dark and light within him.

Kingsley Martin.

FIFTEEN

Schuyler

*T*he look on Jack's face when she broke the glass was a mixture of shock and pride, but Schuyler only allowed herself a quick glimpse. She had to stop thinking about him and concentrate on what she was doing. She had leaped out of the room and into the sky, landing on a trellis and jumping off the roof to the ground. She was running outdoors, in the middle of the party, a blur of pink to the party guests.

It was past midnight and the festivities had taken a darker turn—that moment at every unforgettable gathering when it seems anything and everything is available to anyone and everyone. There was a raucous feeling of wild abandon in the air, as the Bollywood stars shimmied and shook, their bellies undulating in serpentine curves, and a hundred drummers on wooden-barrel dhol drums beat a steady and seductive rhythm. Schuyler couldn't put a finger on it, but there was something almost sinister about how hypnotic the music was, its attraction bordered on menacing. Listening to it was like being tickled too hard—when the tickling stopped being funny and became a form of torture, and the laughter unwelcome and uncontrollable.

She burst through a line of bhangra dancers, cymbals clanging, and knocked down one of the costumed stilt-walkers, barely missing a crew of torchbearers standing guard by the perimeter.

But everywhere she went, he was right behind her. A heartbeat away.

Schuyler!

She heard his voice clearly in her mind. Jack would use the glom on her. It wasn't fair. If he had said her name out loud, maybe she would forgive him, but to know that he was in her mind—that it came as easily to him as before—was unnerving.

She ran past tiger tamers and fire-eaters, past a group of drunken European nobles fat with blood, their human familiars left to swoon by the river walls. This wasn't a party anymore, this was something else. Something *evil* and depraved . . . an orgy, a paean to monstrous indulgence, pernicious and wicked. And Schuyler couldn't help but feel that there was something—or someone—egging everyone on, right to the edge of disaster. And still she could hear Jack's footsteps, light and quick behind her.

In a way the chase invigorated her: running so fast,

using her vampire muscles and exerting them in ways they had never been used—by god he was fast! But I am faster, she thought. I can outrun you, Jack Force. Just try; you'll never catch me.

I can and I will.

Schuyler closed her mind to the glom as Lawrence had taught her. That would shut him out.

There had to be somewhere she could hide. She knew this place. Cordelia had left her here for hours when they visited, and as a child she had explored every inch of its sprawling grounds. She knew every crevice, every secret hiding place—she would lose him in the residential wing—there were so many camouflaged closets and clandestine compartments—she ran back inside the castle through the servants' entrance.

While she ran she sent a message of her own through the glom.

Oliver!

Oliver!

She tried to locate his signal—*Oliver!*

But humans were not as sensitive to the glom's twilight communications. Oliver had never been able to read her mind, let alone speak to it directly. And while they had tried to practice building the mental bridge that tied a vampire to its human Conduit, they had faltered in their exercise. They were young, and a bridge took a lifetime to build, like the one between Lawrence Van Alen and Christopher

Anderson. Maybe in fifty years they would be able to communicate telepathically, but not now.

She had to find Oliver. He was probably sick with worry. Probably pacing the party, ignoring the fireworks, drinking too many cocktails to steady his nerves. He had given up so much to be with her. Of course he would tell her it was his duty, his very destiny to live and die by her side. But still she could not stop feeling that she was a burden to him, that she had brought too much on him—had fated him to live in an endless chase. He had given her everything—his friendship, his fortune, his life—and all she could give in return was her heart. Her fickle, foolish, guilty, unreliable heart. She hated herself.

A terrible thought struck her: What if they had gotten to Oliver first? They wouldn't hurt him, she thought. Just let them try . . . If anything had happened to him . . . She did not want to think about it.

As she ran through the hallway, everything suddenly went black. Someone had turned off all the lights in the palace. She had a feeling she knew who that someone was.

Fine, but like you, Jack, I can see in the dark. She found the door that led to a secret staircase that led down to the basement, past the kitchens, and into the lower dungeons, a relic from an earlier century. Not many knew that the Hôtel Lambert had been built on the ruins of a medieval castle, and that the castle's foundation hid layers of secrets.

Oh god, please don't let that have been a skeleton I just

stepped over, Schuyler thought as her sandaled foot landed on something that crunched in a disturbing way.

She could see the outlines of the steps, ruined and steep, down, down, she had to go down . . . She had to get away.

Oliver!

Nothing.

She would have to send for him later somehow.

Because she was there at last. In the very lowest depths of the dungeon, in the solitary prison cell that had housed who knows how many prisoners, who knows how many miserable souls behind its iron bars.

He'll never find me here.

She felt dizzy and light-headed, and her whole body was trembling uncontrollably as she stepped inside.

And fell straight into the arms of her former love and current pursuer.

Jack Force.

His grip was like a vise. His voice was colder than the air around them.

"I told you, Schuyler, you're not the only one who knows the secrets of the Hôtel Lambert."

SIXTEEN

Bliss

The good thing about fashion people is that they were usually oblivious to other people's reactions. So Henri never noticed Bliss's agitation as he chatted about the latest gossip back in New York. Most of the news was so gloomy: what magazines had folded, what designers were out of business. "It's awful right now, just awful." Henri shook his head. "But you know, life goes on . . . and our motto is Never surrender. There's still work out there," he said with a well-meaning glance. "I mean, I know it's a lot to ask of you, and I completely understand if you're not ready . . . ?" He peered at her over his glasses.

It was only then that Bliss realized with a start that Henri was talking about her going back to work.

Sensing her hesitation, which he took as a sign of surrender, Henri went straight into business mode, setting down his glass and picking up his BlackBerry. "It's nothing too difficult, just something easy to get back in the swing of things. You know Muffie Astor Carter's yearly fashion show for charity? She hosts it on their estate out on the East End?"

Bliss did. Her stepmother used to complain that Muffie never gave her a front row seat even though BobiAnne always ordered a trunkload of clothes at the show.

"You'd be perfect for it. Can I tell her you'll do it?" Henri wheedled.

"I don't know . . ." Modeling. How precious it seemed now, how trivial. How much fun it would be to go back to that old life—go-sees, fittings, gossiping with the hairstylists and having designers fawn over you, getting your makeup done, going to parties—did this mean that life was still open to her? She had completely given up thinking about it. Had totally assumed that that life was over, given what had happened. But what had the Visitor said? *No one must suspect.* After all, it had been a year. No one would fault her for going back to work, would they?

And wasn't the best way to deal with grief and loss to find something to distract you? And what could be more distracting than a big, silly, frivolous fashion show? As Henri had said, look at those people who had lost a lot of other people's money and caused the crash—weren't they all going about their lives as if nothing had happened? Hosting charity benefits and shopping at Hermès while the victims of their financial recklessness cried into their crystal wineglasses?

She remembered a young widow, a teacher from Duchesne, who had gone back to teaching after her husband passed away suddenly. Going back to work, going back to her old life . . . it suddenly seemed . . . not impossible.

Get rid of him, the Visitor had ordered. Well, giving Henri what he wanted was the surest way to secure his exit. As soon as her agent was assured he had his old client back, he was certain to announce he had pressing concerns elsewhere. Asking about her welfare was probably just a pretense to see if he could book her for the show.

"Okay," she said, taking a deep breath and letting it out in a long exhale.

"Okay?" Henri raised an eyebrow.

"Okay." Bliss smiled.

After saying good-bye to her old taskmaster, Bliss sat alone on the couch for a moment. At some point during Henri's visit she had sensed a change in herself. The Visitor was gone. The backseat was empty, as far as she could tell. Perhaps she had passed the test. In any event, like Elvis, he had left the building. But he had left the door open. He had unwittingly given her back the key to her own body. Or had forgotten to take it back. Like a parent who leaves the keys to the Ferrari on the table. Just like in that old movie she used to watch when she was little when it would run on the USA channel . . . someone's day off. The kid had crashed the Ferrari through the window. She wouldn't do anything that stupid, of course. It was her own body. She had little time and had to use it wisely.

She decided to take a bath, and walked upstairs. Each of the ten bedrooms in the house had its own spacious bathroom, and BobiAnne had allowed Bliss to help design her own. It was a pretty space: all warm travertine marble and flattering incandescent lighting. She turned on the faucet and filled the antique claw tub, squeezing in a generous dollop of her favorite scented bath gel. Then she quickly shed her clothes and climbed in, delighting in the soapy bubbles and the slick sensation of warm water running down her bare back.

Afterward she put on one of the fluffy Turkish robes her stepmother had stocked for the house, and went downstairs to the kitchen, where she asked the cook to make her lunch. She ate a cheeseburger—rare, the juices running out and mixing with the French mustard in a way that always made her happy she was a carnivore.

Only then did Bliss realize she wasn't hungry in the real sense. The vampire sense. The old bloodlust was muted. The craving was gone. What did it mean?

She pushed the empty plate away and ran her hand through her hair. She would have to make an appointment at the salon as soon as possible. The Visitor wanted her to keep up appearances, didn't he? Keeping up appearances was something that came naturally to Forsyth Llewellyn's daughter.

When your father was a senator from New York, scrutiny was impossible to avoid.

SEVENTEEN

Mimi

ingsley's face was unreadable, and Mimi could stand it no longer. "So? What? She's gone to a Miley Cyrus concert? She's written a cell phone novel? What does it say?"

He quieted her with a look and showed them the letter. One line, written in the same beautiful calligraphy. *Phoebus ostend praeeo.*

Phoebus was the name of the sun king in the old tongue, Mimi knew, and the rest was easy enough to understand. "The sun shall show the way," she said. "What does it mean?"

In answer, Kingsley folded up the note carefully and tucked it into his jacket pocket.

He has no idea, does he, Mimi thought. "Why would the Watcher take the trouble to send us a note but then have the note be nonsense?" she asked, annoyed. "And how did she know I was coming? And bringing a stuffed toy?"

"You forget. The Watcher can see into the future. If she was being held by Silver Bloods—as she surely was—she must have felt threatened enough to allow only the most cryptic of communications."

"It's a riddle. A clue," Ted said suddenly. "A clue to her whereabouts. 'The sun shall show the way.'" It was the longest sentence he had said in a year. Even Sam looked surprised to find his brother so garrulous.

Kingsley nodded. "Of course. Sophia always did say wisdom had to be earned."

A riddle. Great. A year of tracking down the Watcher, and when they finally get somewhere, they find some kind of one-eyed sphinx blocking the path. Could it have hurt her to have written *Am being held captive at 101 Favela Lane! Come soon and bring a Luna Bar!* Or was that just too much to ask?

You make light of trivial matters, Kingsley sent.

Just trying to keep things interesting, Mimi telepathed in return. *And get out of my head. You don't belong here.*

Meanwhile, the other Venators were deep in the glom, consulting their memories, trying to ascertain the meaning behind the words. Finally, Ted opened his eyes and spoke. "There's a bar not too far away called El Sol de Ajuste. The Setting Sun."

"So?" Mimi said.

"It's an old Silver Blood expression—the setting sun describes Lucifer's fall to Earth," Kingsley explained. "That could be it."

Right, Mimi remembered. Lucifer was the Prince of Heaven. The Morningstar. It made sense that to the Silver Bloods, his doom was akin to the setting sun.

"Well, what are we waiting for?" Mimi asked. "We've got a missing Watcher to find, and I don't know about you guys, but I need a drink."

EIGHTEEN

Schuyler

"There's nothing to fear. Please don't run from me again." Jack's breath was hot in her ear, and Schuyler felt each word as a caress. But his hands did not release their hold, his fingers gripped tightly around her arms.

"Let me go!" she said. "You're hurting me." She gasped, even though, to her surprise, her tremors had lessened the moment he'd touched her.

She felt his grip loosen, and part of her sagged a little that he had given in so quickly. That damnable, hateful part of her that missed his touch the moment it was withdrawn. She hugged herself, trying not to feel so abandoned. Why did she feel this way? She was the one who had spurned him. She was the one who had left. Jack was nothing to her now. Nothing.

"I'm sorry," he whispered. "What's wrong? Are you okay?" He looked at her carefully. "You're trembling."

"It's just this thing . . . I get shaky sometimes . . . it's nothing," she said. She turned to face him directly. "Anyway, I'm not going back. I'm not going back to New York."

To her surprise, Jack suddenly looked relieved, as if a great weight had been lifted from his shoulders. "Is that why you've been running? Because you thought I was taking you back to New York? That's not why I'm here at all."

Now it was her turn to be confused. "Then why?"

"You really don't know?" Jack asked.

She shook her head.

"You're in danger here, Schuyler," he said, looking around warily. "There are Silver Bloods all around. Can't you feel them? Their hunger?"

The minute he said it, she could feel exactly what he was talking about—that deep and consuming voraciousness, an unabated wanting. So that's what she'd felt at the party, a bottomless appetite of greed and sex and desire, that spellbinding siren call to depravity. It hummed in the background, like a noise you couldn't make out but knew was there. *Croatan.* So she did have reason to be afraid. She had felt it.

Jack had backed her into a corner of the prison cell, and Schuyler was starting to feel claustrophobic in the small space. She knew instinctively that many souls had suffered and died in the same place she was standing now. She could feel the primal pain, an unmistakable sense of injustice. Back then prisoners were sent to the dungeons to die—rotting underground, never to see the sun.

How funny that the Conspiracy made humans believe vampires feared the sun, when the opposite was true. They had loved it so much they had been exiled from heaven because of their love of Lucifer's light.

Schuyler shivered as Jack continued to explain. "The party has been compromised. They're here for you."

"But why do the Silver Bloods even care about me? What's so important about me?" Schuyler asked, trying not to sound petulant and self-pitying. Why her? She hadn't chosen this. All she'd ever wanted was to be left in peace, but it was as if she had been born already a target.

When Jack answered, it was with the assurance and gravity of a much older presence, revealing a small glimpse into the very ancient creature behind the young vampire mask. What had Lawrence called him? *Abbadon.* The Angel of Destruction. The Angel of the Apocalypse. One of the most fearsome of Lucifer's former generals.

"The cycles are the key to our existence; they guarantee our continued invisibility in the human world. According to the Code, the expression of each spirit is closely monitored and recorded. There are lists and rules that govern who is called up, and by whom and when. There was no record of Allegra being allowed to bear a daughter in this cycle. So the mere fact that you were born was already a violation."

From birth she had been a mistake, Schuyler thought. Her mother . . . that still, silent figure in the hospital bed . . . why did she choose to have me? Schuyler wondered.

"But so what? That still doesn't explain it. Why would they even care about that? What's it to them? It doesn't make sense."

"I know," Jack sighed.

"You're not telling me everything," Schuyler realized. He was protecting her. "Tell me the truth. There has to be a reason why they've been trying to kill me."

Jack hung his head. Finally he spoke. "A long time ago, during the crisis in Rome, the Pistis Sophia saw the future. She said that one day, the irrevocable bond between the Uncorrupted would break. That Gabrielle would spurn Michael and bear a daughter with a Red Blood. And that daughter would be the death of the Silver Bloods. Sophia has never been wrong."

"So I'm their death?" Schuyler found it absurdly funny. "Me? They're scared . . . of me?" A half-hysterical yelp escaped before she could stop herself. It was so absolutely ridiculous. What could she do to harm *them*? As the Inquisitor had pointed out, she had used her mother's sword and *missed*. She might be fast and strong and light, but she was not a fighter, not a warrior, not a soldier.

Jack crossed his arms. "It's nothing to laugh about. Leviathan would have killed you right there that night in Rio if he had known who you were. And now that he knows he was so close and failed to kill you, he's tracked you down here to finish the job."

"But how do you know Leviathan has tracked me?"

"Because I have been tracking Leviathan," Jack said grimly. "My father and I have been tracking him for months."

"Charles is here?" she asked. She wondered why the news did not make her feel safer. Charles Force was the greatest of them all. He was Michael, Pure of Heart, the Valiant, Prince of the Angels, Supreme Commander of the Lord's Army. She had been looking for Charles herself, and to know that he was here in Paris, and as her protector—or one of them, anyway—should have gladdened her heart. But it did not. Charles Force was not a friend. He was not an enemy, but he was not a friend either.

But maybe now she would be able to find out what Lawrence had asked her to do. Charles would have to tell her about the Van Alen Legacy. Schuyler had to know. She owed her grandfather that much.

Jack nodded. "Yes. He decided to come himself when the Conclave would not send the Venators after Leviathan following your testimony. We have been one step and two cities behind him for months. When Leviathan led us here, to this party, we thought he was after the countess, as she was instrumental in bringing about his imprisonment on Corcovado. But when we saw you in the ballroom, we suddenly knew what his real intentions were. Charles sent me to make sure you were safe while he took care of Leviathan himself."

So basically she was in danger from the baddest demon

around. Wonderful. She was running from the Venators when she probably should have been running *toward* them, now that she knew what was truly after her.

"So you believe me? You believe that I didn't kill Lawrence like the Conclave thinks?" Schuyler asked.

He looked down. "I can't speak for the Conclave. But I have always believed you. I've always believed in you," he said softly.

"Right." She nodded, trying to appear businesslike, to hide the fact that she had been moved by his faith. Jack believed her. He was on her side. He didn't hate her, at least. He didn't hate her for breaking his heart. "So what now?"

"First things first," he said briskly. "Let's get out of this dungeon. I was worried you would choose this place to hide. And I think you've noticed it smells pretty awful down here."

NINETEEN

Bliss

uffie Astor Carter (real name Muriel) was a Blue Blood in every sense of the word. She was educated at Miss Porter's and Vassar, and had worked in the publicity department of Harry Winston before marrying Dr. Sheldon Carter, who had found fame as *the* plastic surgeon to the Park Avenue set. Their bonding was one of the more controversial ones in recent memory, as it had taken each quite a few attempts to find the other. He was her second husband and she his third wife.

She was also one of New York's most popular socialites. Jealous rivals sniped that the public just took a liking to her name. It was so outrageously preppie it sounded like a joke. But it was not; it was the real thing, like Muffie herself, who embodied a horsey, Bedford, WASP authenticity in an age of brash nouveau-riche hordes adding "von" or "de" to their names and who didn't know a Verdura from a Van Cleef.

Every year Muffie opened up her sprawling Hamptons estate, "Ocean's End," for a fashion show to benefit the New York Blood Bank. It was the highlight of the August social calendar. Located at the end of Gin Lane, the property sprawled over six acres and included a manor house with a separate and equally lavish guesthouse, a twelve-car garage, and staff quarters. The sweeping grounds featured two pools (saline and freshwater), tennis courts, a lily pond, and professionally maintained gardens. The Bermuda grass was cut by hand, with scissors, every other day, to keep it at just the right length.

When Bliss arrived for the event early on Sunday afternoon, she found a caravan of European sports cars idling on the valet line. It had been a week since Henri had come to the house. So far, the Visitor had not found disfavor in her actions to reclaim her identity and to keep their cover. She had been able to get a haircut, shop for a few new clothes, and even attend a pilates class or two. Even if vampire muscles were supernaturally strong, they still needed to be *toned*. While the Visitor seemed content with the new arrangement, there were times when he would suddenly return, sending her back to the empty void. He was like a carjacker, Bliss thought, waving a shotgun and rudely shoving her to the backseat of her mind.

But he had been gone since morning, and Bliss was glad to be among people again, *getting out of her own head*, so to speak. Bliss found the only way to deal with what was happening to her was to laugh about it. She'd discovered a streak of black humor she didn't know she had. She was still smiling as she handed her keys to the valet. She'd driven up in one of the house cars—what the family called the cars "assigned" to each of their homes. In Palm Beach the Llewellyns kept a stable of classic cars—a Rolls Royce Phantom, a 1955 Bentley, and a pristine 1969 Lincoln Continental. In New York they had added a fleet of black SUVs, once BobiAnne realized the Silver Shadow Rolls was too showy for Manhattan.

In the Hamptons they kept several Mercedes SLK convertibles of early-nineties vintage—somehow the most ubiquitous car on the East End. BobiAnne always tried to fit in as much as possible. Bliss had chosen the candy-apple red one to match her good mood. Might as well enjoy the cars now. She had no idea how much longer they would own them, as Forsyth was selling them along with the house so they could at least keep their penthouse in the city.

She walked toward the front of the house, where Balthazar Verdugo, the designer whose fall collection was being shown that day, stood at the head of the receiving line next to the party's hostess. Balthazar was very popular with his clients—he had even married one. He smelled of coconut oil and too much hair gel. Bliss had never liked him or his clothes—they were a bit fussy for her taste—but she made the usual small talk. "Isn't it a lovely day? So looking forward to wearing the clothes! Thanks so much for having me! Who's this little cutie?" she said brightly, petting the miniature Chihuahua nestled in the crook of the designer's arms.

Balthazar shook Bliss's hand with a limp handshake and passed her on to Muffie with a wan smile.

"I'm so glad to see you looking so well, my dear," Muffie said, giving Bliss the most insubstantial of embraces. Muffie had a broad, recessed forehead with nary a wrinkle (her plastic-surgeon husband's most effective advertising) and the perfect blond coif pervasive on the Upper East Side. She was the epitome of the breed: tanned, slender, graceful, and appropriate. She was everything BobiAnne had wanted to be but could never match.

"Thank you," Bliss said, trying not to feel too awkward. "It's good to be here."

"You'll find the rest of the models in the back. I think we're running late as usual," Muffie said cheerfully.

Bliss walked toward the backstage area of the tent, swiping a canapé from a tray and a glass of champagne from one of the buffet tables.

Henri was right: this was an easy gig. It wasn't a real fashion show, merely a presentation to wealthy clients in the name of charity. Whereas a real fashion show was a chaotic commotion of energy and anxiety, attended by hundreds of editors, retailers, celebrities, and covered by hundreds of media outlets around the world, the Balthazar Verdugo show on Muffie Carter's estate was more like a glorified trunk show, with models.

It was so odd to be back in the real world, to be walking on damp grass (sinking in her heels, really), munching on appetizers, and looking out at the Carters' amazing ocean view—an unbroken line of blue stretching over the horizon—and to find out that in some parts of the world, even *their* world—the world of the Committee and the Coven—there were some who remained indifferent and downright *disinterested* in what had happened in Rio.

Muffie and the other women on the Committee whom Bliss bumped into at the party did not bring up BobiAnne's death or the massacre of the Conclave. Bliss understood that they simply went on about their lives: planning parties, hosting benefits, doing the rounds of couture shows, horse shows, and charity causes, which filled their days. They did not seem too worried or distressed. Cordelia Van Alen had been right: they were in the deepest denial. They didn't want to accept the return of the Silver Bloods. They didn't want to accept the *reality* of what the Silver Bloods had done and were planning to do. They were satisfied with their lives and they didn't want anything to change.

It had been so long since any of them had been warriors, soldiers, arm-in-arm and side-by-side in battle against the Dark Prince and his legions. It was hard to imagine this group of underfed overly Botoxed socialites and their slacker children as hardened warriors in a war for heaven and earth. It was as Cordelia had said to Schuyler: the vampires were getting lazy and indulgent, more and more like humans every day, and less inclined to fulfill their heavenly destiny.

It dawned on Bliss that this was what had set Cordelia and Lawrence apart—they *cared*. They had kept their vigilance against the forces of hell and had sounded an alarm. An alarm that no one was too keen on hearing. The Van Alens were the exception to the norm. It only made sense that Schuyler would be just like them. Her friend had never felt comfortable in the world of the leisured rich, even though she had been born into it. But Schuyler wasn't the only one. Even Mimi and Jack Force were different. They had not forgotten their gloried past. Just one look at the way Mimi flaunted her extraordinary vampire abilities was enough to convince anyone that there was more to that skinny bitch than just the capacity to shop.

But these people—this self-satisfied group of elites who had barely even blinked at the news of the massacre—*these* people called themselves vampires?

Exactly. Just like the members of the Conclave, they will be easy enough to overcome when the time comes.

Bliss shivered. She had gotten used to being alone, and had forgotten that the Visitor could pop in at any time.

What do you mean? What is in store for them?

But the Visitor did not respond.

TWENTY

Mimi

El Sol de Ajuste was located in Cidada de Deus, The City of God, the notorious slums in the western part of the city that had inspired a major Hollywood movie and a subsequent television show, *City of Men*. Of course, the real city was nothing like the cleaned-up Hollywood version, which was the equivalent of a "slum tour" arranged by hotel concierges: showcasing fashionable grittiness. The reality of poverty was much harsher and much uglier—the towering mountains of trash, the stench of sewer and garbage, the bare-bottomed children languishing on the streets, smoking cigarettes; the way no one batted the flies away—they were way past caring about something so simple as *flies*.

The bar was nothing more than a tin shack, a lean-to with a roof and a wooden counter pocked with holes. When Mimi and the boys arrived, a group of rowdy toughs were harassing the barback, the boy who cleaned the counters and sopped up the spilled beer with ragged towels. Mimi recognized the fierce-looking tattoos branded on the gang members' cheeks: they were members of Commando Prata, Silver Command, a notorious street gang, and responsible for most of the criminal activity in this part of the ghetto. This was going to be interesting.

"*Você deve três pesos!*" the barback insisted. You owe me three pesos.

"*Caralho! Vai-te foder!*" The fat one laughed and cursed at the boy, pushing him against the wall.

The elderly proprietor stood behind the table, looking frightened and annoyed to find his employee being harassed, as well as finding his small establishment suddenly crawling with strange, black-clad foreigners.

"Can I help you?" he huffed in Portuguese, keeping an eye on the kid. "You! Leave him alone!" he cried as one of the gangsters tripped the boy, sending him falling facedown on the floor.

In answer, the fat bully gave the cowering boy a sharp kick in the head. There was a sickening crunch of a steel-toe boot against bone, and in a quick movement, one of the gang had a knife to the bartender's throat. "You got something to say to us, old man?"

"Put down the blade," Kingsley ordered in a quiet voice.

"Piss off," the leader said. He was a skinny kid with a

pockmarked face sitting in the back. He held up his automatic weapon as casually as a soda can. The local drug lords acted as an unofficial police presence in the shantytowns, playing judge and executioner at their whim. But the only law they upheld was their own.

"Happy to, as soon as you let these good people go," Kingsley said smoothly. There were twenty gang members and only four Venators, hardly a fair fight for the sorry group of Red Bloods. If the vampires wanted to, they could destroy everyone in the room without warning. Mimi could see it already: a pile of corpses on the floor.

She felt her blood rise to the challenge, but it was a superficial rise—the kind of shallow excitement one felt upon watching a boxing match when you already knew the outcome. These thugs thought they were so tough, but they were nothing: fleas on the backs of buffalo, hyenas before lions. Mimi wished for better sport, a bigger challenge.

The street gangs were not afraid of the foreigners, however, and were faster than the Venators gave them credit for. Before Kingsley could turn around he was cut with a blade, a tear on his sleeve revealing an ugly wound.

That was enough. Mimi spun around, kicking two of them to the ground and forcing another to his knees. She was about to draw *Eversor Lumen*, Light-Destroyer, when she heard Kingsley's voice in her head.

No weapons! No deaths!

As much as it pained her, she kept her blade sheathed. Two burly gangsters tried to bum-rush her, but she ducked from their assault, sending them crashing against the rickety tables. Another drew his gun, but before he could shoot, Mimi had kicked it away with her heel. *Cake.* She could tell even the Lennox brothers were enjoying themselves as they knocked heads and vanquished their attackers. Watching dreams and validating memories didn't compare to a good old-fashioned fistfight.

One of the thugs picked up a chair leg and pointed it straight at Kingsley's chest, but Mimi slashed it into pieces before it could meet its target.

"Thanks," Kingsley said. "Didn't know you cared so much." He grinned as he made quick work of a boy holding an Uzi.

Mimi laughed. She'd hardly broken a sweat, although she was breathing heavily. As Kingsley ordered, their combatants would live to see another day. She stepped over the heap of bodies, Ted helping her over to join them by the bar.

The bartender came out from underneath a table, bowing in gratitude. "What can I get you?"

"What's the specialty of this place?" Kingsley asked.

"Ah!" The bartender shot them a toothless grin. "Get the Leblon," he told the barback, whose cut had stopped bleeding. The boy disappeared into the back closet and came out bearing a bottle of *cachaça*: sugarcane rum. The bartender poured it into four shot glasses.

"Breakfast." Kingsley nodded and picked up his glass.

"*Saude*," Mimi said, downing her drink in one go. To your health.

"We're looking for this girl. Have you seen her?" Kingsley asked, showing their new friends Jordan's photograph. "Tell us," he said, using a small compulsion.

The boy shook his head, while the bartender looked at the picture for a long time. Then he too shook his head slowly. "I have never seen her in my life. But this is not a place where people bring children."

Mimi and Kingsley exchanged glances, and the twins' shoulders slumped slightly. They left the bar after finishing the bottle. It was midday. The sun was high and the weather was at a broil. A few curious onlookers had crowded around the bar entrance, drawn by the fight, but they kept a fair distance from the foursome. The stares were respectful. No one had ever lived to defeat the Silver Command.

"For you," an elderly lady said, handing Mimi a water bottle. "*Obrigado*." The woman crossed herself, and Mimi understood it as a gesture of gratitude for bringing a small measure of justice to a lawless place.

"Thank you," Mimi said, accepting the water with a nod. Once again she was struck by how helpless she felt.

These people's problems are not your own, she told herself. *You cannot help them.*

She felt very far away from the sheltered, exclusive world of the Upper East Side as she stood on a dusty sidewalk in the slums, her muscles still tense from the encounter. This was why she had signed up for the mission, to shake up her life a little bit—to see a side of the world that wasn't available from the backseat of a limousine. She might be a spoiled princess in this incarnation, but she was a warrior by nature. Azrael *needed* this.

But it was frustrating. They'd set out a year ago to find the Watchers and still had nothing to show for their efforts, save for a letter that didn't tell them anything.

"Maybe the Watcher doesn't want to be found," Mimi said, taking a chug of water and passing it to Kingsley. "Ever think of that?"

"It's possible," he said after taking a gulp and throwing the bottle to one of the Lennoxes. "But unlikely. She knows how valuable her wisdom is to our community. She knew they would send me to find her. Believe me, she wants to be found."

"Let me see the note again," Mimi said. Kingsley handed her the piece of paper. She reread the note. As she held up the paper, she noticed something she hadn't seen before. Something that had been hidden in the dawn, when it had been too dark to see clearly.

"Look," she said to Kingsley, holding the note up so it was facing the direct rays of the sun.

Sunlight shone brightly through the paper, revealing something that had formerly been invisible, like a water-mark. *Phoebus ostend praeeo*, indeed. The sun shall show the way.

In the middle of the page was a map.

TWENTY-ONE

Schuyler

"It's this way," Jack said. "When I was a kid, the cooks used to chase me out of here." He showed Schuyler the secret passageways that twisted through the building's vast storerooms underneath the castle.

Historically, the home had been built to accommodate an entire court of nobles. There was a full servants' wing, and the kitchens and pantries went down three levels. When the count was still alive, the royal couple had hosted lavish monthlong parties for guests and their entourages. The castle was meant to sustain what had become an increasingly outdated, not to mention incredibly expensive, lifestyle. No wonder the developers planned to chop it up into apartments—living with a staff of sixty had become untenable even to the countess, who was moving to her villa in Saint-Tropez with a much more moderate household.

But while the property boasted dozens of hidden rooms

and mazelike passageways, in the end there was only one way out of the Hôtel Lambert. Everyone, from the highest ranking nobleman to the humblest kitchen steward, had to go through the central courtyard and out the main gates. Jack and Schuyler found they didn't have a choice: they would have to walk through the vipers' nest to freedom.

The staircase from the servants' quarters led straight into the main hall, where Jack and Schuyler could hear the sounds of hysterical laughter and uncontrollable gaiety, which sounded more overwrought and frantic as the dizzying music gained speed and volume.

"What are they doing?" Schuyler whispered as they huddled behind one of the fluted columns. "Why do I feel . . . like . . . like I want to . . . to hurt someone?"

"It's what the Silver Bloods do—they *push*—they use the glom like we do, except they push in the opposite direction. They bring out the worst in people."

"Shouldn't we warn everyone?" she asked.

"This isn't Rio. There are too many of us to overpower; the Silver Bloods will not risk anything more dangerous than compulsion. They are only here for you," Jack said, trying to blunt the difficulty of their situation with another reassuring smile.

Schuyler did not want to be swallowed up by her fear, and steadied herself by concentrating on fighting the rising overwhelming sickness she felt from the Silver Bloods' spell.

They had to find Oliver, and then they had to get out of here as quietly as possible. She had made a huge ruckus in running away from Jack, but the over-the-top antics of the Bollywood musical numbers had covered up most of that. The guests had figured she was part of the show, especially given the way she was dressed. In her sari she had blended right in.

"Here," Jack said, handing her a small silver crucifix on a chain. "It should help." He pulled out a similar one from underneath his shirt. "Part of the Venator uniform."

They crept out to the garden and found Oliver standing by himself under a majestic beech tree, holding a drink. If he was surprised to see Schuyler with Jack, he didn't show it except for a slight raise of his eyebrows, although it pained Schuyler to notice that a little light went out in his eyes when he saw them together.

It's not what you think, she wanted to tell him. *I love you.*

Regardless, when Oliver turned to Jack, he was genial and gave him an overly hearty handshake. "Good to see you, man. Been a long time."

For his part, Jack shook Oliver's hand with a firm grip. The two of them were intent on acting as if they had bumped into each other at the Senior Fling. Just a bunch of Upper East Side preppies catching up on news and gossip. "So what brings you here, Force? Not the Conclave I hope," Oliver said, his light tone masking a wary undercurrent.

"Not at all," Jack said, as Schuyler quickly brought Oliver up to speed.

Once apprised, Oliver immediately understood the danger they were in. "So, what do you guys have in mind?" he asked them. "I have a feeling we're not going to be able to get out of here quietly."

"So far they haven't noticed that Schuyler is not in that room waiting for the countess anymore," Jack said, looking around. "I think we can make it to Lu—" But before Jack could finish his sentence, he stopped, looking up with a startled expression on his face.

Schuyler glanced over his shoulder. The Baron de Coubertin had reappeared on the other side of the courtyard. But there was something different about him. Changed. Even from afar, Schuyler could see that his eyes were rimmed in crimson fire. Silver pupils.

Leviathan.

He stood immobile, scanning the room with those dreadful silver eyes.

Schuyler turned to Oliver and saw that he had noticed him too. Oliver's face was ashen. "I let you go off with him—I was so stupid—I knew something was wrong. . . . When I spoke to him at the boat he was different, jolly even. I should have known something wasn't right."

"I didn't see it either, Ollie. There's no way you would have known," she said. Silver Bloods were agile shape shifters,

Schuyler remembered her grandfather telling her. Leviathan had locked her in that room, probably intending to dispose of her later. She shuddered to think of what they were planning to do with her.

"Listen, I'll only slow you down, but maybe I can slow them down," Oliver said, taking off his turban and throwing it on the ground.

"No!" Schuyler said. "We're getting out of this together or we're not getting out at all! Oliver! Listen to me!" she begged, a dawning horror as she realized what he was planning to do.

"Too late," Oliver said as he picked up a nearby torch and ran toward the entrance guarded by the elephants. "Come and get me!" he cried, waving it back and forth in a crazed manner. The elephants reared back on their hind legs, throwing off the King and Queen of Siam, and ran amuck through the bushes, chasing Oliver. The mahouts yelled, and befuddled party guests ran in every direction, trying to get away from the rampaging beasts.

"Quick!" Jack said. "Before they close the gates." He held out his hand.

"But . . . Oliver!" Schuyler lurched around. "Oliver, no! Oliver!"

"He's human; they don't want him—Schuyler, we've got to get you out of here! Please!" Jack said, holding out his hand.

"No! I can't! I can't leave him!" She watched as Oliver ran farther and farther away, the elephants charging right behind him.

But staying there wouldn't help Oliver. Not right now. And she was just putting them in more danger by hesitating. She wanted to run after Oliver, but she let Jack lead her away. They ran, ducking confused torchbearers and catering staff, dodging rampaging elephants, screaming party guests, and dazed servers. She could feel the wrath of the demon Leviathan, could feel his eyes boring at the back of her skull, a heavy, deliberate malevolence.

In a moment he would be upon them.

But unlike fighting, running was something Schuyler could do well, and together she and Jack flew across the cobbled courtyard and through the main gates. She looked over her shoulder one last time and caught a glimpse of Oliver's raised arm as he disappeared into the rioting throng.

He was waving good-bye.

TWENTY-TWO

Bliss

*T*he fashion show went well. Bliss managed to do her two turns on the runway without incident, even though she was still rattled by hearing the Visitor's menacing voice in her head. What was he planning? What did he mean "they will be easy enough to overcome . . ."? But then, she knew what he'd meant, didn't she? Wasn't she just in denial about everything? Because there had to be a reason for the Visitor's presence in her life; it wasn't as if he was just hanging around so he could get to know his dear daughter better, was he? There was a reason he was here.

And whatever reason that was, she was involved because, for all intents and purposes, *she* was him. Whatever the Visitor did or did not do, they wouldn't see Lucifer behind it—they would only see Bliss. Well, maybe she could do something about it. Maybe she should make the effort to find out what the Visitor was doing when he was away.

Maybe it would be a good idea not to be left in the dark so much.

She massaged her temples. Thankfully, most of the other models had left her alone. They knew her story, and no one ventured to give her more than a few sympathetic looks. Bliss thought she might as well have the word "SURVIVOR" stamped on her forehead from the way the girls whispered about her. *Stepmother murdered. Sister missing . . . presumed killed . . . Awful . . . These things do happen in Rio, don't they?*

Bliss thought that was terribly unfair. What had happened to her family had nothing to do with the country they were in, but of course she couldn't tell anyone that. She just wanted to get out here. She changed out of her final outfit—a tulle ball gown that some grande dame would wear to the opening of the ballet in the fall—and put her plain white sundress back on. She was walking across the green lawn, ducking a few familiar faces and hoping she could just get back home without having to talk to anyone, when she heard her name being called.

"Bliss? Is that you? Hey!" A pretty girl with long blond hair, wearing a floppy straw hat and a chic one-shouldered dress, walked over.

Bliss recognized the girl immediately. She was Allison Ellison—or Ally Elli, as she was called—one of the Red Bloods from Duchesne.

Ally was a scholarship kid; her parents lived in Queens or

something, and she had to take some kind of two-hour bus to get to school. Bliss had assumed that meant Ally would be terribly unpopular, but she was the complete opposite. The Upper East Side kids dug her crazy outerborough stories and her funny way of looking at things. Bliss remembered that one time she and Mimi and a large group of people went out with Ally, and Ally made sure everyone paid exactly what they owed at the table—down to the last cent. No one got away with the whole "I forgot my wallet; you know you can hit me up next time" crap that trust-fund kids like Mimi always pulled.

It was one thing to see Ally at school, and another to see her at Muffie Astor Carter's annual Shopping, Champagne, and Charity party. What was she doing here, wearing an original Balthazar Verdugo, sure to have cost five figures at least, looking like she had always summered in Southampton?

Bliss got her answer when Jamie Kip came up to give Ally a hug. So. Ally was a human familiar to one of the most popular Blue Blood boys. Now Ally's expensive outfit and presence at the party made sense. "Hey, Ally." Bliss nodded. "Jamie."

Jamie excused himself with a cough, and the two girls were left alone. "How are you?" Allison asked. "It's good to see you again." The pretty blonde put a hand on Bliss's arm.

Bliss was touched by the unexpected warmth in Ally's voice. "I'm okay. . . . Thanks," she told her.

"You were missed at Dylan's memorial service," Allison said. "But don't worry, no one expected you or anything. Your dad said you needed to rest."

"Memorial? There was a memorial? For Dylan? When?" Bliss asked, trying not to sound like she was about to freak out.

Allison looked uncomfortable. "Almost a year ago now. Yeah, I know. Weird, right? I mean, the guy disappeared, right? Supposedly his parents moved to Grosse Point or something, but then it turned out he was staying at Transitions but he had some sort of forty-eight-hour leave and he died from an overdose."

Another cover-up, Bliss thought. The Blue Bloods covered their tracks well. Easy enough to explain Dylan's death as another rich kid drug overdose. Especially since he was in rehab. An entirely plausible story, except that it wasn't at all true.

Allison shifted uncomfortably. "I didn't even know him that well, but you guys were friends, weren't you?"

"We were," Bliss said. "Was it . . . How did . . . Was anyone else there?"

The Duchesne girl looked embarrassed. "No. Not really. There weren't that many people. I think I was the only one from Duchesne. There were some people from the rehab center, but then they were the ones who organized it. I just happened to find out about it from Wes McCall. He'd been staying at Transitions too. I just thought . . . well, Dylan and

I used to have English together and he was . . . a nice guy. A character. But nice, you know?"

"Yeah," Bliss said. She found that her eyes were suddenly full of tears.

"Oh god, you're crying. I'm so sorry. I didn't mean to upset you," Allison said. "Here." She handed Bliss a scented handkerchief from her handbag.

"I'm okay . . . it's just . . . it was complicated," Bliss stammered, gladly taking the hanky and wiping her eyes.

"Life sure is." Allison nodded. "But it's good to see you . . . out. I mean, it must be so hard. I'm saying all the wrong things, aren't I?"

"Not at all. It's nice to be able to talk to somebody." Bliss smiled.

"Well. You can always talk to me. You coming back to school in September?"

Bliss nodded. "Yeah. It's weird to be held back. I don't really know anyone anymore." The Visitor had agreed that Bliss should go back to school. It would be odd if the senator's daughter suddenly became a high-school dropout.

"Well, you know me, and I'm in your class," Allison said. "It won't be so bad," she said, giving Bliss a hug.

"That's good to hear. Thanks, Ally. See ya." Bliss smiled.

"See ya."

Bliss walked back to her car, wanting nothing more than to be alone as she absorbed this news. There had been a memorial for Dylan and no one had come. To the Red Bloods he was just some troublemaker; to the vampires, collateral damage. No one cared or remembered him.

She hadn't even been there to pay her respects. To see him for one last time before they put him in the ground. He was gone forever, and she would never see him again.

TWENTY-THREE

Mimi

*T*he directions on the map led them to the Tijuca Forest, located smack-dab in the heart of the city, not too far from the smart beach districts along the coast. Rio was a wonder, Mimi thought. Where else in the world could you go so quickly from the glass towers of a modern financial district to a lush tropical rain forest?

In the cab up to Barra da Tijuca, Kingsley studied the carefully drawn map again. "It looks like there's some sort of cabin in the woods next to a waterfall. That must be where they've brought her."

"Do you think she's still alive?" Mimi asked.

Kingsley didn't answer at first. He just folded the note back into his pocket. "They kept her alive for over a year, that much we know. If they were going to kill her, why would they wait so long?"

"I have a bad feeling about this," Mimi said. "Like we've

come too late." The note had been dated four days ago. The little girl's words echoed in her mind. *Bad people. They took her away.*

The cab driver took them to the parking lot by the entrance near the Cascatinha de Taunay waterfalls, which was as far as he could take them. The parking lot was a small plateau ringed by the tallest trees Mimi had ever seen. They had a panoramic grandeur, the kind of natural beauty you only saw in movies, so tall and green and wide they looked unreal.

She stepped out of the cab and took a deep breath of the clear mountain air. It almost had a taste—like dew and sunshine mixed with an earthy green smell. Mimi looked around—there were several decent-looking trails, but they disappeared sharply up the mountain, twisting away to what looked like some sharp rocks. It looked like it would be a pretty arduous trek, no matter what, and she cursed her vanity once more. If only she had worn the regulation shoes. She was never going to make it up that trail in her high-heeled boots.

There were several battered-looking Jeeps whose drivers were trying to entice the small groups of day-trippers and hikers to hire them for the day. But Kingsley had read Mimi's mind and nixed the idea before she could even suggest it. "No, let's not put anyone else at risk," he said. "Silver Bloods think of humans as sport. A guide would only make our mission more vulnerable."

Fine, she thought. It's been forty-eight hours since we left the hotel. Forgive me if I want to ride instead of hike. Even vampires got exhausted if you pushed them too hard. Meanwhile, the Lennox brothers had found a naturalist guide.

"Fastest way to the hidden falls?" The guide was so deeply sunburned his skin was mahogany. He had a British accent, and explained that he was part of the Natural Geographic Society. "Best way is probably up the Pico trail; there's an unmarked path through the woods that you can follow through the jungle. But it's a pretty strenuous climb. Sure you don't want to hire one of the Jeeps? The Taunay falls are right here. They're just as spectacular. . . . No? All right, then, good luck. Park closes at sunset, so make sure you're back here by then."

Mimi looked down at her feet. She knew what she had to do. She sat on a fallen log, took off her boots, and chopped off the spike heels with her blade, wincing a bit at the destruction. Then she put them back on. Much better. She took a big gulp of water from her plastic bottle, wishing not for the first time that she was on that beach in Capri.

"Catch!" Kingsley said, throwing her something.

It was a small bottle of coconut water. "What's this for?" she asked, pressing down on the tab. She took a sip. Surprisingly refreshing.

"Found it at the gift shop," he said. "I know it's not a limoncello, but I hear it's really good for you."

Why did he always seem to know what she was thinking? She was annoyed and grateful at the same time, a strange combination of feelings.

They set a quick pace, soon leaving most of the other hikers on the main trail behind, and reached the mountain-top in short order. The air was so quiet, it was like entering a sort of natural church. From the top they could see all the way across the city, down to the coastline. It was a magnificent and awe-inspiring view.

"This must be that path the guide was talking about," Kingsley said, leading them through the shrouded greenery to the other side of the hill. "I think I can hear the water."

Mimi stopped and listened. She heard it too: a rushing, whooshing sound—just slightly audible and probably miles and miles away. Walking downhill was easier; they were almost gliding—one of the advantages of the vampire agility. They hiked in silence into the dark, desolate heart of the jungle, trusting the map to lead them. The heat was oppressive and overwhelming, the air so humid it was almost like breathing underwater. The dense vegetation was primordial, the tree roots looking like the claws of an immobilized beast, the sky completely covered by a canopy of green, and everywhere, the rustling sound of animals in flight. Mimi glimpsed one or two of the wildly colored macaws, but was disappointed she didn't see any monkeys.

Finally they came to a clearing that opened up to the hidden waterfalls, just as the map directed. A torrent of water ran down through rocks, an elemental, awe-inspiring majesty rushing down to a swirling river that ribboned through the jungle.

"According to the map we'll have to cross the river to get to the bank on the other side," Kingsley said, untying his laces and removing his shoes.

The Lennoxes were already in the water. Their nylon pants were unzipped at the knee, and they carried their backpacks over their heads. Kingsley did the same, except he also removed his T-shirt, showing off his broad chest, tanned and smooth. When had Kingsley had time to work on his tan? Mimi wondered.

Well, at least she wouldn't have to wear her uncomfortable shoes anymore. Even with the heel surgery, they didn't provide adequate support. She kicked them off and stripped down to her camisole and underwear, and slipped into the water, holding her bag over her head.

The water must have come from a mountain spring, because it was cold, almost freezing, but it felt wonderful after almost two days of walking around a hot city without a proper shower. The river current was strong and threatened to wash Mimi away. She used every inch of her muscles to make it to the other side. When she reached the shallow end, Kingsley held out his hand and pulled her up, but she lost her step and fell into his arms, her body crushing momentarily against his.

Mimi blushed at the unexpected intimacy, and to her

surprise found Kingsley looking slightly embarrassed as well. For all his talk and flirting, he handled himself like a true gentleman. "Sorry about that," he said, straightening up.

"Nothing to worry about." Mimi smiled a smile that said no one could resist her in a wet camisole—not even the great Kingsley Martin. But her breezy facade was just that—a facade—because she felt a spark pass between them when Kingsley touched her. Something that she didn't want to acknowledge right then, or *ever*, but she felt a connection to him . . . and not just that—a *desire*—quite unlike her usual voracity for human familiars: those red-blooded toys that she disposed of at will (she'd already left two of them back at the hotel). No, this was something deeper, stirring something inside her. . . . A memory, perhaps? Had they known each other in a prior lifetime? And if so, what had happened between them? Nothing? Everything? She didn't have time to dwell on it, though, because the boys were already scrambling up the edge of the bank.

She removed her clothes from the waterproof pack and began to dress, averting her eyes from Kingsley, who was doing the same.

"We shouldn't be too far," Kingsley said, checking the map once they were ready.

They made their way through the wilderness until they arrived at a cluster of trees and greenery that created a curtain around a small, wooden dwelling. Not quite a shack but not quite a house either. There was a strange symbol on the doorway—a five-pointed star. The mark of Lucifer. Mimi shivered and noticed that the rest of the team looked tense as well. This would not be as easy as fighting off a gang of drug dealers.

"This is it," Kingsley said. "Force and I will take the front; you two cover the back exit," he ordered.

Mimi followed Kingsley into position as they crept up toward the front door.

"On the count of three." Kingsley nodded. He had brandished his sword. Its silver blade glinted in the sun.

Mimi removed hers from the wire in her bra, the needle unfolding to the full length of her weapon. A sudden image came up: hunting demons through a tunnel of caves, the shrieking and then the silence. A memory? Mimi blinked. Or a projection? Wasn't that Jack's voice? She couldn't be sure. The connection between them was not what it used to be.

Focus. Kingsley was counting down.

"One, two . . ." He nodded to Mimi and she kicked at the door, which opened with a bang.

Twenty-four

Schuyler

*J*ack led Schuyler through the residential streets of the Île Saint-Louis and over the bridge connecting to Île de la Cité, where she caught a glimpse of Notre Dame as they flew past the square and into the nearest Metro station. "Where are we going?" she panted as they jumped the locked turnstiles. The trains had stopped running an hour ago.

"Somewhere we'll be safe," he said as they ran to the very end of the empty platform: Schuyler had become familiar with the aesthetics of the Metro, but she was still struck by how beautiful even something like the subway could be in Paris. The Cité tunnel was lit by Art Deco–style globe lights that curved over the tracks with a charming flair.

"There's an old station below this one; they closed it off when they rebuilt the Metro," Jack said, opening a hidden door located at the very end of the station and leading her down a dusty staircase. The station underneath appeared to be frozen in time, as if it had been just yesterday that travelers had waited for steam engines to take them to their destinations. Schuyler and Jack walked on the old railroad tracks, until the tracks stopped and the tunnels turned into caves leading farther and farther underground. The darkness smothered them like a blanket—Schuyler was glad for the *illuminata*—it was the only way she could see Jack.

The twisted narrow underground paths reminded Schuyler of something she had seen in an old Repository book. "Is this . . . ?" she asked.

"Lutetia." Jack nodded. The ancient Gallic city. When they had conquered Gaul, Blue Blood Romans named the place after the marshlands that had surrounded the area. The vampires had built a massive underground network of tunnels below the city. Red Bloods believed that all that was left of Lutetia were the remains of an amphitheater in the Latin Quarter. They did not know that most of city had survived intact, deep down in the catacombs.

Unlike the dungeon underneath the Hôtel Lambert, the catacombs of Lutetia were unexpectedly filled with fresh air. They were clean. Protected by some sort of spell, Schuyler guessed. There were no rats skittering in the walls, no smell of sewage and rot.

"Do you think he's still following us?" Schuyler asked, keeping up with Jack. She felt as if her entire being were a tuning fork, vibrating with fear. As they walked deeper into the caves, she found she was unable to pierce the total darkness, even with the vampire sight.

"Hopefully," Jack replied.

Hopefully? As they ran, Schuyler realized the tunnels created a maze, a hundred different corridors leading in a thousand different directions. "You could get lost in here forever," she said.

"That's the point," Jack replied. "Only the Blue Bloods know the way out. These tunnels are enchanted against the *animadverto*. Try to remember the way we came. You will not be able to."

He was right. She couldn't remember the way, which was strange and unsettling because having vampire sight was like watching a show on a DVR: you could rewind to exactly the same place and remember everything—every detail in the room, every nuance, every expression on anyone's face, every word that was uttered. So that's why Jack said he hoped Leviathan had followed them, although Schuyler wasn't convinced a mere maze could stop a demon.

"What about everyone we left behind?"

"Charles is there. He won't let any harm come to them," Jack said. "He was keeping an eye on Leviathan while I fetched you from the room. He should be more than a match for the demon."

They ran for what felt like miles underground. Schuyler had no way of knowing where they were, and she hoped Jack knew what he was doing. Schuyler thought her heart might burst from exertion, and her muscles were starting to flag. How much farther could they run?

Not far, Jack sent. *We are almost to the intersection. Come.*

He led them through a narrow tunnel—it was almost like a cut in the rock, so thin and sharp they had to walk sideways, inching along the wall—and finally they stepped into a crossing of some sort, an open space that pinwheeled away to seven different corridors.

"Where are we?"

"Underneath the Eiffel Tower. This is the center of the old city and the beginning of the new. All the tunnels eventually lead here."

"'All roads lead to Rome,'" Schuyler quoted. "Same idea, right?"

"Sort of." Jack allowed a smile.

Schuyler looked around. Carved above each of the seven corridors were symbols that looked familiar. She wondered where she had seen them before, then realized: they had been flashing on the banners of the Chinese junks. They were the emblems of each Great House, in the sacred language. Above the middle tunnel was a symbol Schuyler carried on her own wrist. A sword cutting through clouds. The archangel's sigul.

Also next to each tunnel opening were seven wooden torches leaning against the wall. Jack reached for one and waved his hand above it, making a small white flame appear. "This is called the breath of God. Any Blue Blood can bring light to the tunnels. C'mon, it's this way to the exit," he said, heading down the leftmost corridor. He lit the way, just as a dark figure came charging out from the other side.

Schuyler almost screamed, but her voice died in her throat when she recognized the man in black. Like Jack, he was dressed in a Venator's uniform.

"Father!" Jack said.

Charles Force nodded curtly. He gave Schuyler the usual distant, contemptuous look that seemed to be reserved especially for her. She wondered why he even deigned to help her when it was so apparent in his every gesture that he could not stand to look at her. "Good work, Jack. They are behind us, trapped for the moment by an *obsido* at the southern junction, but it will not hold them forever. Hurry—up the stairs. To the intersection where they cannot cross. Now."

A small door led to a stairway. Schuyler began to run up two, three steps at a time, until she was suddenly pulled downward, away from her companions, by something that had a viselike grip on her legs. She fell against the stone steps, and the shock dealt a severe blow to her head, and she blacked out for a moment.

When she came to, she discovered she was trapped in a dense, gray smoke, and a feeling of intense, voracious joy filled her. It was the enemy's joy, Schuyler realized; they were feeding off her fear: consuming it, devouring it. The fog was impenetrable, solid to the touch—it looked amorphous but it had a physical density, an impossible weight, as solid as the bars of a cage or a prison cell.

Then she heard them: a sound like the whistling of the wind through the trees, or like chalk rubbing on a blackboard the wrong way: piercing. It was accompanied by a strange clicking noise, like the clattering of claws against a surface. *Clickclickclack* . . . devil hooves on a rooftop.

The Silver Bloods were going to take her. She was surrounded and overwhelmed. No. She would not give in to despair; she would fight . . . but with what? She had to stay awake, couldn't give in to the heavy drowsiness that was overtaking her. Then she saw the eyes shining in the darkness, their otherworldly, ominous, crimson gaze—eyes brimming with hellfire itself. Leviathan had come to finish what he had started.

A blazing light cut through the smoke. At first Schuyler thought it was the torch, but then she saw it was a sword. It was completely unlike any sword she had ever seen before. Her mother's sword had shone with a bright white flame: as pure as ivory and as beautiful as sunlight. This blade was different. It was almost the same color as the smoke: a dark gray edged with silver, and there were terrifying black marks on it. It looked less like a sword than an ax, rough-hewn and primitive, with a battered leather holster for a scabbard.

"Schuyler, run!" Jack bellowed. "GO!"

He slashed his ugly blade across the creature—or was it more than one? Was it just Leviathan or more than that?

The monster screamed in pain, and now Schuyler could feel *its* fear. Saw the reflection of what it saw in its eyes.

Because Jack had transformed. He was no longer there. Only Abbadon.

Schuyler did not want to turn around. Did not want to see what Jack had turned into, but she caught a glimpse of the black fire that surrounded him, that lit up his image and made him glorious and terrible, like a vengeful, wrathful god. Frightful and awful to behold, a power that was not of this world, not of this kind.

Schuyler would not want to admit it, but Abbadon didn't look all that different from Leviathan, the demon that had sprung from the earth.

But she couldn't think about that now.

Instead, she ran.

TWENTY-FIVE

Bliss

Of course, just because Bliss was allowed to have control once in a while did not mean that things were back to normal. She would start taking her life for granted, but then the Visitor would return, and it was out, out, out again till next time. She would keep track: Monday to Wednesday, then out for much of Thursday, then the weekend blending into a blur—then back!—she would still be confused by dates, think it was Thursday when it was really Saturday. As the days passed, it was becoming more difficult to adjust to the times when the Visitor returned, to suddenly find herself thrown out of the light and the world, and back into that cold, empty void of memory and restlessness.

She decided that the next time it happened, she would not allow him to shut her out. There had to be a way to *stay*. She had to find out what the Visitor was planning—where this was all going. Sure, the Visitor had allowed her to have part of her life back, but who knew if it would continue? Plus, Bliss didn't want to share. She wanted *all* of herself back. She couldn't live like this, like a crazy person. There were other people to think about—the Visitor was dangerous, evil. She couldn't let what had happened in Rio happen again.

The thought made her insides turn to ice. If only there were more fashion shows to book, or more parties to distract her; but things were winding down in the Hamptons, and there were fewer excuses for her to be out in the world.

She spent the afternoon sunbathing in the backyard. She was so pale, she always burned, and had lathered up with some French sunscreen that was like, SPF 100—you might as well be wearing a blanket. She basked in the sun, enjoying how the heat slowly warmed her body. After a year of being nowhere, it was heaven to be outside again, to sit on a chaise lounge, bobbing gently in the middle of the pool, her hand skimming the warm water.

Then she felt it: a darkening . . . like a shadow passing over the sun, and then the *push*, the Visitor coming back. But instead of dutifully letting him take over, Bliss forced herself to remain. Inside her mind, Bliss made herself very, very quiet, curled up like a ball, like a shadow against the wall so that the Visitor would not notice that she was sticking around. She knew, instinctively, that he must not realize she was still there. She tried to become an ocean of stillness, with nary a ripple on the surface.

She forced herself to hang on. Somehow, it worked. The Visitor was in charge, but she was *still there*. This time, she could see everything he could see; she could even hear him speaking (through her voice).

They (she had to think of them as two people now) were getting up, putting on a robe, then striding into the house. They took the steps two at a time and practically charged into Forsyth's study.

The senator was home for the congressional summer recess. He was sitting behind his desk with a cigar, and he jumped at their unannounced entrance.

"Didn't I teach you to knock?" he snarled.

"It is me, Forsyth," the Visitor said in Bliss's voice.

"Oh! My lord, I am sorry. I am so very sorry. I did not know you were returning so soon," he said, throwing himself at Bliss's feet.

It was discomfiting to see Forsyth through the Visitor's perception—a lowly worm cowering before her.

"Tell me how I can be of service, my lord," the senator said, still on his knees.

"News, Forsyth. Tell me of the Conclave."

Forsyth practically *chuckled*. Bliss had never seen her "father" look so smug, which was saying a lot for a politician. "We have nothing to fear from that group, my lord. Half of them are relying on Red Blood 'hearing aids' to listen to reports. It's highly entertaining, really. Did I tell you Ambrose Barlow is now a voting member? Of course you know him as Britannicus."

"Britannicus . . ." the Visitor said. "He does sound familiar."

"He was once your foreman. He took the children to the baths."

The Visitor found this incredibly funny. "Very good. I take it everything is set in motion, then? The Venators aren't giving you any trouble?"

"Not at all. Everything is proceeding as planned. Charles Force is in Paris as we speak. He is easier to manipulate than a puppet," Forsyth said with a sharp bark of a laugh.

A deep sense of satisfaction settled over Bliss. The news had made the Visitor very happy. Like an overstuffed cat who had just devoured a cage of canaries. "Very good. Very good. And my brother?"

Forsyth removed a bottle of scotch from underneath his desk and poured two shots into crystal glasses. "Say the word and Leviathan will strike. The girl is within his reach. It will be easy enough for him to infiltrate the party. By the way, you may find this amusing: my sources tell me that Charles was unable to get an invitation to the ball."

"How fortunate that the schism still holds." The Visitor nodded, sounding very pleased. "I could always count on my dear sister to harbor such a long grudge. It works to our favor." The Visitor downed the scotch in one fluid motion. "And my other sister, Sophia?"

"Alas, she refuses to divulge information about the Order. She swears she does not know. You know, after a year with Harbonah, she might just be telling the truth."

"I see."

"The good news is Kingsley and his team are still in the woods. They've been misdirected for months, with no idea they were sent on a useless mission."

"Kingsley," the Visitor snorted. "That traitor. We'll deal with him soon enough."

"What shall we do about Sophia? Do we continue to hold the Watcher?" Forsyth asked.

"No." The Visitor ran a finger over the rim of the empty glass, making a small, high-pitched sound. "If my sister truly does not know the identities of the Seven, then she is nothing to me. I grow bored of her stubbornness. Take her away. Kill her." His words had a rash, impulsive cast to them, but there was something else that had made Bliss feel suddenly frightened.

When the Visitor had called Sophia "sister," an image had come to her mind: Jordan.

Was the Visitor speaking of Jordan? And if so, did that mean Jordan was still alive? Where? How? Bliss could feel herself starting to get agitated. She had to calm down. She wanted to hear more . . . She had to . . . She had to find out . . .

But it was too late. She was tossed out of the light and back into the cold, alone and helpless to do anything about what she had heard. What was going to happen in Paris? Why had they wanted Charles Force to go there? And Sophia—was that Jordan's real name? What did the Visitor have planned for her? And who was the girl Leviathan was after?

Was there anything she could do to prevent any of it? Or was she going to be doomed to know that the end of the world was coming—and yet be completely helpless to do anything about it but watch from a front-row seat?

TWENTY-SIX

Mimi

*S*he'd kicked the door so hard it had clattered to the floor, making a tremendous noise. But afterward, all was silent. There was no reply to her challenge. Mimi crept up against the doorway, feeling along the edge of the wall for a light switch. When she turned it on, she saw that she was standing in a filthy mess; everything in the place was ransacked and disorderly. "Um, like, ew?" Mimi said, making a face at Kingsley, who in turn was surveying the squalor with a flinty stare. Mimi held her nose and tried not to breathe. "What is that?" she asked, almost choking. It smelled sweet and rancid. Like something left to rot.

Kingsley shook his head. Mimi decided she didn't really want to know.

She could hear the Lennox brothers breaking down the other door. They edged around the explosion of clutter.

There was something pathological about the scope of the disaster, from the upturned sofa, where someone had hacked at the cushions, leaving a mess of feathers everywhere, to every drawer in every table and bureau being wrenched open, contents spilling out onto the floor. There were empty bottles and newspapers scattered all around, remnants of food—plastic wrappers, dirty paper plates, a half-empty bag of M&M's, unopened cans of Red Bull.

Something about the disarray looked familiar. Mimi realized she had seen it before—the Force's town house had been burglarized a few years ago, and her parents' rooms had been ransacked in just this manner: everything turned over, upside down, everything picked through. She remembered how odd it had been to see Trinity's jewelry box in the middle of the bed, broken and empty, among the jumble of clothing and old family photographs that the thieves had unearthed from the closet.

This was the same: the methodical way every item in the room had been assessed and discarded. Someone had been looking for something.

Kingsley signaled to Mimi to keep moving, and they continued to inch along the hallway. They found two bedrooms, both just as messy and overturned as the rest of the house. Sam and Ted came in from the kitchen.

"Anything?" Kingsley asked, still holding his weapon at the ready.

"Nothing, Cap."

"This isn't that old," Kingsley said, picking up a paper bag with the McDonald's logo. "It's still warm. Eyes up," he said, ordering them to stay sharp.

Mimi continued to look around. During their burglary in New York, the thieves had made off with four million dollars' worth of her mother's diamonds. But the robbery hadn't been the worst of it. She remembered how violated she had felt, to think that strangers had been in their house. One of them had left a coffee cup on the dining room table, leaving an ugly ring on the wood.

It wasn't so much the loss of the stones, although Mimi had been upset not to inherit the jewels—it was the principle of the thing: to know that someone had been in your space. An uninvited, *unwelcome* someone who had used your house as their own personal playground. There had been a muddy footprint on her headboard, cookie crumbs on the white rug, a smear of chocolate (Mimi hoped it had been chocolate) on her silk bedspread.

The police had come, taken fingerprints, and filed a report—not that anything ever came of it, of course. Charles had said most of the jewel thieves dealt with the black market, where pieces were broken down, the stones disguised and laundered through the system, sold to shady dealers on Fifth Avenue. Luckily, insurance had covered most of the damage, as well as the stones, so there was no real financial loss, just sentimental value and a nagging feeling of injustice.

Mimi's parents had had the whole apartment repainted that night and over the weekend. The housekeepers put everything to rights. Once the insurance check came in, Trinity had kept Harry Winston and several auction houses on their toes. After a few months, Mimi had completely forgotten about it: life went on.

But seeing the momentous mess the Silver Bloods had made took her back to that awful night. Charles looking ashen, Trinity tearing up a bit, and Jack punching his fist into a couch pillow. Mimi had taken one look at the rape and pillage of their beautiful home and declared, "I'm getting us a suite at the St. Regis."

What could they have possibly been looking for here? Mimi wondered. This was a shack in the middle of the jungle. What on earth could it possibly have that was of any value to anyone? And where was Jordan? If they had taken her here, why were they looking for something? Mimi knelt down and rummaged through the disorder, trying to make sense of things. She pushed away a pile of rotten cardboard and unearthed a strange pattern on the carpet.

Footprints.

Small ones.

Leading toward—or coming from—the bathroom. Mimi entered the small space. This room had also been turned upside down, the cheap plastic shower curtain pulled off the rings, a mountain of towels in the bathtub, the mirror over the sink smashed to bits—there was blood on the glass.

There were signs of struggle, the remnants of a fight. . . .
Mimi pushed the towels around.

There was something here. . . .

Hidden underneath the fallen shower curtain . . .

Mimi pushed the crumpled plastic off with her foot, her
heart beating. . . . Could it be . . . With trembling hands she
picked away the piles of broken glass and removed the pile
of dirty towels.

There was a small, dead body in the bathtub, wearing dirty flannel pajamas. No. No. No. No. No. NO! They
were too late; she'd felt it. They'd been walking in a fog, too
slow . . . They were too slow. . . . But still, she didn't want to
believe it. NO!

"Kingsley!" she cried. She didn't want to be by herself
when she turned the body over.

Twenty-seven

Schuyler

he was used to being alone. She had been alone for much of her life. Her grandmother had not advocated the current hovering, anxious practice of modern helicopter parenting. There had been no one from home to watch the few school plays she was in, no one to cheer her on from the sidelines at the Saturday soccer games. It had been sink or swim with Cordelia: no risk of drowning from too much attention. Schuyler's childhood looked lonely from the outside: no siblings, no parents, and until Oliver came into her life, no friends.

But here was a secret: Schuyler hadn't been lonely. She'd had her painting, her drawing, her art, and her books. She liked being alone. It was company that flagged her; she had no idea how to make casual chitchat, or how to interpret and emulate the fluid social gestures that drew people together. She was forever the Little Match Girl at the window, shivering out in the cold. But while people scared her, she had never been afraid of the dark.

At least, not until now. The darkness that surrounded her was absolute: so complete, even vampire sight was useless. She hid in a tunnel until the screams and sounds of the skirmish subsided, fading into blackness.

She should have stayed; what had she been thinking? Why had she left him there alone? She had left Oliver and now Jack. But she had had no weapon; she had nothing. Jack had wanted her to run, and so she had.

"Jack? Jack?" she called, her voice echoing down the length of the tunnel. "Are you all right? Jack!"

There was no answer.

The silence was even more unsettling. It was so quiet she could hear the sound of rain falling somewhere above the catacombs, could hear the drip-drop-drip of every trickle that fell through the cracks in the walls and hit the floor. She hugged herself tightly, unsure of what to do. Her shoulders ached, and it felt as if her muscles were frozen. So this was what it was to be afraid of the dark. To be afraid and alone in the dark.

Schuyler called Jack's name for what seemed like hours, but there was no answer. There was no sign of the Silver Bloods either, but that didn't mean anything. Maybe they had withdrawn, only to return later. She didn't want to think about what might have happened to Jack. . . . Could they have taken him? Was he destroyed? Lost? Broken?

Jack was gone. *No.* Schuyler shook her head even though she was only arguing with herself. There was no way he could have fallen. Not him. Not that dazzling fearsome light that he was. No. She had seen his true form and it was awesome to behold. A pillar of fire. A thousand magnificent suns burning with flames the color of the deepest night. Terrible and wonderful and more frightening than anything she had ever seen.

No!

He will return for me.

She believed it. She looked around at the maze of tunnels. She had no idea where she was, or where she had come from. You could get lost in here for centuries, Schuyler had told Jack.

That's the idea.

What am I doing? I'm such an idiot. The intersection! It was the only natural place. What had Charles said? The intersection. *The place where they cannot cross.* All the tunnels led there. Where was it? She couldn't see, so she felt along the wall. There was an opening. She felt another. Two tunnels. A fork in the road. She would have to choose. But which? She felt along the grain, trying to sense something. If she could not see, maybe she could smell. . . .

It had smelled clean in here, she remembered thinking. She had expected the underground cavern to smell moldy, like a damp towel that had been left too long on the floor. But when she and Jack had first disappeared into the catacombs, she had been surprised to breathe fresh air.

This one, she thought. This one smells just a bit fresher, as if maybe it would lead to more fresh air, maybe to the stairs that led upward and out. She made a decision. She walked into the dark tunnel, with only her fingertips as her guide.

It felt as if she had been walking in the dark for miles, but her nose had not failed her—the air had cleared, and from far away she could see it . . . a light shining in the darkness. Jack. It had to be Jack.

Finally she reached the intersection.

But the light was from the torch Jack had been carrying before they were attacked.

And there was no one there.

TWENTY-EIGHT

Bliss

*I*t was the last week of August, and Cotswold had finally sold after the price was reduced another hundred thousand, give or take. A Russian oligarch bought the Hamptons house and everything in it, down to the last nautical cushion and including the car collection. The new family wanted possession right away, so there was a very short escrow period. And ever since the day Bliss had overheard the conversation in Forsyth's study, the Visitor had retreated for his longest absence yet. Saturday, their first day back in New York, made it the fifth straight day that he had been gone. Almost an entire week.

It was a relief to be back in the city again. She had gotten tired of the Hamptons, as everyone ultimately does. And while she had her freedom, Bliss tried to find out what was going on. She had called the Force household, not sure of what she could say exactly—not that it mattered anyway since their maid told her that no one was around. Charles was gone, Trinity was in D.C., and the twins were away as well. Then she called Schuyler's cell, but her service had been disconnected. She called the house on Riverside Drive, and Hattie told her Schuyler was . . . away. The house-keeper sounded too frightened to tell Bliss anything else. The Hazard-Perrys were spending the summer in Maine, but when Bliss called that number, no one picked up. There wasn't even an answering machine. It was all very strange and not promising.

She had raided Forsyth's study before it had been packed up and had tried to call Ambrose Barlow. She had decided that if Forsyth and the Visitor had mocked him, then maybe Warden Barlow was one of the good guys. But when she called the Barlow residence, the warden wasn't there. And she didn't know what kind of message to leave that wouldn't find its way back to the Visitor. She had to make sure he was kept in the dark about what she was planning as well.

Finally she decided she would mail an anonymous note. Not an e-mail that could be traced back to her computer, but a note on some nice stationery so that the Barlows would pay attention to it and not think it was junk mail. BobiAnne had kept a nice collection of card stock, and Bliss selected one.

Dear Warden Barlow,

You don't know me, but I have to warn you about something. Beware of Forsyth Llwellyn. He is not who you think he is.

—A friend

God that sounded lame. But what else could she do without giving herself away? It had as much teeth as a BEWARE OF DOG sign on an unguarded lawn, but Bliss had no idea what else to do. She couldn't risk the Visitor being aware of her actions, and if anyone from the Conclave came around asking for her, Forsyth would know what had happened.

It was better than doing nothing.

Maybe it would even help. She hoped so.

After posting the note, she walked aimlessly up Fifth Avenue past the Guggenheim Museum. The weather was sticky and hot, one of those fry-an-egg-on-the-sidewalk New York days, but Bliss didn't care. She was just glad to be home. Back in the city she had grown to love so much.

Then she wandered back down to the Metropolitan Museum of Art. She walked up the grand steps, dodging picnicking crowds of tourists sitting out under the bright sun. As she entered the grand marble foyer and passed the security bag check, waiting patiently as a bored security guard poked at the contents of her handbag with a baton, she felt a pain in her heart.

This was where Dylan had taken her on their first date.

It was too keen to be anything but grief, as she remembered how Dylan had paid the entrance fee for the two of them with a dime. But as she walked up to the ticket counter, she found she did not have his audacity, and surrendered the entire "suggested" fee.

It had been almost two years ago when he had brought

her to the museum. He had been so excited to take her to the Egyptian wing, and unconsciously Bliss began to walk toward it, passing by glass display cases of scarabs and cartouche jewelry. She passed the display of sarcophagi. She remembered how Dylan had asked her to close her eyes and led her through the passageways, and when she had opened them she was standing in front of it. The Temple of Dendur. A real Egyptian temple rebuilt in a room at the Metropolitan. It was like having a piece of history come alive.

So ancient and beautiful.

And so romantic. She remembered how Dylan had stood in front of it, his eyes shining like bright stars. Bliss walked softly in front of it, remembering. . . . The light slanted into the room, making shadows on the memorial. She was struck by a sadness so overwhelming she had to steady herself or she would have fallen.

"Are you all right?" a girl asked.

"I'm okay." Bliss nodded. She sat down on the steps across from the ruin and took a deep breath. "I'm okay." The girl gave her another curious look, but left her alone.

Bliss was still rooted to the same spot four hours later, when the lights started to blink and an announcement came over the speakers. "The Metropolitan Museum is closing in thirty minutes. Please make your way to the exit." This announcement was repeated every few minutes in many different languages.

Bliss didn't move from her seat. Everyone else in the

room—art students, a handful of tourists, a docent-led group—dutifully walked toward the exit. What am I doing? Bliss wondered. I should go home.

But the minutes passed and the overhead lights continued to blink in warning, and when Bliss heard the footsteps of the museum guard, she hid in the temple's crevice and made herself invisible to human sight. After what seemed like an incredibly long time, the lights finally went out, it was completely silent, and a ghostly moonlight streamed into the museum.

She was alone.

She walked right up to the temple, touching the rough stone, putting her fingers in the grooves of the etched hieroglyphics. Dylan had kissed her right here, for the first time.

She missed him so much.

I miss you too.

What was that?

She looked around the empty room. The light made weird crazy shadows on everything, reminding her of how she used to fear the willow tree outside her bedroom when she was a kid.

She walked up to the fountain on the perimeter of the room and threw a quarter into the water, watching it fall. For a moment she had thought she'd heard his voice—but now she was really going crazy, wasn't she?

You're not crazy.

She was annoyed, agitated. Whoever was talking to her had to stop it. "Is anyone there? Hello?" Her voice echoed throughout the still chamber.

All that answered was an echo of her question: *HelloHelloHello* . . .

But if the voice wasn't out there . . . then maybe . . . maybe . . . it was coming from somewhere . . . *inside.* . . . But that wasn't the Visitor's voice, she was sure of it. She closed her eyes. What was the harm? It wasn't as if stranger things hadn't already happened. She looked inward. There was a void where the Visitor usually was, an emptiness. The Visitor was definitely still away.

But for the first time she sensed *another* presence, and another and another—so very many others—hundreds of others. . . . Oh god, what was it that the Silver Bloods did? They took the blood—the undying consciousness—so that their victims lived on inside their captors. Many souls trapped in one body. *Abomination.*

There were hundreds of souls just below her consciousness—just like her, they had been trapped in the backseat (maybe even the trunk?). It was like looking down into one of those mass graves . . . but instead of corpses, they were all still alive. . . .

She wanted to scream. . . . This was so much worse than having the Visitor. This was . . . She almost lost it, but then . . . that voice again. . . .

Low, husky, and raspy, as if it had smoked too many

cigarettes and had spent too many nights shouting in a packed downtown bar. It was the voice of a boy who had seen it all and had lived to tell a funny tale about it—deep and rough but with a sweet edge that went straight to your heart.

Could it be?

How could it?

"Dylan?" she whispered. "Is that you?"

There was silence.

Then, out of the darkness, she saw him materialize in front of her—saw his shape, saw his face—his beautiful sad eyes, his crooked grin, his dark disheveled hair. He stepped out of the void and into the light.

"I don't have much time," Dylan said. "That Visitor of yours is coming back soon."

TWENTY-NINE

Mimi

*M*imi felt someone come up behind her, but when she turned around, it was not the handsome Venator she saw, but a wraith. A blackened, burned figure. A walking corpse with sockets for eyes and a slash for a mouth, and a bandaged torso. Burned, disfigured, but somehow stomach-churningly . . . alive.

"You . . ." The wraith pointed a bony finger at Mimi, and spoke in a whistling, raspy whisper reminiscent of rustling dead leaves. "You dare . . ."

That voice. Even in its present, eerie iteration, Mimi recognized that voice. It had once made speeches behind podiums, had once welcomed elite groups of guests to a particularly spectacular Park Avenue co-op.

"Warden Cutler?" Mimi whispered. "But I . . . I killed you." It sounded absurd even as she said it. But she had cut Nan Cutler in two, had left her to burn in the black fire in the Almeida villa. How could the warden have survived? It was ridiculous. And it was equally absurd of Mimi to parry or banter with a walking and talking death wraith.

"One more step and I'll have your blood," the faceless horror croaked. What was not charred or blistered on her body was bone, a sickening sight.

Mimi's hand twitched a little. She should not have put her blade away. Did she have time? Where the hell was the rest of the team? Had Kingsley heard her? Where were the boys when she needed them? Why had she strayed from the group; Venator training taught that you always stayed in twos. How stupid of her to have followed those footprints. . . . It had trap written all over it.

Would she have enough time to arm up before Nan made a move on her? No time to think—she unsheathed it—but even as she did, in that same moment, Mimi found herself locked in a death grip with the half-dead Silver Blood.

The monster who had once been the most sought-after hostess in New York was ferociously strong, and as much as Mimi kicked and clawed, the demon would not release her hold. Mimi could feel its foul breath on her neck, knew it would not be long before its fangs would puncture skin and draw her blood. . . .

No!

She slammed the warden backward against the wall with all her might. But Nan had gotten the upper hand and knocked Mimi against the concrete floor. It would have felled many a vampire, but Azrael was made of a tougher substance. Still, it made her dizzy, and she could feel a crack in her skull and the wound bleeding out. . . . She was losing consciousness. . . .

At that moment Kingsley appeared. Mimi thought she had never been so happy to see anyone in her life. "Croatan!" he ordered. *"Absed! Absed abysso!"* Go back to Hell! With a mighty thrust of his sword, he stabbed it straight through the heart.

There was a hissing sound, like the wheel of a tire deflating—somewhat anticlimactic until the figure suddenly burst into a bright silver flame, a momentarily dazzling, blinding light, and the temperature in the room rose to solar levels, as the spirit collapsed into itself in a supernova.

Mimi shielded her eyes until it was safe to open them. She thought the warden would have disappeared, but the corpse was still there. Only now there was nothing menacing about it. Just a mere heap of bones.

Kingsley wrenched out his sword from the pile, and it transformed back into the short jackknife he carried in his pocket. "Are you all right?" he asked, kneeling beside Mimi. He took a look at her head wound, his hands gentle as he held his thumbs against her temples and slowly massaged them. "Cracked like an egg, but you'll be okay. It's already starting to heal."

"How did she live? I cut her in two," Mimi choked.

"You didn't stab her through the heart. It's the only way. It was my fault. I should have made sure. I thought you knew," Kingsley sighed. "Lawrence was right. The Conclave doesn't bother to teach anything anymore, and the new crop of vampires has forgotten too many things."

"I thought that was just a myth . . . you know, like in the movies, when humans think they can kill us with a stake through the heart," she said.

"There is always some truth to a myth," Kingsley said kindly. "The Conspiracy saw to that. So that the Red Bloods feel no need to look for the actual truth."

"Well, *someone* should have told me. I owe you one," Mimi said. "What took you so long anyway?"

"We found two dead Silver Bloods out back," he said. "But those had been taken care of properly. What did you find?"

In answer, Mimi stood up. "I found something. Someone. In the bathtub." She led him to the room and showed him the body.

When Kingsley saw the small figure in the flannel pajamas, he crossed himself. They exchanged a look of anguish and sorrow. "Do it," he said. Mimi nodded.

Slowly she turned the body over.

It was Jordan Llewellyn. Mimi recognized the girl's gray eyes. They were open and staring at the ceiling. In death she looked even younger than her eleven years. She was wearing a grubby pair of pajamas—the same ones she had been wearing the night she was abducted. From the girl's sallow complexion, Mimi knew without having to be told: every drop of Jordan's blood had been drained. Full consumption.

Mimi felt as if she was going to throw up. Nothing had prepared her for this. This was so much worse than almost being taken by the half-dead warden. She had joined the Venators to find adventure, to get out of New York. . . . She had never once thought they would fail in their search. Never. And to know they had come so close, only to be so very far. . . . She was not prepared to see the dead body of a child. It was an image that she would carry with her forever.

Mimi was a confident person. She had an unshakable belief in herself and in her abilities, and she had believed in Kingsley's power to find Jordan. She had believed he would not let them down. She looked at him now, with the deepest sense of betrayal.

But Kingsley was doing something odd. He had taken out a magnifying glass from his Venator kit and was looking into the dead girl's eyes. "Lennox, what do you think? Can you see it?" he asked Ted, who was hunkered by the doorway.

Ted peered through the glass. After a few minutes he handed it to his brother, who did the same. "No. I don't see it."

"I didn't think so," Kingsley said, and there was a note of triumph in his voice. "Force, take a look—closely—do you see it? Or more correctly, do you *not* see it?"

She took the magnifying glass and looked into Jordan's eyes. What was she looking at? What was she supposed to not see? This was morbid. Jordan's expression was a blank, remonstrative gaze. Finally she noticed it. Jordan's eyes were missing their pupils. In the space in the middle, where they should have been, there was nothing—her eyes were one simple surface. She looked like a doll.

"What happened to her? What does it mean?" Mimi asked.

Kingsley's drawn face broke into a grin. "It means, Force, that we haven't failed just yet. The Watcher is alive."

THIRTY

Schuyler

aiting was the hardest part. Schuyler remembered
how she used to sit in the apartment on Perry Street
waiting, just like this, for Jack to arrive for their secret ren-
dezvous. It always seemed like such a miracle every time he
walked through the door. So unbelievable that he was hers,
and that he had been looking forward to seeing her as much
as she had been longing to see him.

It was as if she had left him only yesterday, the emotions he stirred up in her were so dizzying, the memories
he brought back to the surface so strong. She had loved
watching him walk inside the apartment. She remembered
how his face wore a look of anxiety as he appeared in the
doorway—as he too had always readied himself for disappointment. The question lingering on his features . . .
Would she be there waiting for *him*? She had loved him so

much for that. To know that he was just as vulnerable, just as nervous, as she had been. He had never once taken her for granted.

Now she waited for him again. He would return for her, she believed that. Believed it so much more, as she waited, sitting on the cavern floor in an underground catacomb in Paris, than she ever had sitting on a couch in an apartment in New York.

She believed he would return for her, because if he did not, it meant—no. No. There was no way he could have been killed. But what if, what if he had been harmed? What if he was somewhere down one of those dark tunnels—the tunnels she had not chosen—what if he was somewhere down there, bleeding and unconscious? What then?

She couldn't even begin to think about what had happened to Oliver. She hoped Jack had been right, that the Silver Bloods had left him alone. . . . The Croatan weren't interested in humans . . . were they? How could she have left him? She would never forgive herself for deserting him. And now, Jack too . . . Jack was gone as well. Was she fated to lose both of them in one night?

She should go. She had waited long enough. Jack needed her. She had to go looking for him; she couldn't just wait around doing nothing.

She took the torch off the floor. But just as she stepped toward the first tunnel, she heard a noise from behind her.

Footsteps. She turned around, brandishing the flame. "Stay back!" she called.

"It's me—don't worry—it's just me." Jack stood in front of her. He looked untouched, unharmed. Not a single hair out of place. No cut on his cheek. His clothes were clean, and looked freshly pressed. He looked perfect, the way he always did, and not as if he had just battled a pack of monstrous Silver Bloods.

She did not put down the flame. Was it Jack? She remembered the baron's crimson eyes. She had not seen the Silver Blood underneath the human disguise at first. Was this Jack Force or was it something else? Another shapeshifting enemy?

"How do I know you're you?" she asked, holding her torch as if it would save her from whatever creature stood before her.

"Schuyler, I've just narrowly escaped with my life. You've got to be joking," Jack said.

"Stay away from me!"

A thought occurred to her: What if this was all part of the Silver Blood scheme? A deadly ploy? A masquerade? What if they had planned for Jack to "rescue" her so he could gain her trust? A year had gone by—loyalties changed. How did she know he had not been turned? They had been so far away from all the news in the Coven—what if . . . what if . . .

"Schuyler, I am not a Silver Blood!" Jack looked angry

now, and a vein on his forehead was throbbing. His voice was hoarse from shouting. "Stop this. You need to trust me! We don't have much time—my father can only hold them back for so long. We've got to get out of here!"

"Prove it!" she hissed. "Prove you are who you say!"

"We don't have time for this! You really want me to prove who I am?" he asked.

"Yes!" she challenged.

In answer, he took her in his arms, lifting her up and against the wall. He pressed his lips against hers, and with each kiss she could see into his mind, into his soul. She saw a year of hate . . . saw him alone, alienated, hurt. She had lied to him and had left him. With every kiss he made her see, made her feel . . . every emotion, every dream he had of her . . . every ounce of his wanting and his need . . . and his love . . . his all-consuming, life-affirming *love* for her. In the darkness they found each other again . . . and she kissed him back, so greedily and hungrily, she never wanted to stop kissing him . . . to feel his heart against hers, the two of them intertwined together, his hands in her hair, then down the small of her back. She wanted to cry from the overwhelming emotion that engulfed the two of them. . . .

"Now do you believe me?" Jack asked huskily, pulling away for a moment so they could look into each other's eyes.

Schuyler nodded, breathless. Jack. Every fiber of her being tingled with love and desire and remorse and forgiveness. Oh, Jack . . . the love of her life, her sweet, her soul . . .

But how?

How could he still feel this way about her? He was already bonded to his vampire twin, wasn't he? Wasn't he? She had seen the invitations. Mimi in her white bonding dress.

"The bonding . . ." she croaked.

It never happened. I am not bonded to my twin.

He was still free. He was still himself, still the boy she had fallen so deeply and irrevocably in love with that even a year apart could not quench her love for him. And he loved her still, she knew that now. They looked at each other—suddenly understanding everything between them that had gone unsaid.

Jack let go first. He looked at the rubble with a frown. The Silver Bloods had destroyed the stone steps that led to the exit ten stories up. Schuyler could see a small pinpoint of light from the hole above.

"That's the intersection. If we get past it, they cannot follow. Hold on," he said, unspooling a coil of rope that was attached to his Venator pack. He swung the hook over the edge and took her by the waist. "Don't look down," he said as he zoomed them up through the air like a couple of superheroes.

"Wait! Someone's down there! I think—I think it might be your father—Yes! It's Charles! Wait, Jack!"

The rope slipped, caught; there was a struggle as they were suddenly pulled downward again, back down to the depths . . . and Schuyler could see, far in the distance, Charles Force battling Leviathan himself, the demon taking the form of a basilisk, a dragon, and a chimera, changing shape and taunting its attacker with mirthless glee.

"GET OUT OF HERE!" Charles Force bellowed when he saw them dangling on the wire above him. "SAVE YOURSELVES!" And she felt it—felt his ferocious might push them out of the hole, send them flying through the air and sprawling out onto the sidewalk. They made it to the surface just in time.

Just behind or underneath—she wasn't sure—she felt a huge wave, as if a lightning bolt had just missed her by a centimeter. Then the universe wobbled.

A ripple.

A tear.

A wound.

For a moment the world was not in focus. Schuyler could see into the vastness of space and infinity. Alternate universes. Alternate endings. Alternate outcomes.

She felt a trembling deep inside herself as well as out, as if every atom in the known universe were shaking, as if time itself were being unhinged, as if the very earth, the very world they lived in, were in danger of being destroyed.

But then, just as suddenly, everything snapped back into place. Time fixed itself. The universe stopped trembling. The world was the same as it ever was.

Schuyler was sprawled on the sidewalk. She couldn't feel

anything: her legs, her arms, everything was numb. Jack lay on the ground beside her.

With the last of her remaining strength, she reached for him, brushing her fingertips against his cold ones, and then she felt his hand grasp hers in his strong, firm grip. He was alive. Her heart rejoiced. He was alive.

They had survived.

But there was no sign of Charles Force anywhere.

THIRTY-ONE

Bliss

"Is it really you? How is this possible?" Bliss asked, marveling at how well he looked. The Dylan she remembered had been skin and bones, but this Dylan looked healthy. His cheeks were pink, and his dimples were back.

"It's really me," Dylan assured. "You know, the Corruption—the thing that turns vampires into demons—works by drawing out the soul through the blood, and so the times that, uh . . . you know . . ."

Bliss nodded. The times that the Visitor had been in control, and had sucked Dylan's blood, she had taken enough of his spirit into her own, so that a shell image, or a faded version, a piece of his consciousness, lived inside of hers.

"So . . . you're alive?" Bliss asked.

"In a way," he said. "In that I can think, and I can still feel."

"But you're not *real*, are you?" she asked.

He shook his head sadly. "No. I'm not. Not in the way that you are. I mean, no one else can see me but you."

"Is that bad? Does it feel weird?" she asked.

For a while, Dylan merely smiled, and it was his same crooked sad little smile. "I don't know how to explain it, but part of me is here—with you—and another part is . . . somewhere else. I don't know, but I know I am not complete. I'm like . . . like a . . . template . . . you know, like a virtual personality trapped in a computer," he explained.

He confirmed what she already knew: that there were dozens, possibly hundreds of other souls living within her. "The Croatan are insane because none of the spirits have the body for enough time to make it work. They become imbalanced and unpredictable—*schizo*, as the humans call it. Usually because the original host spirit loses control to a strong and forceful personality."

She shuddered. "Like I have."

"The Visitor. Yes. But you are aware of the transgression, which means you've been able to resist it. And there's something else that's different about you. Do you know what it is?"

"Not really."

"Your human familiar, Morgan. Remember him?"

Bliss remembered the cute young photo assistant from the Montserrat shoot.

"The Red Blood is poison to Croatan, and yet it did not harm you. Which means, part of you is still uncorrupted. And also, you have me," he said.

"What do you mean?"

"I keep them from you. I guard the wall," he said. "That's the best way I can put it. Imagine there's a curtain that stands between your consciousness and the others. I'm that curtain."

"So basically all that stands between me and the crazies is . . . you?" she asked.

"Yeah." He shrugged. "Me."

Bliss cracked a smile. Suddenly she didn't feel so alone anymore. She had someone to talk to, and someone who understood exactly what was happening to her. "I like those odds," she said.

She was about to say something else when she was suddenly overcome with rage, a debilitating, inchoate rage— she felt as if she were frothing at the mouth, choking on her own bile—she gasped for air—doubled up and clutched her stomach—what was this? What was going on? Why was she so angry? Then she realized. It was not her anger, this was not her fury. She could feel it, but it wasn't coming *from* her.

"What's going on?" Bliss whispered. "It's him, isn't it? The Visitor? He's upset."

"Yes," Dylan said, looking worried. "Try not to feel it so much. Push back. Do not let his emotions control yours."

She nodded, gritting her teeth, trying to fight back as a garbled mangle of violent emotions washed over her. ANGER! HATRED! HOW COULD THIS HAVE HAPPENED—WHO IS RESPONSIBLE—I SHALL SLIT THEIR THROATS AND DRINK THE BLOOD OF THEIR CHILDREN—THE GATE WAS THERE! WE HAD THE GATEKEEPER IN OUR HANDS! THE PATH WAS WITHIN OUR REACH! FOOLS! FOOLS! She pushed back—*No. No. Not me. Not me. Him.*

Shut him out. Shut him out. Shut him out. Get away from me, from my thoughts, from my life. I am not you. I am not you. I am not you.

"He's gone," Bliss said, exhaling. She opened her eyes. She was still in the museum, and Dylan was sitting on the steps across from her.

"Good," Dylan said. "It's very important that you keep him away—that you don't . . . you don't let him take over."

"I won't." She told him about how she was able to *remain* even when the Visitor came back. "He was trying to do something, I think, but I have a feeling it didn't work out. It didn't happen. Something went wrong. That's why he was so angry just now."

"Yes, but I have a feeling it's not over. You must continue what you are doing. Resisting him. Remaining, as you say. Watch and observe. And you must act when the time is right," Dylan said.

"But what if he finds out?"

"I will help you as much as I can. I promise."

"And what about you. Will you always be here?" she asked him.

"I can never leave," Dylan said. "You're stuck with me."

"Can I?" she asked, holding out her hand. She put it up against his, *hoping.* But she felt nothing. Air. He was smoke and mirrors. Air and light. A memory. A ghost.

He wasn't real. This wasn't real.

"I want to kiss you so bad," she whispered, looking into his dark eyes. "But there's nothing here. You're not really here, are you? I'm just crazy. I probably just invented you to feel sane," she said, and before she could help it, she started to sob. The tears came flooding down her cheeks.

The enormity of her responsibility overwhelmed her. She didn't know if she was going to be able to do it. It was too much to ask. She couldn't stand up to the Visitor. To Lucifer. He was too powerful.

Dylan put a hand on her shoulder—she could see it but she couldn't feel it. But she could hear his voice. "It's all right, Bliss." His voice was gentle. "It's going to be all right."

THIRTY-TWO

Mimi

imi wanted to scream. Riddles and clues and a dead body and now yet another mystery. She wanted explanations and she wanted them now. "What do you mean she's not dead?" she cried. But Kingsley and the team were more interested in examining the bodies of the Silver Bloods right then.

A man and a woman. Mimi recognized them from the Committee. The couple had lived next door to the Forces on Fifth Avenue. My god, Mimi thought, her heart racing. The hidden Silver Bloods were like terrorist sleeper cells; who knew how many more of them were in the Coven?

Ted examined the wound on the woman's chest. There was a mark in the middle of it that had been obscured by all the blood. It was a tattoo of a sword piercing clouds, right where the heart would be.

"Is that what I think it is?" Mimi asked.

"The archangel's sigul." Kingsley nodded. "You see that gold crust around the wound? There's only one sword in the world that can do that. Michael's."

"I don't understand," Mimi said. "I don't understand any of this."

Kingsley closed his eyes in fierce concentration. "They took her from the hotel a year ago. For some reason, they must have wanted her alive. Nan Cutler survived and posed as Jordan's grandmother, hiding her in the favela, where Jordan must have been able to befriend those children. But Sophia knew we were coming—she left us the note—told the children who to give it to. And she knew the Silver Bloods would take her here, but I think we were supposed to save her. That's what she saw. That's why she sent us here—to prevent this from happening. But somehow her timing was off. They decided to kill her sooner than she expected."

"But she succeeded in fighting them off. She found Michael's sword—that must have been what she was look-ing for. It had been stolen from my father's study, you know. The Silver Bloods must have had it," Mimi said, thinking of the burglary. "So we know what killed these two," she said. "But then something else happened. . . ."

"Yes. Nan came back, and that was a surprise. Jordan didn't see that one coming," Kingsley said.

"So Nan killed her, or at least she thought she did."

"Yes."

"But her pupils—you said she isn't dead," Mimi said. "But Jordan *is* dead."

"Yes. But Jordan was just a physical shell for the Watcher." Kingsley looked at Mimi. "You really don't remember any of this? You should be ashamed."

"I don't have to apologize for anything!" But she felt as if she should.

"The Watcher is not exactly one of us. While her spirit can be called up in the blood to be born in a new cycle, there's something that the Silver Bloods don't know. In Rome, when Sophia was the first of us to recognize Lucifer in the Emperor Caligula, when her cycle was completed, the Coven decided she was too valuable to be bound by blood alone. So Michael set her spirit free. She is more than vampire. She is like a ghost. She inhabits a body, a machine, but she can leave it—and exchange it—at any time."

"So, Nan Cutler killed her body, but Jordan had time to release her spirit into something else? What?"

Kingsley looked out the window, at the colorful birds hanging in the trees. "My guess is she went into one of those macaws out there. An intelligent bird. But that would just be a temporary shelter. She would look for a Red Blood as soon as she could."

"So you mean to tell me . . . she's out there? Living in another body?" Mimi asked skeptically.

"Yes."

Mimi crossed her arms. "A human. A Red Blood."

"Yes." Kingsley's patience was wearing thin. "They are made from the same physical shell as we are. A human host."

"And you know all this—that she's still alive—just by looking into her eyes?"

"If the Watcher had truly been destroyed, Jordan's eyes would have pupils. You know what they say . . . eyes . . . windows . . . soul. Do I have to put it together for you, Force?"

They buried Jordan near the waterfalls. Kingsley fashioned a cross from two branches and stuck it in the mound. The four of them clustered around the grave while he said a few words.

"We give to the earth the body of Jordan Llewellyn, who carried the spirit of the Pistis Sophia. We ask the earth to take what is hers, and send it back with gratitude and love and sorrow. Rest in peace."

Mimi and the Lennox brothers murmured soft Amens.

Afterward, they stacked the bodies of the dead Silver Bloods in the backyard and made a funeral pyre. It was only when the first flames caught the wind that Mimi realized it was getting dark. The sun was setting. More than forty-eight hours had passed with no sleep. Mimi was a vampire, but she would have really loved a comfy bed right then. She watched the fire engulf the bodies and send sparks up toward the night sky.

All this and still no Watcher. So what if the Watcher was still alive: this time they didn't even know what she—was she still a she?—looked like anymore. She could be anybody.

"Where would the Watcher go for safety?" Kingsley asked. He was talking to himself. "To the one who called her. But with Cordelia gone, and Lawrence dead, she has only one recourse. Allegra Van Alen."

"But Allegra's in a coma. She's not going to be much help to anyone," Mimi pointed out. "Unless, don't tell me . . ."

"The Watcher has other forms of communication at her disposal, even deeper than our forays into the glom, which have not been able to pierce the wall Gabrielle has erected around herself." Kingsley nodded. "Besides, I have a feeling that after a year in the Rio slums, I'm sure she's feeling it too. . . ."

"Feeling what?"

"I think the Watcher wants what you want, Force," he said softly.

"What's that?"

"She wants to go home."

THIRTY-THREE

Schuyler

Oliver tracked Schuyler and Jack to the bottom of the Eiffel Tower, having triangulated their location from the GPS signal on Schuyler's phone, which was now working since they were outside the Île Saint-Louis. His costume was torn and singed—it seemed a year ago since he and Schuyler had stepped off of that bus. Schuyler's heart leapt when she saw him. Oliver! Safe! Whole! This was more than she dreamed possible.

They were both weeping as they hugged, and held each other close. "I thought you were dead," she whispered. "Don't you ever, ever do that again. Ever."

"I could say the same to you," Oliver said.

He told them that after they had left the party, there had been chaos. Leviathan and the Silver Bloods had begun to set fire to everything, scorching treetops and coming dangerously close to the building itself. It looked as if the massacre in Rio was happening all over again. But then Charles Force appeared and fought them off one by one, leading them out of the grounds. Then they had disappeared. It looked like they had all gone underground.

"Yes," Jack said. "Charles was leading them to the intersection. A portion of the glom that the Silver Bloods can enter but can never leave. A space between worlds."

"Limbo." Oliver nodded.

"So what happened back there?" Schuyler asked, remembering the strange phenomenon they had experienced.

Jack shook his head. "I'm not really sure. But whatever it was, I think Charles somehow managed to reverse the process—to stop the tearing and repair the wound. Otherwise none of us would be standing here."

But Jack did not say what they all knew. That while the Silver Bloods had failed, it had not been without a small victory. Charles Force was gone. He never made it to the surface, and the catacombs were empty.

"So is he dead?" Schuyler asked dully.

"I'm not certain. I think he's just lost," Jack replied.

"What will you do?"

"I don't know just yet," he sighed. "The Conclave is not what it was. I don't foresee garnering any help from that direction. But they're all we've got." Jack looked exhausted. "What about you? What will you do?"

"Run," Oliver said firmly. "We'll keep running."

"You can't run forever, Schuyler. The tremors—your

sickness—you can't hide it. It's part of your transformation. You must go to the right doctor who can help you. You're only endangering yourself by keeping away. I can vouch for you with the Conclave. I will make them understand. They will call off the Venators. Trust me. You'll be safe in New York. You can't risk being alone anymore. The Coven is weakened and leaderless right now, but we will regroup. Come back to New York."

Come back to me. Jack did not say it out loud, but Schuyler heard it loud and clear nevertheless.

She shuffled on her feet. The two boys stood on either side of her, both of them with their hands jammed into their pockets. Oliver's chin was almost at his chest, his head was bowed so low. He couldn't look her in the eyes. Jack was looking at her directly, with that overpowering stare. She loved them both, and she could feel her heart breaking over them. She would never be able to choose. It was impossible.

Oliver was telling her to keep running, while Jack wanted her to go home. More than anything, she wanted to go back to New York; to stop, to rest, to recover, but she could not make the decision alone. As much as she still loved Jack, and as much as it would make her miserable forever to leave him again, there was Oliver to consider. Her gentle truehearted friend.

"What do you think, Ollie? What should we do?" she asked, turning to the boy who had kept her safe for more than a year.

THIRTY-FOUR

Bliss

*I*t was the night before the first day of school. It had been a week since Dylan appeared to her, and sometimes Bliss was convinced she was just dreaming about him. A good dream, but just a dream. But then he kept coming back and talking to her, telling her things she didn't know (which never happened in a dream: somehow she always knew she was just talking to her subconscious), and she finally decided that it *was* Dylan whom she was speaking to, or at least a version of him.

She never knew when he would come back. Sometimes she would close her eyes and wait and nothing would happen. Other times she would be in the middle of something—ordering coffee or trying on shoes—and she would have to get out as fast as possible and find someplace she could be alone. That day she was arranging her books for class. She loved the smell of new textbooks, and liked to run her fingers over the glossy pages. The start of a school year always promised so many good things. She was glad to be going back.

"I liked it too," Dylan said, looking over her shoulder. It startled her to see him standing next to her, with a hand on her desk.

"God! You scared me."

"Sorry. Tricky, getting to the front you know. I have to make you see me, although now that you know I'm here it's a little easier." He continued to look over her shoulder. "What are you taking this year?"

"The usual. A bunch of AP and honors classes. I might check out that Individual Art Study." Dylan nodded and hoisted himself up on the edge of her desk so his long legs swung off the floor. "Wanna see something cool?"

"Sure."

And without warning, suddenly Bliss was sitting with Dylan on the roof of the Cloisters, a museum on the uppermost edge of Manhattan. Of course they were only there in her mind—or in his mind. In reality she was still sitting in her chair at her desk in the apartment. Dylan explained it was his memory that had brought them there. Bliss had never been to the Cloisters.

Dylan explained that they could be anywhere. They didn't have to be in a black void, with nothing surrounding them, or wherever Bliss happened to be at the moment. They could go anywhere as long as one of them had already been there. It was like having a passport to anywhere in their past. And Dylan loved the Cloisters. The view from the roof was pretty amazing.

"Uh-oh," Bliss said. "He's back."

Dylan looked over his shoulder, at the storm clouds that had suddenly gathered over the city. Even in their self-contained bubble they could not escape the Visitor. "You know what to do," he said.

"Do I?" Bliss asked. But Dylan was already gone, and Bliss had left their happy moment on the rooftop.

The Visitor had taken charge, and slipping into the darkness, Bliss assumed the stillness of a statue. While outside, her body was pacing the room, barking orders at Forsyth. "And the Conclave?"

"Barlow has passed a resolution offering Charles Force the leadership of the Conclave again, should he return," Forsyth said nervously. "He was quite adamant."

The cobra quivered, hood up. This was agitating. *Michael!* Always they turn to Michael! They forget who brought them to Paradise!

Forsyth loosened his tie anxiously. "Ah . . . and about Paris. Leviathan has confirmed it—there is no longer a gate in Lutetia. Only an intersection. That was why the *subvertio* did not work, because there was no gate to destroy. We were deceived. Charles had laid a trap for us. But Leviathan's releasing of the white death into the intersection created a time vacuum. Leviathan was almost pulled inside it himself.

But the good news is, he believes Charles's trap was also his undoing. The archangel has been destroyed."

"He can prove this?"

"No, my lord. But there has been no sign of Charles Force since Paris."

"So. Michael was playing games with us as well," the Visitor ruminated. "I was there, you know, the day he forged the key to the gate. The day he anointed himself keeper."

"He is tricky, my lord. Michael was never to be trusted."

"Crafty is what he is. But now we know. The gate is no longer at Lutetia. He must have found a way to move it." The Visitor brooded for a while. "This Barlow resolution must be crushed. But do it gently. You shall convince the Conclave they cannot go on without filling the position. The spirit of the Coven demands a Regis. You shall refuse at first, but they will press you to accept. You will be named Regis."

"As you wish, my lord."

"Once installed, our real work can begin. Without Charles, without Lawrence, they will be looking for a new leader. You shall step into that vacuum. They will come back to me. They will *beg* me to lead them once again, and through you, Forsyth, our real work can begin. . . ."

Without warning, Bliss was suddenly thrust back into the void.

"What happened?" Dylan asked. "Why are you back here?"

"I don't know . . . I got upset . . . He must have felt something. . . ." She told him what she'd heard.

"You have to go back there. Make yourself. Do it."

Bliss concentrated. She tried as hard as she could. She wrenched away the line that separated her from the real world—forced herself to see the world as the Visitor did.

And this time, she was right in his mind.

But he wasn't talking to Forsyth anymore.

Instead she saw what he saw. Bodies. Corpses. Piled on each other. Children, really. They were lying in the desert. They had drunk something. A potion. A poison. Mixed by a devil. She saw a thin spectral boy holding a guitar, and a beautiful but hard-looking girl with dark hair, and another boy—handsome and clean-cut and worried. They were all that stood against this disaster. This massacre of innocents. So many kids . . . Red Bloods . . . slaughtered.

Then she saw the demon: he was in the form of another boy. A good-looking kid but with an ugly sneer to his lips. He had caused it. Another of Lucifer's children.

The images continued, one after another: death, destruction, hate, war. The devil's handiwork.

Then, just as abruptly, the visions stopped. Bliss woke up. She was sitting at her desk, alone. She was shaking so much she had dropped her pen.

What had happened to Charles Force? Had he been destroyed as they thought? What were they talking about? What gate did the Visitor want to destroy?

And those visions she saw—who were those children? Was that the future? And what would the Visitor do once Forsyth was named Regis? What were they planning? Horror did not even begin to describe what she was feeling. Dylan was right: she had to find a way to stop it—whatever it was—from happening.

She closed her eyes. "Dylan?" she called. "Dylan? Are you there? Where are you?"

But there was no answer, inside or out.

THIRTY-FIVE

Schuyler

"*S*ky, wake up! Wake up! You're having a nightmare! Wake up!"

Schuyler opened her eyes. She was sitting up, the bed a messy hurricane of blankets and sheets. Oliver sat next to her, a hand on her shoulder. "You were dreaming," he said. "That dream again?"

She nodded, pulling her knees up to her chin. "The same one. Always."

Ever since she had escaped from Leviathan that night in Paris, Schuyler had had the same dream, the very same one every night, as if her subconscious were stuck on one channel, repeating the same eerie television show.

She could never remember what it was about, only that in the dream she was filled with the deepest, most agonizing despair. For days she had woken up crying.

"You okay?" Oliver asked. His eyes were puffy from sleep,

his hair tousled and messy, a little part of it in the back sticking straight up, as soft as a baby duck's down. He was wearing a Duchesne sweatshirt and flannel pajama bottoms—his usual bedtime attire. Schuyler had teased him once about his surprising school spirit. Oliver had never worn anything branded with the school name in the daytime in his life, as far as she had known.

"I'm okay," she said. "Go back to bed."

They were in a capsule hotel in Tokyo. It had been a week since they'd left Paris. They had spent three days in Berlin first. Tokyo seemed like a safe place to go—as far away from France as possible.

When they'd arrived in Japan, Schuyler had been drained, with no energy even to perform the ritual that would invigorate her. She was beyond exhausted, but after seeing Jack again, and having all the old feelings stirred up, it felt disloyal to rely on Oliver so much. So she had restrained herself from performing the Sacred Kiss.

For once she wished that she had taken a docile stranger as her human familiar instead of her friend, but it felt like a betrayal to even think it.

That night in Tokyo, Oliver lay back down, his head on the pillow, facing away from her as he curled up on his side, the way he always did. This was how they slept, how they had always slept ever since their journey had begun—in one bed, yet back to back, facing outward to their enemies, having each other's back, literally. This was the way Oliver had been taught. This was the way the Conduits had protected their vampires for centuries during times of war. In the middle of the night when Schuyler woke up, she was always comforted by the feeling of warmth from Oliver's back pressing against her own.

A year of sleeping back to back, never once turning to each other, not even for the *Caerimonia*. In bed, it would have been too intimate . . . too much like the other thing that they had resisted so far, an unspoken agreement to wait for the right time. Because what else did they have but time? They would be together always. That much they knew.

"Are you awake?" Schuyler asked. Their room was approximately the size of a small coffin. She could only just sit up. The pods were little boxes stacked on top of each other, with a fiberglass door and a curtain for privacy, and one window. The capsules were popular with Japanese businessmen who were too drunk to go home. It was the cheapest accommodation Schuyler and Oliver could find. They had stored their packs in a locker in the lobby.

"Uh-huh."

"I'm sorry I keep waking you up. It must be tiring."

"Uh-huh."

"Do you not feel like talking?"

"Mmm . . ."

Schuyler knew that Oliver was upset. And she understood why he was being cool with his one-word answers. Something between them had shifted after Paris. Something had changed their easy friendship; something had come into the hermetic little world they had made.

Schuyler had believed Jack Force was part of her past—that after she had left him in that apartment on Perry Street, that would be the end of things. But seeing Jack again in Paris had not felt like the end. Especially when they'd kissed. She didn't know what to think. She felt so guilty about it, sometimes she couldn't even face Oliver. But sometimes when she remembered the kiss, she would find she couldn't stop smiling. It had felt like a beginning, like a promise of a brighter future, even as that future had begun to dim. And so every night as she lay against Oliver's back, when she closed her eyes she would dream of a boy whose eyes were green and not hazel, and she hated herself for it.

So what if Jack was still free? So what if he was not bonded? She had made *her* choice. And she loved Oliver so much, the thought of being away from him would break her heart, shattering it into a million pieces.

She had to stop dreaming of Jack. That kiss. How did that song go in that movie she and Oliver used to watch all the time? *A kiss is just a kiss. A sigh is just a sigh.* It was nothing. It meant nothing.

Maybe she was confused because she was tired of waking up in a different city every three days. Maybe that was all it was. She was so very tired of airports and train stations and hotels and bland, overpriced hotel food. She missed New York so much it was like a physical ache.

She had tried to forget how much she loved the city. How invigorated it had always made her feel—how much she belonged there.

Outside the porthole window, Schuyler could see a view of Tokyo's neon cityscape: endless blinking lights, skyscrapers lit up like video games. Her eyes were closing, she was about to drift off, when Oliver suddenly spoke.

"You know, when I sent you off with him in Paris, it was the hardest thing I'd ever had to do."

Schuyler knew he was talking about when he had sent her off with Jack, not with the baron.

"I know," she said, speaking to her pillow.

"I thought you would run away with him," he said, addressing the wall.

"I know."

She knew all this: she had read it in his blood, but she understood he had to tell her. Had to say the words aloud.

"I thought I would never see you again." His voice was calm, but Schuyler felt his shoulders shake a little.

Oh, Oliver . . . Her heart slid into her throat, and tears came to her eyes. He loves me so much, she thought. I can never hurt him. I can't.

So in answer, Schuyler turned and slid her arm through his and intertwined their fingers. She pressed her chest against his back, and her knees and legs rested against his so they lay like two spoons. She had never done that before, and now she wondered why. It felt so comfortable to rest against him. To put her mouth on his neck so that he could feel her breath on his skin.

"Ollie, I would never leave you," she whispered, and she knew she was telling the truth. She would keep his heart safe.

But he did not reply, and neither did he turn around, even with the implied invitation in her embrace. He kept his back to her all night, as he did every night.

She fell asleep to the steady sound of his breathing.

THIRTY-SIX

Mimi

*T*o many people, Rockefeller Center *was* New York. The steel, concrete, and glass compound in the middle of Midtown was home to a number of the city's most famous and beloved institutions. There was the Rainbow Room on the top floor, and the iconic ice-skating rink below. The middle of the square was a favored place to show off new art exhibits—a giant puppy made of blooming multicolored flowers, or an oversized mirror pointed to the sky. A popular television show had even taken its address for its name. Mimi had always loved walking past the row of brightly colored flags on her way to Saks across the street. But what many people did not know, of course, was that Rockefeller Center had an even older history.

In vampire lore, it was consecrated as the place where Michael had first taken the title of Regis when the Coven had moved to the New World. The land was blessed with part of his spirit, which was probably why Rockefeller Center had become so popular with the Red Bloods. Humans, as dense as they were, could still feel the charged atmosphere that surrounded them, the electricity in the air from the sacred ground.

The sanctuary had stood right where the venerable Christie's auction house was today. It was nine thirty in the morning when Mimi walked through the glass doors of the front entrance. The auction was to start at ten, but she wasn't there to bid on a collection.

She had arrived from Rio the week before, and was missing the first day back at school to attend this ceremony. Duchesne would just have to understand—she had responsibilities that went beyond the classroom. The school had welcomed the Force twins back after their "sabbatical" so they could start their senior year and graduate from high school. The Committee had decreed that the young vampires finish their education before joining another Venator mission, as they were still in a vulnerable time of their transformation. Elders were forever trying to keep the young ones from growing up too fast, Mimi thought. It didn't even matter that she was a voting member of the Conclave! No. She had to get her diploma.

She collected her paddle from the guard and took the elevator to the public auction room. The auditorium was half empty when she arrived. A sign of the times, maybe? Or of the many foreign buyers who bid online or through agents sitting at the phone banks in the back of the room? Mimi wasn't sure. She did remember the auctions being a little more social in nature when her parents used to attend. There would be a cocktail party in the anteroom, and the women would wear jewels as precious as the ones they were bidding on.

She spotted a few of her colleagues sprinkled around the area. The Conclave was down to seven, but seven was all they needed for a quorum. Josiah Archibald was studying the art catalog closely. Abe Tompkins tottered in and took a seat in the back. The auction would begin promptly at ten, and so would the meeting of the Conclave. For they had come to this ancient spot to name their new leader. Forsyth Llewellyn had called for a White Vote.

The installation of a new Regis was no trivial matter, and no one in the Coven could remember having so many new ones in such quick succession. They had been led by Michael in his various incarnations since the dawn of time, and just last year had put Lawrence Van Alen in his place. But now Lawrence was dead, Charles Force was missing, and Forsyth was pressing his case for the position.

Mimi looked surprised when two of the members, Minerva Morgan and Ambrose Barlow, entered the room and made a beeline in her direction. Minerva and Ambrose were among the oldest living vampires of their cycle, and while vampires' minds did not lose their sharpness, the flesh deteriorated on a human schedule without the requisite maintenance. What did the two mottled old geezers want?

"Madeleine," Minerva said, taking a seat next to her, "Ambrose would like to show you something."

Ambrose Barlow carefully removed an envelope from his coat pocket. It was folded in quarters, and when Mimi opened it, the note inside was creased, and the paper so thin—as if from endless re-reading.

Beware of Forsyth Llewellyn. He is not who you think he is.

It was signed "A friend." Mimi handed it back to Ambrose with distaste. Her father had told her never to put any stock in anonymous notes.

"Do you think it's real?" Minerva asked.

"I don't know. I don't really pay a lot of attention to those kind of things," Mimi sniffed. "It's probably just a prank."

"But why would someone send it? Obviously it's some-one from in the Coven. But who? And why? And why send it to Ambrose? He'd been retired from the Conclave for at least fifty years. Plus, Forsyth has no enemies, and he's the only one keeping us together," Minerva said, looking agi-tated. "Don't you think so, Ambrose?"

Ambrose Barlow nodded. "I agree, anonymous notes are the work of cowards. But somehow I feel that we must pay attention to this one. It is a strange time for us . . . and with so much change going on . . ."

Mimi noticed that Forsyth Llewellyn had slipped into

the room, and the three of them stopped talking. The senator was looking particularly robust and even more pompous than usual, considering what had happened to his family not too long ago. He saw the three of them huddled together and took a seat next to Ambrose. "Hello, hello," he greeted Mimi as Ambrose folded the note quickly back into his pocket.

"Hello, Forsyth. I was just telling Madeleine that I still don't understand why we have to do this so soon," Minerva said. "Charles is sure to return and to name a Regis while he is still alive. I don't like it. After what happened in Paris, I feel it is hasty of us."

"Dear Minerva, I do hear your concern, but *my* concern is that after what happened in Paris, time is now of the essence. We cannot dawdle as we have," Forsyth said.

Minerva grunted, while Mimi kept her face neutral. The Red Blood papers were filled with gory stories of the Paris disaster—none of the vampires had been killed or harmed, but there had been a few human familiars who had been trampled during the riot. The tragedy was blamed on the unlicensed Thai circus unable to control its animals, and fire code violations due to overcrowding.

Jack had told Mimi the real story when he had returned the other night, and how Charles had stopped the worst of it. But even with Charles's efforts, the Hôtel Lambert had scarcely escaped being burned to the ground. The new owners were incensed and threatened to pull their bid, but had been placated by the countess, who had offered them some of the historical furnishings free of charge.

The twins decided they would not share the news of Charles's apparent demise with the Coven. Jack continued to believe that regardless of the evidence to the contrary, their father lived, and Mimi agreed it would be best if the community continued to think that Charles was deliberately keeping away. Best not to start a panic; the Blue Bloods were edgy enough as it was.

Seymour Corrigan entered the room, sending a look of apology for his almost-tardiness. They were all accounted for. Seven wardens symbolizing the original seven families, as tradition dictated.

The auctioneer, a sober-looking man in a blue blazer and a red tie, walked up to the podium. "Welcome, my good ladies and gentlemen, to the Impressionist and Modern Art Sale," he said. The audience clapped politely, and a screen behind him displayed a portrait of Kurt Cobain, immortalized in vibrant, jewel colors. Mimi thought it looked like one of those images from a prayer book. Grunge rocker as saint. "First up—an Elizabeth Peyton. The opening bid is five hundred thousand dollars."

As the gavel came down, the Conclave meeting began in earnest.

THIRTY-SEVEN

Schuyler

hey were in Sydney when it happened. Right in the middle of Chinatown, in a little apothecary shop that sold the organic green tea that Schuyler liked to drink in the morning. The trembling began in her legs, then her arms, then her whole body was convulsing and she fell to the floor, dropping the tin she was holding as she writhed and thrashed against the cold linoleum tile.

"Stay back—it's okay—she's . . . she's epileptic!" Oliver said, pushing everyone away. "Just give her room to breathe! Please! It'll pass."

It was strange for Schuyler not to be able to control her body, to find it was in revolt against her wishes, almost as if it had been possessed by an evil spirit. She felt as if she were watching herself from a distant place—as if this was not happening to her, but to another girl, who was lying down while her arms and legs moved jerkily, and she frothed at the mouth.

"Sorry, I'm sorry," she whispered when it finally stopped. The shaking had ceased, but even if her limbs weren't moving anymore, her heart was still beating a mile a minute.

"It's okay. You're okay," Oliver said, gently helping her to her feet by giving her his shoulder to lean on.

"Here . . . water," the shopkeeper said, bringing a paper cup to her lips.

Schuyler was glad for the kind eyes of the man and of the other customers. She kept leaning on Oliver as they walked out of the shop and to the bus stop, where a bus back to The Rocks was already waiting. "This was a bad one," he said, as they paid their student fare and found seats at the back.

He was being kind. It was probably the worst episode she'd experienced. The massive headache, the frothing, the way her tongue had almost choked her . . . What had Dr. Pat said during her last visit? That the vampire strength was a gift, but in her case was also a burden. Her human body was treating the transformation as a disease, as something it wanted *out* of her. . . .

"Are you sure you're all right?" Oliver asked again, as Schuyler leaned forward with her head in her hands.

"I'm okay," she said. "Really I am." It was the last thing she said before she fainted.

* * *

Back at the hotel, and feeling much better, Schuyler sat on the little balcony outside their room, wrapped up in a bathrobe. Inside the tiny kitchenette, Oliver was putting the final touches to his curry. He brought out a steaming bowl and set it in front of her with a spoon. They had both learned to cook while on the run. Oliver's specialty was an Indian banana-and-chicken curry, while Schuyler liked to make interesting concoctions out of pasta and whatever she could find in the fridge. (Sometimes Oliver said they were too interesting.)

"Thanks," she said, gladly accepting the warm bowl of yellow curry and rice. She lifted a spoonful to her lips and blew on it before eating, so it wouldn't scorch her tongue. Outside, sailboats and cruise ships dotted Sydney's harbor. The ocean was a deep sea-green—not unlike Jack's eyes, she thought, then stopped herself. She would not think about him, or what he was doing, or if he was missing her too. She focused on her food. Oliver was watching her through the sliding glass door.

He had that look on his face, and she knew what it meant. He walked out, set a cup of tea next to her, and sat on one of the plastic chairs. "Sky, we need to talk."

"I know what you're going to say, Ollie, but the answer is no." She took a sip of the tea. Amazing that even with everything that had happened, Oliver had still managed to buy a tin. He really was a good Conduit.

"Sky, you're not being reasonable."

"I'm not? They're going to put us in jail, or whatever they do to people like us." Schuyler shrugged. She knew the punishment for evading Conclave justice: a thousand years of Expulsion. Your spirit locked up in a box. But what if she wasn't immortal? What would they do to her then? And what would happen to Oliver?

"You heard what Jack said. The Conclave has bigger problems than the two of us right now. Besides, maybe this time they'll believe you. The fire at the Hôtel Lambert was all over the papers, and the European Conclave is up in arms—they have witnesses who saw Leviathan! They can't deny it anymore."

"Even if they believe me now, they won't let our actions go unpunished. You know that better than I do," Schuyler pointed out.

"True, but that was when Charles Force was Regis. No one is leading the Conclave right now. They're frightened and disorganized. I think it would be safe to go home."

"Frightened people make the worst judgments," Schuyler argued. " I don't trust an organization that would make policy out of fear. And how about you? You're a traitor too, you know. What about your parents? They'll go after them." So far Oliver's family had been left alone, aside from their every move being tracked by the Venators: phones bugged, accounts analyzed. Oliver's parents told him on one of their rare satellite phone calls that they couldn't go to Dean & Deluca without feeling they were being watched.

Oliver took a gulp from his big Foster's can. "I think we can buy them."

Schuyler stacked her empty cup into her empty bowl. "Excuse me?"

"Pay them off. The Conclave needs money. They're pretty much broke. My parents have a ton. I can buy my way out of it, I know I can."

Why was she arguing? Oliver was telling her what she wanted to hear—that they could go home, and yet it frightened her. "I don't want to go."

"You're lying. You want to go home. I know it. And we are. End of discussion," Oliver said. "I'm booking us on the next flight back. I won't hear anything else."

Oliver didn't speak to her for the rest of the evening. She fell asleep with a crick in her neck from the tension. Why was she being so stubborn, she wondered as she drifted off to sleep. Oliver only wanted the best for her.

Why are you being so stubborn?

Schuyler opened her eyes.

She was in New York, in her bedroom. The faded Broadway *Playbill* covers that lined the walls were yellow and curling at the edges.

Her mother was sitting on her bed. This was a dream. But not the usual one. A dream about her mother. She didn't think about her much anymore. She hadn't even had time to say good-bye when they had left New York last year.

It was the first time she'd seen her mother since Allegra had appeared on Corcovado holding a sword.

Allegra looked at Schuyler sternly. "He is right, you know. The Conduits always are. You cannot live this way. The Transformation will kill you without the proper guidance and care. You cannot risk your life like this."

"But I can't go home," Schuyler said. "As much as I want to, I can't."

"Yes you can."

"I can't!" Schuyler rubbed her eyes.

"I know you are afraid of what will happen when you return. But you must face your fear, Schuyler. If you and Abbadon are meant to be, then there is nothing that any-one—not him, not even you—can do to stop it."

Her mother was right. She didn't want to go home be-cause then Jack would be so, so, so very close. Jack, who was still free . . . Jack, who had kissed her so passionately . . . who could still be hers. . . . But if she kept away, then she wouldn't be tempted to see him and betray Oliver.

"You cannot be with someone just because you don't want to hurt him. You have your own happiness to think about," Allegra said.

"But even if we're together, it will only kill Jack," Schuyler said. "It's against the Code. And he'll diminish . . ."

"If he will take the risk to be with you, who are you to tell him what to do with his life? Look at me. Look at how much I risked to be with your father."

"My father is dead. And you're in a coma. I practically grew up an orphan," Schuyler said, not even trying to keep the bitterness out of her voice. She had never known her father—he had died before she was born. As for Allegra—well, there wasn't much of a relationship anyone could have with a living corpse, now was there. "Tell me, Mother, was it worth it? Was your 'great' love for my father worth what has happened to your family?" She couldn't keep herself from saying such hurtful things. But everything spilled out after years of living alone.

She loved her mother, she did. But she didn't want an angel who only appeared once in a lifetime to give her some enchanted sword. Schuyler wanted a real parent: one who was there for her when she cried, who encouraged and prodded and annoyed her—a little bit—only because they cared so much. She wanted someone ordinary. Like Oliver's mom. She had no idea how Mrs. H-P knew where they would be, but every few months a package would arrive at their hotel, and inside would be chocolates and new socks and things they didn't even know they needed, like flashlights and batteries.

Allegra sighed. "I understand your disappointment in me. I hope that one day you will understand and forgive. There are consequences to every action. It is true, I have deep, deep regrets sometimes. But without your father I would never have had you. I was only with you for such a brief moment of time, but I treasured every moment—with you and your father. I would do it all over again if I had to. So yes. It was worth it."

"I don't believe you," Schuyler said. "No one in their right mind would choose your life."

"Be that as it may, come home, daughter. I am waiting for you. Come home."

THIRTY-EIGHT

Mimi

When Mimi opened her eyes, the auction room had slipped away and she was in the sanctuary, a small room with four walls made of stained glass. Of course, in the glom, it had never been destroyed.

She stood in a circle with the five other members; Forsyth, the seventh, stood in the middle. They were dressed in long black hooded robes. Like a bunch of grim reapers, Mimi thought. So much of the Blue Blood ways had seeped into popular culture—but twisted and stripped of their gravity.

"Welcome, everyone," Forsyth Llewellyn said, looking very puffed up and self-satisfied. Perfectly natural, Mimi thought, as he was assuming the highest office in the land, as head of a secret government the Red Bloods didn't even know existed. His work as a senator was completely perfunctory. Mimi heard he had done only superficial work toward helping to resolve the financial crisis that held the country in its grip.

Mimi had not been a full-serving member of the Conclave when Lawrence had been elected, but she had a vague idea of the proceedings.

Seymour Corrigan called the roll and started the ceremony. "Since the early days of this world, our Regis holds the soul of the Coven in his heart. But before he is chosen, he must be blessed by the Seven, and so we have gathered here today for the benediction." It was a ceremony that went back to ancient Egypt. Except this time there would be no false beard of goat's hair, no magic scepter, no symbolic leather whip, no crown of ostrich feathers. But the fundamentals were the same.

Warden Corrigan began the tabulation, calling out to the great houses by their names from the Sacred Language.

"What say you, Domus Magnificat?" The House of Riches was represented by Josiah Rockefeller Archibald, whose family had built the center on which they stood.

"We say aye," he murmured.

"What say you, Domus Veritas?" Of course the Venators were represented on the council, but Mimi was curious as to why Abe Tompkins spoke for them. He hadn't been an active Venator for many years.

"We say aye," old Abe responded.

"What say you, Domus Preposito?" The House of the Stewards was a title that had always been given to the family nearest to the Regis. The Llewellyns currently had that honor.

Forsyth Llwellyn smiled. "We say aye."

"What say you, Domus Stella Aquillo?" The House of the Northern Star was one of the biggest benefactors of art programs in the country. Ambrose Barlow looked nervously at Minerva Morgan. He bowed his head and whispered, "Aye."

There were only three houses left. Next to her, Mimi felt Minerva Morgan's anxiety. "What say you, Domus Domina?" The House of the Gray Lady. Death House, but no one called it that. The family that was in charge of the records, of the cycles of expression and expulsion.

Minerva Morgan did not respond.

"Domus Domina?" Seymour Corrigan cleared his throat. "Domus Domina!"

Minerva Morgan sighed. "Aye."

"Domus Lamia says aye," Warden Corrigan said, a bit grumpily. The House of the Vampyres; an old title, and the head of the Conspiracy.

Mimi braced herself. She was next.

Warden Corrigan coughed. "What say Domus Fortis Valerius Incorruputus, House of the Pure Blood, of the Uncorrupted, of the Valiant and the Strong, Protector of the Garden, Commander of the Lord's Armies? What say you?"

That was Michael's line. Gabrielle's line. The Van Alen

line, now bastardized by the Force name. Mimi raised her voice. "We say . . ." She wavered. She thought of Minerva Morgan's uncertainty. Ambrose Barlow, who was so old they had all thought he was senile. And yet he had brought in that piece of paper. Had brought it to her. They were counting on her. An anonymous note, but an important one. They were right. They could not discount its message.

Mimi suddenly understood that Ambrose and Minerva could not do it themselves, but they very much wanted her to. She was young, but she outranked them by far. She represented the house that had led this Coven of immortals for centuries upon centuries. The house that would now be stripped of its power by the very ritual they were undertaking.

She hadn't thought about it until today, but it suddenly hit home that they were just going to hand over the Coven to Forsyth Llewellyn. Who was Forsyth Llewellyn anyway? Mimi scanned her memories. A minor angel. A minor deity. A *steward*. He was no Regis.

She could do this. She had battled Silver Bloods and sent demons back to Hades. She would stand up when others could not. "The House of the Pure Blood would like to render their objection to this proceeding," she said clearly and confidently.

"Objection?" Seymour Corrigan looked confused.

"We say no." Mimi said.

"No?" Corrigan asked again.

"No." More clearly this time.

Forsyth, for his part, looked composed.

"I just don't understand why we need to do this—move the spirit of the Coven to a new leader when my father is still alive!" Mimi burst out. She took a deep breath. "Therefore I must object."

"The White Vote must be unanimous," Warden Corrigan said worriedly. "We cannot move the Coven to Forsyth's safekeeping unless it is a unanimous vote by the seven families." He looked lost, while Ambrose and Minerva looked relieved. Everyone else looked to Forsyth for guidance.

Mimi noticed that, White Vote or not, he was already their leader.

"We shall stay the installation as Warden Force wishes," Forsyth said smoothly. "I have no desire to assume a role that not everyone agrees is mine. And I too am distressed by Charles's disappearance. We shall wait."

One by one they popped back into the proceedings at the auction room. Mimi realized she was still holding her hand up, as she had been in the glom.

The auctioneer gave her a brilliant smile. "And *Portrait de Femme (Françoise Gilot)* goes to . . . the beautiful young lady in the front row!"

She had just bought a Picasso.

THIRTY-NINE

Bliss

*T*he fall semester at Duchesne always unrolled in the same tradition, never wavering from a schedule of activities that had been set a hundred years ago, or so it must have seemed to the students who were indoctrinated into the soothing, predictable rhythms of cushy private-school life. It started with the last week of August first-year orientation, when incoming freshmen were mildly hazed by their final-year tormentors with shaving-cream pie–throwing contests in the cortile, water balloon fights from the balconies, and an epic game of Murderer. On the final orientation day, there was a solemn presentation of class rings and the singing of the school song, culminating in a decidedly extracurricular after-hours party on the roof of the head boy's house, when the first of the May–December romances would blossom, usually between an "old girl" (what the school called female seniors) and a "new boy" (a male freshman), and not, as one would think, the other way around.

Bliss walked up the steps into the main building, nodding to a few familiar faces. Everyone was still a little tan from a Hamptons or Nantucket summer, the girls not quite ready to give up sundresses and sandals for wool and plaid, while the boys wore their broadcloth shirts untucked and their ties askew, holding their jackets over one shoulder with a rakish air.

Bliss had heard the Force twins were also back at school. She would have to try to contact them as soon as possible. Mimi and Jack had to help her.

As she walked to the locker room, noting the names engraved on each metal plate, she saw that Schuyler's and Oliver's names were missing. Facing the truth of their absence made her sad. She'd found out finally what had happened to them—something about the Conclave doubting Schuyler's version of events surrounding Lawrence's death, and how the two teenagers had decided to run from the Venators rather than face judgment.

But somehow she hadn't really believed they would be gone. During the course of the day she half expected to see Oliver sitting by the radiator in her AP European History class, or Schuyler looking up from her clay pots in Independent Art. Bliss walked to her third class before lunch period, Ancient Civilizations and the Dawn of the West. The first week of school was a shopping period, when students hopped from class to class until they decided which ones they were going to register for. The course had sounded intriguing—a mixture of history and philosophy, studying the Greeks, Romans, and Egyptians. She took a seat in the middle row, next to Carter Tuckerman, who always smelled like the egg sandwiches he ate for breakfast.

The teacher was a newbie, of a different type than the usual Duchesne faculty. Most of the teachers had been at the school forever—and looked it. Madame Fraley taught French, and the students were convinced she'd been at the school since the 1880s. (She probably had, since Madame was a Blue Blood.) Or else they were recent college grads, kids who had somehow flubbed their Teach for America applications and were stuck with a bunch of preppie brats instead of needy hardship cases. This one was different. Miss Jane Murray was an apple-cheeked sturdy woman of early middle age, with bright red hair and a ruddy Irish complexion. She wore a plaid skirt and a yellow shirt with an argyle vest. Her hair was cut in a blunt pageboy and her blue eyes twinkled when she spoke.

Miss Murray (she wrote it on the blackboard, and it was decidedly "Miss" not "Ms." She had gone to Miss Porter's, and in her mind a lady was not called by a buzzing sound) did not look like she had been around during the dinosaur era, nor did she have that lost fearful look of the post-collegiate.

"This is a mixed-class elective, and it is seminar-style, which means I will expect my students to participate in discussions and not just doze off or text each other. I don't promise not to bore you, but you may bore each other if you don't bring your own thoughts and ideas to the table," she said brightly, looking around with a cheerful smile.

When the sign-up sheet came around, Bliss decided to put her name down on the list, noticing that almost everyone in the room had done so as well. Bliss could read the room's reaction: Miss Murray was going to be a charming new addition to Duchesne life.

The bell rang, and as Bliss gathered her things, she overheard two girls talking animatedly as they jostled their way to the door.

"Omigod, our senior year is going to rock!" said Ava Breton.

"Totally!" squealed Haley Walsh. "The best!"

Senior year is going to rock. What a funny sentiment, Bliss thought as she followed them out of the room. *These were the best years of their lives.* Good lord, hopefully that wasn't true.

So far, Bliss's adolescence had, to put it frankly and literally, *sucked.* She'd moved to a new city, discovered she was a vampire, fallen in love and lost her love, all in one crazy year. And now she'd spent the last year possessed by a demon, who, by the way, was also her father—however that worked, she had no idea.

The Visitor had been gone for most of the week. And after Bliss had glimpsed the hellhole that was his mind, she was glad he was away. His visions had given her nightmares.

She could hardly sleep without thinking about what she had seen. Much worse, Dylan hadn't come back after that fateful day. She kept hoping he would suddenly show up somewhere—or else take her back to the Cloisters—but there was nothing but silence. It was as if she were all alone in her head again, and she knew that wasn't the case.

School finally let out at three, and Bliss went home. She entered the apartment and found Forsyth slumped at the kitchen table, surrounded by empty bottles of alcohol, and a dazed-looking woman draped on the couch. He was usually more discreet with his human familiars, and Bliss averted her eyes.

He jumped when she came in, and his face looked ashen. He looked at her fearfully.

"What's wrong?" she asked. "What happened?"

As soon as she spoke, he looked relieved. "Oh, it's only you," was all he said. Then he poured himself a pint of whiskey into a beer glass and downed it in one gulp. For a vampire, he was curiously affected by alcohol.

Bliss gave him a look, then went up to her room and shut the door. She had homework to do.

FORTY

Schuyler

ack was right. When Schuyler and Oliver returned to New York, there were no Venators waiting to arrest them at JFK. Still, neither of them was going to put their faith in the Conclave membership anytime soon. The plan was to keep Schuyler's return a secret, while Oliver would testify to the Conclave that Schuyler had deserted him so he would be able to go back to his family. Hopefully the Elders would believe him instead of handing him over to the Venators for a truth-telling session. It was a risk they had to take, but Oliver was confident he could "sell" his story.

Oliver had not been too keen on the idea of their pretend estrangement, but Schuyler had convinced him it was the only way to secure their freedom in New York.

Kennedy Airport was its usual chaotic mess as they maneuvered their way through the bustling terminal, looking for the bus that would take them to the subway.

"Welcome home." Oliver yawned and rubbed his stubble. It had been a twenty-hour flight from Sydney. Not fun in a too-small economy seat. The two of them had been squished in the middle row of five seats, bounded by a honeymooning couple, who noisily kissed the entire flight, and an adventure-tour group, who kept the stewardesses hopping with their cocktail orders.

Once outside the terminal, Schuyler took a deep breath and smiled. They had arrived in the middle of September, and the weather was still mild, with just a faint tinge of cold in the air. Fall was her favorite season. The hustle of the city, the limo drivers seeking their fares, the long line for yellow cabs, the taxi dispatcher barking at everyone to hurry up. It was good to be back.

They checked into a nondescript hotel by the West Side Highway, one of those big corporate institutions that was filled with weary business travelers. The room looked out into a light shaft, and the air-conditioning was noisy. Nonetheless, Schuyler slept soundly for the first time in months.

The next morning, Oliver reported to Conclave headquarters with his story, pledging his life to the Blue Blood community at large. Just as he'd predicted, once the Conclave got wind of what he was really offering (money), no questions were asked.

He told Schuyler afterward, back at their hotel, that the wardens didn't even seem concerned about her disappearance, or about enforcing any disciplinary action. What happened in Paris had changed the game. It had forced the Conclave to reconsider its actions concerning Leviathan's return. They had much bigger problems to deal with, and they just didn't care about her anymore. Or so it had seemed.

"You ready to go, then?" he asked. He had made an appointment for her at Dr. Pat's clinic. Patricia Hazard was the Conclave's most trusted doctor and also happened to be Oliver's aunt. "What did you do while I was out?"

"Nothing. I got an egg-and-cheese and a coffee from the deli across the street. Then I read the *Post*," Schuyler told him. "It was heaven."

Dr. Pat had redecorated. The last time Schuyler had been there, the office had looked like the lobby of a very white, very minimal, very modern hotel. This time the office resembled a bizarre but fabulous fun house. There were crystal vitrines filled with glass eyes. There was a lounge chair made out of stuffed animals that had all been stitched together; it was cute to the point of craziness. Venetian mirrors lined the walls, and fur throws were folded over white sofas. It still looked like a hotel lobby, but this time, instead of an ice queen, one expected Willy Wonka to appear.

"Hey, Dr. Pat, what happened here?" Schuyler asked as she followed the good doctor into the examination room (which she was glad to find still looked like a standard exam room).

"I got tired of all that dry-cleaning. White is really hard

to maintain." Dr. Pat smiled. "Oliver, your mother wants to know what you'd like for dinner," she told her nephew before closing the door.

Dr. Pat had gone to their hotel room the night before to give Schuyler a thorough physical examination, taking blood samples, but she had asked Schuyler to come to the office for the results.

"So. What's wrong with me?" Schuyler asked, hopping onto the table.

Dr. Pat referred to her chart. "Well, all your bloodwork came back normal—for a human as well as a vampire. Blood pressure, thyroid, everything. Normal."

"But there must be something."

"Oh, there is." Dr. Pat put down the clipboard and leaned against the wall, crossing her arms. "Isolation is not good for the immortal soul," she said. "You must be among your own kind—you have been away too long. Your body has become tense, toxic."

"That's it?" Schuyler asked. "That's the reason why I've been so sick lately? Because I've been away from other vampires?"

"Strange as it sounds, yes." Dr. Pat nodded, tapping on her stethoscope. "The blood calls to same. You have been alone, stressed, and alienated from vampire society. My nephew tells me you went to the Bal des Vampires in Paris. Did you feel better when you were there?"

Schuyler thought about it. She hadn't noticed in the

adrenaline of the moment, but Dr. Pat was right. During the time when she was surrounded by Blue Bloods she had experienced none of the uncontrollable shaking and trembling. Except, of course, for those few minutes she had spent alone in the dungeon. A hundred feet belowground, away from everyone, until Jack arrived. The tremors had returned once she and Oliver had hit the road.

"They say no man is an island," Dr. Pat mused. "It's the same for Blue Bloods."

"But what about my grandfather? Lawrence was exiled. He lived alone for many, many years, away from his people. Yet he never exhibited any of my symptoms," Schuyler argued.

"Your grandfather, as I recall, was an Enmortal. A rare breed. Capable of long periods of isolation from the community. He chose exile because he knew he would be able to handle it. Physically and mentally."

Schuyler absorbed the diagnosis. "It just . . . seems . . . too easy an explanation," she finally said.

"You know, Schuyler, the Red Bloods have a word for it too. Homesickness isn't just a state of mind. It has physical symptoms as well. Your vampire self makes you stronger and faster than any human being. But the vampire in you also exaggerates every human ailment you might feel. You've got the best of both worlds, so to speak."

FORTY-ONE

Mimi

*T*wo weeks after the White Vote was called, Mimi found a note in her Conclave e-mail asking her to visit Forsyth at the Repository in the Force Tower that afternoon. Her last class was a free period, so she finished early and took a cab.

She had to be at the Repository anyway. The other evening she had been looking for her favorite fountain pen and thought to rummage around Charles's study. She remembered she had left it there the last time she had needed a quiet space to do her homework. Her father's office was as tidy as always, with nothing on his desk but a Tiffany clock and a desk calendar. Mimi had checked drawers and cabinets, but did not find her treasured Montblanc.

She had sat in his leather swivel desk chair and spun, looking around the room. A few unmarked cassettes shoved toward the back of a shelf caught her eye. She stood up and examined them. What was Charles doing with such old audio equipment? They were marked *RH: Audio: Ven. Rep.* Repository of History Audio Archives. Venator Reports. Usually tapes from the Repository came with written transcripts, but Mimi couldn't find any. She turned the tape over to see which Venator had filed them. *MARTIN.* These were Kingsley's reports, from his assignment two years ago. The one that had sent him to Duchesne.

What were they doing in Charles's office? They belonged in the Repository. And if Mimi wanted to listen to them, she would have to borrow an old tape recorder from the archives. She knew the Conduits were uploading everything onto digital files now, but they had obviously missed these. She had put the tapes in her pocket and taken one final look around the room. Where was Charles anyway? What had happened to him? Jack was convinced he wasn't dead. If Michael's spirit was gone from Earth, they would know for certain, he had argued.

At last night's meeting, the Conclave had voted to send Venators after the missing former Regis, and a team was being assembled. She knew her brother was disappointed not to have been picked for the assignment. But Forsyth had been adamant: they needed the twins here, he said. They couldn't leave the Coven so unprotected.

As she walked into the Force Tower that afternoon, she wondered what the senator wanted to talk to her about. Forsyth had never sought out her company before, and they had not spoken about her objection to his crowning.

"You wanted to see me?" Mimi asked, walking into the light-filled corner office after Forsyth's secretary announced her arrival. She noticed that he had set up shop in the same office Lawrence had chosen when he was Regis. Talk about overconfidence. Charles had used the one in the old building under Block 122.

"Madeleine. Thanks for stopping by," Forsyth said. "Doris, hold my calls, will you dear?"

His secretary closed the door, and Mimi took a seat across from the expansive walnut desk. She noticed that even though Forsyth had taken over Lawrence's office, he still kept the former Regis's photos of Schuyler on his desk. Mimi wished she had dressed up more; she had come straight from gym, and hadn't bothered to change out of her ratty Duchesne Athletics T-shirt and red running shorts. She put her bags on the floor and waited for him to speak.

"I just wanted to commend you on your work with the Venators. You did a fine job in Rio." He beamed.

Mimi scoffed. "Yeah. Right. We didn't find her."

"Only a matter of time, my dear. Kingsley will find her. I have no doubt. He's quite . . . resourceful," Forsyth said, with a hint of annoyance Mimi could not help but notice.

"All right. Well, thanks. I did want to go on another mission, but the Conclave says I have to finish Duchesne first. The school isn't going to hold my place for that long."

"Alas, that is true. It is unfair, is it not, that we have to go through the rigamarole of a human childhood and adolescence. But it is in the Code," Forsyth said, getting up to fix himself a drink from the bar cart. He picked up a carafe and poured a shot of whiskey into a glass. "Want one?"

"No thanks." Mimi shook her head."Um, is that all? May I be excused now?"

"Oh, I am carrying on as usual. Bliss likes to tease me about being a big blowhard." Forsyth smiled, taking a sip and walking around his desk so he could lean on the edge of it and look down at Mimi.

Mimi sank lower in her seat. Llewellyn rarely spoke of Bliss. The bemused-father act didn't suit him too well: it felt bogus, like he was trying to sell her a used car, or get her to believe he cared an iota about his daughter. At least Charles and Trinity had *tried* to be there for Mimi and Jack during their Transformation. As far as Mimi knew, Bliss's parents never bothered to explain to her what was happening.

"How is Bliss?" she asked. Mimi had bumped into her a couple of times, and Bliss had seemed friendly enough, but their conversations never seemed to go anywhere. She didn't know why that was, but something about Bliss made her feel nervous and giggly.

"She's much better." Forsyth Llewellyn nodded. "Anyway, I called you in today to discuss a rather delicate situation . . . and forgive me if I offend . . . I realize this may not be the right time for such an occasion, but I feel that after everything that's happened with the Conclave . . . the community needs something to lift its spirits right now, and perhaps, if I may . . ."

Mimi made a motion to let him continue.

"A simple favor . . . for the betterment of the entire community. I know you and Jack canceled your bonding because of the tragedy, but now is the time to renew morale, to show our people that we are still strong, and to see the two of you together. Our strongest, our best, will bring them hope."

A wry smile played on Mimi's lips even if her heart suddenly clenched and an image of Kingsley's smirking face came to mind.

"So what you're telling me is, the bonding's on?" she asked. It took no effort to keep her tone light and breezy. After all, she was still the same Mimi Force whose image was plastered on a billboard across from Times Square. The Mimi Force who tortured freshmen for sport, making them fetch and grovel. (How she had missed orientation week!)

Hopefully she would still fit into her dress. . . .

FORTY-TWO

Bliss

*I*f Dylan wasn't going to come to her, maybe she could go to him. The Conclave urged its newest members to perform the regression therapy to access their past lives and learn from the accumulated knowledge that was available to them from the vastness of their prior experience.

Bliss sat cross-legged on her princess bed. She closed her eyes and began the deep sorting through many lifetimes of memories. This was the knowing. The practice of finding out who you really were. She was in the void, in that space in between her conscious and subconscious self—who had she been before? What shape had her spirit taken in its prior histories?

She was dancing across a crowded ballroom. She was sixteen years old, and her mother had let her wear her hair up for the first time . . . and she was laughing because tonight she would meet the boy who would be her husband—and even before he came to stand in front of her to ask her to dance, she knew his face.

"Maggie." He smiled. Had he always kept his hair that way?

Even in the nineteenth century, Dylan—or Lord Burlington—made her heart pound.

But then, something happened at the party—the Visitor whispering lies in her ear. Telling her to kill. Maggie could hear him. Maggie did not want this, did not believe it . . . and before Bliss could open her eyes, she could feel the cold water surrounding her.

Maggie Stanford had drowned herself in the Hudson. Bliss saw the dark murky river, felt her lungs burst and her heart collapse.

As Bliss went backward, it was all the same. Goody Bradford had set herself on fire, pouring oil over her head, and then she had lit a match and let the flames consume her. Giulia de Medici "accidentally" walked off the balcony of the family's villa in Florence, her broken body splayed in the center of the square.

Quick as the flutter of a butterfly's wings, every image, every "death" Bliss had ever experienced came to the forefront. But then . . . Maggie walked out of the funeral home. Goody Bradford survived the flames. Giulia got up from the fall.

None of them had been successful in ending their lives,

or successful in exorcising the demon that possessed them. They had all tried and they had all failed.

Bliss understood.

I have to die.

Because if she died—truly died—if she found a way to never come back, then the Visitor would die as well. He would never have a chance to do what he was planning.

That was it. That was the only way. She knew it.

There was no getting out of it. There was no surviving it. She and the Visitor were locked in a fatal embrace. If she was able to kill her spirit, the undying blood in her arms, she would bring death to him as well.

She would have to make this sacrifice, or else those horrible visions, that terrible future, would be unavoidable. She was a vessel for evil, and as long as she lived, so did he.

"Dylan, you knew, didn't you? You knew what I would have to do. All along," she whispered.

From the darkness, Dylan appeared at last. He looked at her mournfully. "I didn't want to tell you."

FORTY-THREE

Schuyler

*I*t had been a few days since Schuyler had visited Dr. Pat's clinic, and her new life in New York was finally starting to take shape. That afternoon she and Oliver stopped by the real estate office that was holding the keys to the small studio apartment in Hell's Kitchen, which Oliver had secured for her, paying a year's rent in cash. To obscure her identity, Schuyler would pretend to be the only daughter of a single mom: an ex-hippie folk singer who was usually on tour with her band. With Schuyler's ability to transform her facial features, she could even pretend to be the mom on occasions that demanded it. *Mutatio* was easier now that she felt like herself again.

They took the subway across town and ended up in a bustling section of Ninth Avenue, a neighborhood that was a mixture of corporate dormitories for Wall Street newbies as well as shabbier walk-up buildings next to strip clubs and triple-X video stores. But there was a grocery store not too far away, and Schuyler and Oliver loaded up on a week's worth of food: organic vegetables, a loaf of raisin bread from Sullivan Street Bakery, cans of beans. Oliver pushed her to splurge on the Spanish ham and a block of French double-cream cheese. The clean, wide aisles of the supermarket gladdened her heart; it was good to be back in America again, where everything was so easy and convenient.

The studio was located in one of the shabbier buildings, as Schuyler had wanted, and it was very small: if she stood in the middle of the room, she could almost touch all four walls with her fingertips. The apartment came furnished with a hot plate, a microwave, and a futon that rolled into a corner. The lone window opened up to a view of the light shaft. Still, it was better than living in a hotel. It was New York. It was home.

"Are you sure about this?" Oliver asked. Schuyler had entered the building wearing the hippie-mom mask, and she felt her features relax back into her own as soon as he had closed the door. "You don't have to stay here, you know. My dad has a place downtown—for when he works late. You could stay there," he told her.

"I know it's not as nice as your house. Or even my old one," Schuyler said, looking through the empty cupboards and finding little black plastic roach motels in the corners. "But I don't think we should be seen together at all. We can't jeopardize your status in the Coven."

The house on Riverside Drive was a mere cab ride away. Hattie would be there with her homemade pot roasts, and Julius to show her card tricks. But she could not go back. Not yet. She knew the minute she stepped through the doorway, the Conclave would know. She had no idea how she knew this, but she felt it instinctively and knew she was right. She had to keep away. They might not be interested in her right now, but she had a feeling that would change.

She felt safer in the studio already. Already she felt she was Skye Hope—not Schuyler Van Alen. She and Oliver had decided it was a name a former flower child would give her offspring. Plus, if people called her by a name she was used to answering to, there was less of a chance Schuyler would slip up.

Alexander Hamilton High was the local public school, and they had accepted Schuyler's last-minute registration with no questions or complaint. Oliver had pushed for one of the other private schools: Nightingale, Spence, Brearley. But even he had to agree it was too dangerous. Those institutions were crawling with Blue Bloods. At Hamilton High, there would be little chance of anyone from the Conclave finding out she was there. The elite might give lip service (and donor money) to their commitment to public education but never went so far as to actually send their children there. For the Conclave to believe the story of Schuyler and Oliver's estrangement, Oliver would have to return to Duchesne without her.

But she would have to continue her education somehow. What had Lawrence always said? School was more than academics; an education prepared you for the humdrum of real life: working with others, tempering one's personality to assimilate with the group but without losing your individual identity, understanding the factors of logic, reasoning, and debate. For a person—vampire or human—to succeed in the world, unlocking the mysteries of the universe was insufficient. One would also need to grasp the mysteries of human nature.

"Are you sure there isn't another reason I should be here with you?" Oliver asked.

But she didn't want to answer him right then. She was still sorting out her feelings, starting to wonder if maybe her mother could be right. If maybe love was something you had to fight for—no matter what the cost. She didn't want to hurt Oliver. She would rather die herself than see him suffer. But she needed time to think. Alone.

"I'll be okay; I'm in New York—see—the shaking, it's gone," Schuyler said, raising her hands to her face in wonder. Had she simply been homesick, as Dr. Pat had said? That her blood had called to her own kind? Was that all it was? Truly? That she was close to a coven once again?

"Good," Oliver said. "Well. You have my cell. You can call me anytime. You know that."

"I'll miss you," Schuyler said. "I already miss you." But they had to do this, to keep the other safe.

"Well. Have fun," he said reluctantly, and with one final hug, he was out the door.

As she unpacked the groceries, she noticed Oliver had left his mail among the stack of papers for Schuyler's new apartment.

There was a thick white envelope stuck in the middle of the bills and magazines. It didn't have a stamp, which meant it had come directly from someone in the Conclave. They always hand-delivered their correspondences.

It was an invitation to a bonding, Schuyler saw, and without having to check, she knew that the address embossed on the back would be the Force town house.

FORTY-FOUR

Mimi

*T*he Starbucks at the corner of Fifth and Ninety-fifth had closed, so Mimi had to walk a few more blocks to EuroMill, a fancy new coffee "boutique" that had recently opened. The EuroMill had taken the gourmet coffee culture to a new level. They had a fat binder where a customer could choose the bean, the roasting, even the way the flavor was "extracted" (hand-drip, siphon, French press, or "solo").

The place resembled an art gallery: white walls with square blackboards, the coffee grinders and espresso machines polished to a gleam, mirroring the artwork on display.

"How can I help you?" the nose-ringed barista asked.

"La Montana, slow clover," Mimi said, meaning she wanted a cup of the El Salvador roast through the no-sediment French press. "Two of them. To go. Oh, and one

257

of those," she said, pointing to a chocolate croissant behind the glass display.

A sharp whistle drew her attention. At one of the middle tables, among the writers typing on laptops and the private-school crowd angling for their breakfast lattes, sat the rest of her former Venator team.

"Hey, guys," Mimi said with a smile. Had it only been a month since the four of them had battled Brazilian drug gangs and Silver Bloods in the jungle?

She was gifted with a rare grin from the Lennox boys, who soon took their leave. Ted slapped her on the back, even. "Force." Kingsley nodded. He kicked the chair next to him away from the table so she could sit down.

"Let me guess. Café con leche? Four sugars?" Mimi smirked as she tried to still the butterflies in her stomach. They hadn't seen each other since landing in New York. What happened in Rio stayed in Rio, wasn't that how the saying went? If she'd thought Kingsley would seek her out afterward, she'd been wrong. What did she care anyway? It hadn't mattered back then, and it sure didn't matter now.

Kingsley raised his cup to hers. "Back to school, I take it? Senior year?" He teased. "You know, it's a funny thing . . . I never did go to high school. I mean, not in any real sense. The first time I went was when I got assigned to the Duchesne case."

"Don't tell me you miss it," she joked. She wondered how old Kingsley was. Silver Bloods were like Enmortals, they were free of the cycles. They didn't age, almost as if they were frozen in time. She knew a little about Kingsley's history: he had been corrupted by a Silver Blood in Rome, but had been forgiven by Michael himself and welcomed back into the Blue Blood community.

"Maybe a little. The little announcements at the start of the day. All that peer counseling. Very self-actualizing." He grinned to let her know he was making fun, but not making fun of her.

The barista yelled from the counter. "Two clovers!"

"That's mine!" Mimi said, collecting her order. Some things didn't change: even if this was no Starbucks, the coffee still came in a cup the size of a pitcher. "I should go or I'll be late," she told Kingsley. She picked up her satchel and swung it over her shoulder, holding the two drinks in a cardboard carrier.

"I heard about the bonding," Kingsley said quietly. He put down his coffee cup and signaled to the waitress for another.

"Forsyth told you."

"Indeed. He explained that since Charles is still MIA, he's giving you away."

"So? What of it?" she challenged.

Kingsley smiled sweetly. "Nothing. I just wanted to congratulate you. You'll make a beautiful bride."

Now it was Mimi's turn to blush uncharacteristically. She didn't know what she had expected. Him to plead with her? To ask her not to bond with Jack? Ridiculous. Impossible. Kingsley was exactly like her: selfish, dangerous, unable to follow rules. Had she wanted him to feel something for her when she felt nothing for him?

She stared at him, her cheeks slowly burning. He returned her gaze steadily.

"Dude, I don't know why I even bother," Mimi said, and she left, storming out of the café.

A year ago, when Mimi had returned from Rio to New York, there had been no time to even think about the bonding. Everything had been canceled immediately. It wasn't the right time, and after what had happened, she and Jack were too shell-shocked to think of it. Deposits were lost, her gown taken to storage. A week later she had confronted him about his little affair with the half-blood, and they had reconciled. In any case, Schuyler had ceased to be a problem: the little wench had left New York and Jack. She was following in the footsteps of her mother, headed to some sad tragic end, Mimi hoped.

But instead of Schuyler's absence leading to a deeper relationship, the two of them being alone together at last had caused an estrangement between them. But this time it was Mimi who had withdrawn. She didn't want to be second choice. She didn't want Jack to be with her only because he couldn't be with the person he truly loved.

Jack in her arms was nothing but a Phyrric victory. Mimi

wanted him to love her and to mean it. But every day, it appeared he was doing the same thing he always did: paying lip service to their bond, placating her fears with lies, while his eyes betrayed the deeper truth: that his heart still belonged to another.

And so she had escaped. She had joined up with the Venators. She had left *him*. See how well he would do without her. She wanted him to miss her. She wanted him to miss her so desperately he would understand exactly how much she meant to him. She thought that if she left, he would realize the error of his ways, and discover the deep bond between them. She might as well have stayed home.

Nothing had changed. Jack had gone his way and she had gone hers. When she had told him about Forsyth's request, he had accepted the new date of their bonding without comment. He would bond with her. But he would find no joy in the process: the groom as dead man walking. She was tired of it.

She found Jack standing at the corner, his messenger bag slung across his broad shoulders. He really needed a haircut, she thought.

"Here you go." She handed her twin his coffee.

"Thanks."

They walked to school, their steps easily matching the other's. Even after a year away, they fell in line together. In a weird way, they would always be bonded even without the official ceremony.

"Here's your croissant. Probably not as good compared to Paris, right?" Mimi asked.

Jack took a bite. "It's okay." He shrugged. When she'd mentioned Paris, his lips twitched, like they did whenever he was upset.

But for the first time in a very long time, Mimi couldn't care less about what was bothering him.

FORTY-FIVE

Bliss

HERE R U? MISS U. AM BACK & WANT 2 C U. WHY
HAVEN'T U TXTD ME?

Bliss read the text. Her thumb hovered over the REPLY
button, but in the end she put her phone away. No. She
wasn't safe to be around. She didn't want any more of her
friends to suffer because of her.

"Sorry," she said, when she noticed Miss Murray looking in her direction.

"Glad you decided to join us," her teacher said with a
stern smile.

Bliss didn't need to be told twice. Ancient Civilizations
had quickly become her favorite class, and she didn't want to
miss any of it. It was like a particularly good program on the
History Channel, except without the cheesy reenactments.
In the past few weeks they had covered such diverse and fas-
cinating topics as Etruscan feminism (those Etruscan chicks

ruled—literally), Egyptian funeral rites and the four types of love according to the ancient Greeks (from platonic to passionate), and how the ideas related to the birth of Western culture.

Today the topic was the reign of the third emperor of Rome. Caligula. When Miss Murray had handed the assignment to Allison Ellison last week, there had been much tittering. Most of the class was familiar with a certain movie that played on cable. Or if not, like Bliss, they knew the basics of the emperor's reputation: sexual perversity, insanity, cruelty.

"My thesis today—please excuse me, Miss Murray— since the class *is* called Ancient Civilizations and the Dawn of the West, is that the West—or the idea of it—truly died with the assassination of Caligula," Allison began. The tall girl stood in front of the blackboard and read confidently from her note cards.

"Interesting theory. Please explain," Miss Murray said, leaning forward from her desk at the front of the room.

"As you all know, Caligula was assassinated by a conspiracy headed by leading members of the Senate. They stabbed him multiple times. By the time his loyal guards came, he was dead. The Senate then attempted to restore the Roman Republic, but the military did not support them—they remained loyal to the empire. With the help of the Praetorian Guard, they installed Claudius as emperor."

"So you are saying Caligula's death did exactly the

opposite of what the Senate intended?" questioned Miss Murray.

Allison nodded enthusiastically. "With the death of Caligula came the death of the idea of the Republic. The empire was infallible. The people grieved for their murdered emperor, no matter how cruel or insane his enemies said he was. And with Caligula's death, the death of the Republic was all but confirmed. The Romans never tried to bring it back again.

"The Senate's greatest achievement, then, in murdering the emperor was solidifying the people's loyalty to the empire," Allison said. "It's ironic, isn't it? Especially since it wasn't the first attempt on Caligula's life. His sisters Agrippina and Julia Livilla had tried to kill him before, but failed. They were unsuccessful and banished. But the Senate succeeded where they did not."

There was a hand up. "I thought Caligula was . . . um, you know, *close* to his sisters," Bryce Cutting insinuated with a smirk.

Miss Murray interjected this time. "He was certainly 'close,' as you say, to his sister Drusilla. She was treated as the head of his household, and when she died, he mourned the loss like a widower. He even had the Senate name her a goddess. But as to whether they were close in a Biblical sense, history is ambiguous on the subject. Understand, class, that just like today, they tried to discredit their rulers with sex scandals and all sorts of salacious lies. If you believe half the things you read, everyone is a sexual pervert in antiquity. Perhaps Caligula and Drusilla were lovers. Or perhaps they simply wanted to solidify their power, to rule as brother and sister, as did the Egyptian despots."

Bliss looked up from her notes. For some reason she had the sense that she was not hearing about distant historical figures safely entombed in the past and in the pages of history books. Instead, when she heard the names Drusilla, Agrippina, and Julia Livilla, she felt her skin tingle. These were people she *knew*.

Dylan, I think I'm getting close. I think this is what I am meant to—

"Thanks, Miss M.," Allison said. "Anyway, for the trivia portion of my presentation, I wanted to add that even though we all call him Caligula, it was just a nickname, which he probably didn't like too much since it meant "Little Boot." His real name was the same as Julius Caesar's. They called him Gaius."

Gaius. Yes. That was what they used to call the Visitor.

And Allison was absolutely right. He had despised that nickname.

Bliss felt as if everything was coming back too fast and too soon—memories were falling like snowflakes, bright and glittering in her mind—but these were the Visitor's memories: Rome, the final days, the deception, the betrayal. First with his sisters—Agrippina he could understand (Bliss was shocked to find the image of Agrippina looking back at her with the eyes of Mimi Force)—Agrippina and Valerius had sided with that damned Cassius or whatever they had called Michael back then. But *Julia!* How could she do this to him—his baby sister, the youngest child—she was so young when she first suspected, and it was she who had called Cassius's attention to his Corruption—Julia Livilla . . . how Julia hated that name—said it reminded her of her awful aunt, whom she despised. She had wanted to be called something else. . . .

Sophia.

He had been so close. So close to having his dream realized. He had come so close, only to have Cassius ruin everything. . . .

In her mind, Bliss saw what the Visitor had seen back then. A path. A winding path deep below the city of Lutetia, through tunnels far beneath the earth, a winding path that led underground, to a coven of demons bowing to his crown. . . . He would rise again, majestic and glorious, the Prince of Paradise once again . . . forever. All the world would shake and cower. The rivers would run with blood and the horsemen would be unleashed. . . . There would be no escape from Satan's army.

This was the crisis in Rome.

Bliss gasped.

The demons. The deaths. The Corruption. All this had happened before.

And it was going to happen again. Unless . . .

She blinked. She was sitting in the classroom, Allison was done, and everyone was stuffing books and papers into their bags. Miss Murray was looking at her curiously. "Are you all right, Bliss?"

"Yes," she said. "I just . . . I think I forgot to eat breakfast."

Miss Murray nodded. "You know, Bliss, that if you find you need someone to talk to, I'm here for you."

Bliss nodded. Teachers at Duchesne were always super-empathic. The school policy was an "all-hands" approach. They didn't wait for troubled students to find their way to the guidance counselor's office. "Sure, Miss M. Thanks." Miss Murray was smiling at her so kindly that she found herself talking, even though she had not meant to say anything.

"It's just . . . I have this problem, see . . . and I'm worried about bringing my friend into it . . . but I have a feeling she's the only one who can help me."

"I see." Miss Murray crossed her arms. "Sometimes it's good to ask for help, Bliss. And friends are the only people we can trust when we are in trouble. That's what they're for, anyway. I'm sure your friend would be glad that you had reached out to her."

Bliss nodded. "I think . . . I think you're right."

"Good." Miss Murray smiled. For a moment, she reminded Bliss of someone, but she couldn't figure out who.

Bliss removed her cell phone from her handbag. Her history teacher had helped her make a decision. She couldn't do this alone, and the Force twins were no help at all. Trying to have a meaningful conversation with Jack was impossible. He stalked the halls of Duchesne with a shuffling, mournful air, as if grieving the loss of something precious. He rarely smiled anymore. Bliss had even seen him barking at the freshmen who got in his way, which was completely unlike him. Jack had always been kind to new students.

As for Mimi, Bliss had felt the temptation to confide in her, but so far all Mimi ever wanted to talk about was lipstick and jeans, and there was no way for Bliss to steer the conversation in a more serious direction. Mimi had once been so interested in the Conclave, but now she acted as if she could care less about what happened to the Blue Bloods.

But there was someone who could help her. There was someone who would understand. Someone who was just as intimately connected to everything that had happened as she was, and who deserved to know everything. She couldn't shield her friend even if she wanted to. She was part of this too.

Bliss punched a quick reply on the screen.

TOMORROW. MEET ME AT THE PRADA SAMPLE SALE.

Forty-six

Schuyler

chuyler was familiar with the horror stories of
American public education: the overcrowded class-
rooms, the violent students, the indifferent teachers. She had
no idea what to expect: graffiti-ridden walls? Metal detectors?
Roving gangs slashing innocent victims in the hallways?

It was early October, and as she walked into the school,
a nondescript building on 22nd Street, she tried not to look
too surprised. It was orderly. The metal detectors were built
into the entrance, so students wouldn't feel like they were
walking into a prison. You had to walk through a metal de-
tector to get into the Met, right? Not that this was anything
like the Met, but it wasn't something out of Jonathan Kozol
either. She had even managed to get in to the few AP and
honors classes offered. She had a locker, a homeroom, and
a pretty good English teacher.

But even though she was relieved that Hamilton High

exceeded her expectations, as she walked through the hallways that always smelled slightly of Pine-Oil cleaner, she realized with a pang how much she had loved Duchesne. Especially now that she could never go back.

At least she would be seeing Bliss tomorrow. Schuyler decided enough was enough. There were *some* people she could trust in this world and Bliss was one of them. She was keen on seeing her friend, and wondered why it had taken Bliss so long to get back to her. Maybe she was mad at her for deserting her—Schuyler hoped not—she had to make Bliss understand, they'd had no choice but to leave. Oliver said that at school Bliss was friendly but uninterested, acting as if they were mere acquaintances and nothing more.

It hurt to think of everyone back at Duchesne without her. She didn't know what the future held, but she had a feeling it would not bring SAT prep classes and early admissions letters. She was here to follow her grandfather's advice: to learn how to move in human society without giving away her vampire ancestry.

One thing Hamilton lacked was a proper library. Oh, it had a tiny library, a room the size of a closet displaying old S. E. Hinton paperbacks, with a bank of computer terminals where everyone checked their e-mails. Studying at home had always made Schuyler feel itchy, and one of the things she loved about her new neighborhood was that she wasn't too far from the New York Public Library.

She liked the reading room on the second floor, where

the writers worked—the ones with the library fellowships. It was always quiet there. She was walking up the grand staircase one afternoon after a long day of classes when who should be walking down but Jack Force.

He didn't look too surprised to see her back in New York. "I'm glad to see you took my advice finally," he said by way of greeting. He did not smile. "Welcome back."

"Thanks. It's good to be back," she said, trying to appear as nonchalant as he was. Jack had let his hair grow out a little since they had seen each other last, now that he wasn't a Venator anymore. It curled behind his ears and over his shirt collar. "What are you doing here anyway?" Duchesne had a wonderful library—on the top floor, with a view of Central Park. And whatever could not be found in the Duchesne library could be found in the vampire Repository.

"Trinity's on the board for the Library Lions," Jack said. "Since she's been in D.C., she asked me if I could fill in during the meeting."

Schuyler nodded. She had come back to New York, but had come back too late. When she'd spied the invitation the other evening, her heart had not thumped wildly in her chest, her mouth had not turned dry, her eyes had not threatened to water. She had almost expected it, somehow. She was resigned to the news by now.

"About the Conclave," she started. "Are they . . . ?"

"Don't worry about them. You are safe for now. Oliver did a fine job with his story of your estrangement.

Thankfully there's no one on the Conclave who knows the two of you well. Because if they did they would realize there's absolutely no truth to it," he said. "He is a good friend to you."

She knew it took an effort for him to say it, and she thought she would return the gesture. "So . . . I hear . . . congratulations are in order. You and Mimi."

"Ah. Yes." He appeared pleased.

Schuyler understood they would not talk about what had happened between them in Paris. The kiss. It was as if Jack were standing behind a block of ice. He was unreachable. His face set in stone. Already he was shutting her out. He had tried so hard so many times, and she had always rejected him. On Perry Street. In Paris. He would not give her another chance, she knew.

She had come too late. She had followed her heart and had come too late, as usual. In two weeks he would be lost to her forever. He would be bonded to Mimi, but at least he would be safe. It's all she ever wanted for him. "I'm happy for you," she said brightly. "Really. I mean . . . I know what it's like to be alone in the world, and I wouldn't want that for you."

"Thank you," he said. "I wish you the same."

Jack lingered on the stairway. It looked as if he were going to say something else, but thought better of it. With a wave of his hand, he was gone.

Schuyler forgot what she had come to the library to find.

She blinked back tears and felt her throat constrict. Soon her whole body was shaking as badly as it ever had, but this was no Transformation-related sickness. She was wrong. She was not strong. Her heart was breaking, she could feel it— nothing would ever be the same. Her eyes watered, and she knew if she did not stop herself, she would soon be sobbing on the staircase.

So this was how a love affair ends: with a random meeting on a public staircase. A few polite words and nothing real said, even though their world was ending. And so, with the most self-control she had ever managed, she dried her tears, picked up her books, and continued up the stairs.

She would just have to endure.

Forty-seven

Mimi

Coordinating a bonding was easier than Mimi expected. Especially since the whole package—St. John's Cathedral, the Met reception, the Boys Choir of Harlem, the Peter Duchin Orchestra, and a dozen other details—had all been decided upon a year ago. It was simply a matter of securing a new date and rehiring vendors, most of whom were more than happy to take her security deposit once again. The bonding was set for mid-October, the earliest date that worked for everyone.

But Mimi wasn't thinking of her upcoming bonding as she sat in the lobby of the Mandarin Oriental hotel, waiting for Kingsley Martin to arrive that evening. It was the farthest thing from her mind, almost as if the whole bonding scenario were simply a role she would step into at the right moment, like a glass slipper that had to fit. But until then, she could do as she pleased.

The Repository aide who had unearthed the tape re-corder that was able to play the tapes from Charles's study had advised her to go easy on it; it was the only one they had left. He couldn't even let her take it out of the building.

"Venators don't like to upgrade," he'd grumbled, hand-ing her the bulky black object. "We've given them the at-tachments for their phones, but they still use their old junk to turn stuff in. Someone gave us a report on parchment the other day. In longhand. You know how hard that is to read? Let alone retype?"

Mimi had murmured sympathies, and then found an empty cubicle and some headphones. She started to listen.

She had spent almost the entire night at the Repository, leaving only so she wouldn't miss her first class.

When Kingsley finally walked in, she wondered why it was that almost every time she was with him, she had been awake for more than twenty-four hours.

As he sauntered over, Mimi noticed how everyone at the bar turned to gape at him. Talk about using the glamour.

"You're late," she said, tapping at her watch.

"No, you're just early." Kingsley smiled and slid in next to her on the banquette.

She inched away from him. "Aren't you staying at this hotel? You don't even have an excuse. I've been waiting for over an hour for you." And Mimi Force did not wait for anyone. It was a new and frustrating experience. She'd read the looks of pity from the cocktail waitress.

Kingsley yawned. "I know you're not here to talk about my inability to master time management. So what's up?"

"Order first," Mimi snarled, as the waitress glided up to their table. Mimi noticed the girl was already making eyes at Kingsley.

"Macallan. Straight. And whatever the lady desires," Kingsley said, winking at Mimi.

"I'll have a dirty martini," Mimi said.

"And I'll have to see your ID," the waitress said with a fake smile.

I have never been carded in my life! Mimi wanted to scream. *This is New York City! Do you even have any idea how old I am?* But before Mimi could say anything, or use the glom to her advantage, Kingsley reached over and snagged her purse and plucked out Mimi's driver's license to hand to the waitress. The girl didn't even bother to look at it. "Whiskey and a martini coming right up."

"Smooth. What did you do? Change the date?" Mimi asked. Some vampires had the ability to transform inanimate objects. Mimi would have loved that talent. Imagine all the knockoffs she could turn into real Birkins! She'd make a fortune.

"Nah. No need. She just wanted to mess with you. It's my attention she was after."

"You're really something else, aren't you?"

Kingsley grinned. "I've missed you, Force. You still mad at me from last time? I hope not. No hard feelings, yeah?"

She snorted, but it was hard to stay mad at him when he was smiling at her like that.

Their drinks came with no further flirtation from the waitress. Mimi took a sip of hers. Meanwhile, Kingsley had somehow managed it so that she was practically sitting on his lap at their cozy table.

"Stop it," she said, pushing off. "I want to talk to you about something serious."

"That sounds boring," he sighed. "I was hoping you wanted to talk about something else."

"Listen. I found the tapes. Your reports from two years ago. They were in Charles's office," Mimi said, looking him square in the eye.

"Spying on me now?" Kingsley cocked an eyebrow and finished off his whiskey in one gulp. But he sat up straight and looked alert. With his right hand he motioned for the check.

"I don't understand!" she whispered fiercely. "What were you doing for Charles? Why did you call the Silver Blood? What were the two of you trying to do?"

"Do you really want to know?" Kingsley asked. He returned her forthright stare, so she could look right into his dark eyes. She could see the hint of silver at the edge of his pupils.

Mimi didn't blink. "Yes. Tell me. Tell me everything."

FORTY-EIGHT

Bliss

he Prada sample sale, while admittedly an exclusive experience (they checked two IDs against the guest list at the door) and filled to the brim with last season's must-haves, struck Bliss as completely anticlimactic. Where were the hordes of fashion-mad women fighting over the last pair of six-inch embroidered platforms? Was the lack of buzz because the economy was in a downturn, or maybe because sample sales were inherently secretly lame? Filled with overstock of designs whose life-expectancy rate was the three months that fashionistas actually wore the stuff? Because who needed a degrade skirt when it was no longer in fashion? Or for that matter, vertiginious pumps in a crocodile pattern that turned a foot into a hoof? Was it still fashion when it was no longer fashionable?

Bliss wandered around the shelves, pulling a bag to look at here and there. Four hundred dollars was still too much to pay for a handbag, she thought. They called this a sample sale? A dress caught her eye—one of those baby-doll dresses that had looked so cute in the advertising campaign. Purple with yellow flowers. She picked it up.

When Schuyler walked in, dressed in her various layers but looking as ethereal and beautiful as ever, Bliss could see the envy from all the other insect-sized fashionistas, which made her feel proud and happy. Seeing Schuyler reminded Bliss that she wasn't some centuries-old freak, some cursed being . . . that part of her was only sixteen years old and still innocent, and no one else, no one else in this room, would understand what she was going through. . . .

Except for the girl in the gray trenchcoat and black sweater.

"Bliss! Oh my god! Oh my god! Oh my god!" Schuyler cried, and soon they were embracing, hugging each other tightly, tears flowing down their cheeks, making a bit of a commotion so that the other shoppers turned away and tried to pretend they weren't gawking.

"Do we have to stay here?" Schuyler asked, looking curiously at Bliss. "Are you buying that dress?"

"I might . . . Why? Do you not like it? But no, I mean yes, it's better if we stay here . . . but I think there's a room where we can talk," Bliss said, leading Schuyler outside to the hallway and into a little anteroom on the side.

They sat side by side, still clutching each other. Bliss noticed how thin Schuyler had gotten. "When I heard you guys had to run away, I was so worried. What happened?" She listened while Schuyler told her about the investigation and all that had happened afterward. As she did, she realized more and more what a danger she was posing to Schuyler. Even without the title, Forsyth was already leading the Conclave. Bliss could feel the Visitor behind it all. But why would he care what happened to Schuyler Van Alen?

"I saw Oliver at school, but we haven't had a chance to get together," Bliss said. She'd had an awkward reunion with him. They were friends-in-law, Bliss thought. Without Schuyler, she and Oliver didn't have too much in common. "It's weird to see him without you. You guys were always joined at the hip."

"I know," Schuyler said, and twisted her thumbs. "It's better this way. If the Conclave knew I was back . . ."

Bliss nodded. Forsyth had been asking her if Schuyler had been in touch, which meant the Conclave was still interested in her whereabouts. Bliss had told him nothing, of course. Schuyler was right to hide. But Bliss had a feeling there was something other than just fear of the Conclave that was keeping Schuyler and Oliver apart. She'd once hoped that Schuyler would find happiness with Oliver, but friendship was one thing, and love was another. The Greeks were right about that. "Have you seen Jack?" she asked.

"Yes." Schuyler hesitated. "It's fine. It's . . . we're . . . it's over." She looked Bliss straight in the eyes when she said it and held her head high.

"I'm glad to hear that," Bliss said gently. The Force twins were finally going to be bonded, and she could imagine how much that had to hurt. Mimi had even asked Bliss to be one of her bondsmaids, which was unexpected since they hardly spoke to each other anymore. Bliss had said yes to be polite.

"And you? I . . . I'm sorry we never got to talk about what happened to Dylan. I can only imagine how terrible . . ." Schuyler's voice trailed off and her eyes grew bright. "I'm really sorry I haven't been there for you. I didn't want you to be alone after that, but we didn't have much of a choice."

"It's okay. I'm all right. I really missed you guys. It's been . . . kind of crazy for me. . . ." she said. Inside Bliss's head a familiar voice said, *Tell her I say hello,* which made Bliss smile. "Anyway, sometimes I feel like he's still with me."

"He'll always be with you," Schuyler said, grasping for Bliss's hand and squeezing it.

Bliss leaned over so they could speak more intimately. She could feel the darkness coming, a sensation not unlike reaching the precipice of a roller coaster. Hanging over the abyss, right before the drop.

"Listen, Sky, I need to tell you something. There's something wrong with me. I can't talk about it too much, or whatever is wrong with me will put you in a lot of danger. But I'm taking this class . . . Ancient Civilizations . . . and I was reading about Rome . . . and I started to remember some stuff . . . stuff that happened before, and I think it might"—she was going to say, "might be happening again," but she never had a chance because Schuyler's iPhone began to ring.

"Hold on. God, I'm so sorry. Bliss, I have to take it. It's my mother's hospital," Schuyler said, checking the number. She put the phone to her ear. "Hello? Yes, this is Schuyler Van Alen. . . . What? Sorry? Yes . . . yes of course . . . I'll come right now."

"What's going on?" asked Bliss.

"It's—it's my mother. She's awake! She's asking for me. Bliss, I'm sorry, I have to go!"

"Allegra? Allegra's awake? Wait—Schuyler! Let me come with you!"

But it was too late. Her friend had gone so fast it was as if she had disappeared into thin air.

FORTY-NINE

Mimi

*O*utside the window the sun was rising over the Hudson. Mimi shrugged on a robe, swinging her legs off the bed so she could take a better look. Or so she just told him. She felt . . . confused. And she didn't like it.

She patted the pockets of the robe for her cigarettes, then remembered she had quit smoking. Somehow chewing gum wasn't the same. She would have to console herself with a tapping of her fingers on the glass. Outside, the sky was a brilliant red and orange, the purple darkness and the yellow of the smog mixing with the horizon. But Mimi was bored with a picture of a pretty sunrise, or even sunsets, for that matter: she found them clichéd, hokey, predictable. Anyone could like a sunset. And she wasn't anyone; she was Mimi Force.

"Come back here."

Half invitation, half command.

She turned. Kingsley Martin was lying on the bed, his arms crossed behind his head. Arrogant bastard. Rio had been a mistake. The torrent of emotions after coming so close to the Watcher, only to have her slip away . . . the two of them had met up later that night at their hotel. Well. What's done was done. She couldn't change that.

She had been far from home and feeling low. But she had no excuse for last night. Okay, so after Kingsley had told her his whole sad, terrible story, and shared the burden of his secret, they had closed down the bar downstairs, and then everything had felt inevitable after that. Hooking up once was a mistake. Twice? Twice was a pattern. The Mandarin Oriental was one of Mimi's favorite places to stay, and the one in New York was especially lovely. If only she could convince herself she was here to enjoy the view.

"Well? I'm waiting," his silky voice announced.

"You think you can order me around?" she said, throwing her hair over her shoulders: a practiced move that she made appear unrehearsed. She knew he found the sight of her hair swinging over her back enticing.

"I know I can."

She moved closer. "Who do you think you are, anyway?"

Kingsley only yawned. He tugged at the edge of her robe, pulling it halfway off her shoulders, before she stopped him. "What's wrong?" he asked.

"I'm getting bonded in two weeks, that's what's wrong," she snapped, belting her robe tightly around her waist. She had asked him that night in Rio if this had happened between them before. And she had asked him again last night. If they had ever been together . . . if . . . if . . . if . . . Of course Kingsley refused to answer. He had been maddening. Do your exercises, he had said. Do your regressions. He had teased and mocked her and refused to answer her question.

If it had happened before, I could forgive myself, she thought. Maybe this is my one weakness. Maybe *he* is my weakness.

"Can I ask you something?" Mimi asked, watching as Kingsley got dressed and walked over to the little dining table. Kingsley had ordered a breakfast suited for a king. Not just the usual plate of eggs and bacon. There was also a seafood platter on ice, a full tin of caviar, toast points, chives, sour cream, and chopped onions. A golden bottle of Cristal was sweating in a wine bucket.

"Anything," he said, scooping up caviar with his fingers and licking them. He filled a plate with food, then popped open the champagne bottle and poured two glasses. He handed her one with a smile.

"I'm serious . . . I don't want you to get offended."

"Me?" he said, balancing his breakfast on his lap as he took a seat on the couch and put his feet up on the coffee table.

"What do . . . what do Silver Bloods live on?" she asked. "I mean, other than caffeine and sugar and prawns the size of your fist," Mimi said, watching him eat. "I mean, do you still perform the *Caerimonia?* On humans, I mean?"

Kingsley shook his head. He looked mournful as he dipped his shrimp into the cocktail sauce. "No." He took a bite. "No, my dear, that is not an option any longer for those of us who have drunk from the undying blood. I'm afraid to the Croatan the only blood that matters is the blood that runs through *your* veins."

Mimi crossed her legs as she sat on the bed opposite him. She arched her neck. "So do you ever feel tempted?"

"All the time." He smiled lazily.

"So what do you do?"

"What is there to do? I can't. I've pledged to honor the Code. I live in restraint. I can still eat food . . . and sometimes some of it even tastes good." He shrugged and wiped his fingers on the edge of his shirt.

She wanted to tell him not to do that, but didn't want to sound like his mother. "You mean you can't taste any of that stuff?"

"I try."

"But all those doughnuts . . ." she said, suddenly feeling sorry for him. He was immortal in the truest sense of the word. He didn't need anything to survive. What a lonely and strange way to live.

"Yeah, I know." He laughed, but his eyes looked sad. "I eat a lot because I can taste only a fraction of what is in front of me. I have a bottomless appetite that can never be filled." He winked. "And that's why the Silver Bloods are cursed."

"You make light of serious matters, you said that to me once," she chastised.

"Well, yes. We are very much alike," Kingsley said. He put down his empty plate and glass and walked over to stand in front of her. "And we have fun together, don't we?" he asked. "Admit it, this is kind of fun . . . isn't it?" He licked her neck, then her ear, gently kissing her back and her shoulders. She could smell the champagne on his lips.

Mimi closed her eyes. A bit of fun, that was all. It meant nothing. Not to him, not to her. Hooking up. That's all they were doing. Purely physical and purely pleasurable. There were no feelings involved, no divine connection, no heavenly conscription . . . This was just fun. Pure and simple.

Kingsley was still kissing her neck when she felt his fangs come out, that slight prickling, tickling her skin.

"What do you think you're doing?" she asked, feeling afraid, but excited too. She had never known what it was like to be treated as a victim. As prey. He was dangerous. A reformed Silver Blood. You might as well call him a reformed Doberman.

"Shush . . . it won't hurt . . . I promise." And then he bit her neck, just a tiny bit—just so she could feel his fangs sink in and pierce the skin, and then she felt his tongue lick a drop of her blood. He licked his lips and smiled at her. "You try it."

Mimi was horrified. What had he just done? And now he wanted her to do it too? "No." But she had to admit, she was

was tempted. She had always wondered what it would be like. Why the Croatan preferred it over the usual *Caeremonia*.

"Go on. You won't hurt me. I dare you."

Being with him made her feel alive and uninhibited. What could it hurt? Just a touch. Just a drop. Just a tease. She did not want to drink his blood—but she did, suddenly, very much want to taste it.

To play with a lit candle. To hold her finger to the flame, taking it away just before it burned. That knife edge that skirted between danger and fun. A roller coaster ride. The adrenaline rush was heady. She pushed out her fangs and buried her face into his neck.

The sun rose, filling the room with light. And Mimi Force was having the time of her life.

FIFTY

Schuyler

*S*he felt bad about leaving Bliss like that. But right then she was too wound up to even think about anything other than the fact that the person she had waited her entire life to talk to . . . was now awake. Alive. Allegra Van Alen was alive. She had opened her eyes a half hour ago, and she was asking for her daughter.

As she walked through the glass doors of New York Presbyterian Hospital, toward the back elevator that would take her to the permanent care unit, Schuyler wondered how many days, how many nights, how many birthdays, how many Thanksgivings and Christmases, she had spent walking down the same fluorescent-lit hallways, with the smell of antiseptic and formaldehyde, walking by the sympathetic smiles of the nurses, by the tearful groups huddled near the surgical waiting rooms, their faces drawn and anxious.

How many times?

Too many to count. Too many to mention. This was her entire childhood, right in this medical center. The housekeeper had taught her to walk, to talk, and Cordelia had been there to pay the bills. But she'd never had a *mother*. There had been no one to sing her songs in the bath, or to kiss her on the forehead to sleep. No one to keep secrets from, no one to fight over her wardrobe with, no one to slam doors on—there had been none of the normal rhythms of softness and disagreements, the infinite ways of mother-daughter kinship.

There was only this.

"You're here so quickly," the attending nurse said with a smile from the nurses' station. She escorted Schuyler down the hallway to the private wing, where New York's most privileged and most vegetative slumbered. "She's been waiting for you. It's a miracle. The doctors are beside themselves." The nurse lowered her voice. "They say she might even be on television!"

Schuyler didn't know what to say. It still did not seem true. "Wait. I need . . . I need to get something from the cafeteria." And she ducked away from the nurse's side and ran down the entire flight of stairs to the first floor. She burst through the swinging door, surprising a few interns sneaking a coffee break on the hidden landing.

She wasn't sure if she would be able to do this. It seemed too good to be true—and she couldn't bring herself to face it. She wiped the tears from her eyes and walked inside the café.

She bought a bottled water and a pack of gum, and returned to the right floor. The kind nurse was still waiting for her. "It's okay," she told Schuyler. "I know it's a shock. But go on. It'll be okay. She's waiting for you."

Schuyler nodded. "Thank you," she whispered. She walked down the hallway. Everything looked exactly the same as it always did. The window looking over the George Washington Bridge. The whiteboard charts with the patients' names, medications, and attending physicians. Finally she stood in front of the right door. It was open just a crack, so that Schuyler heard it.

A voice, lilting and lovely through the doorway. Calling her name ever so softly.

A voice she had only heard in her dreams.

The voice of her mother.

Schuyler opened the door and walked inside.

FIFTY-ONE

Bliss

*W*hat did you say?

Bliss was paying for her new dress when she was jolted by the Visitor's voice in her head. "Do you take Amex?" she asked the salesgirl sitting at the desk. She tried to maintain her composure while inside the Visitor's excitement made her head ache.

Allegra is awake? Allegra is alive?

Why does this bring joy to you? Bliss asked. Why would you care? She's just a coma patient in a hospital room.

"Did you say something?" the salesgirl asked, shoving the purple dress into a plain brown bag and stapling the top with the receipt.

"No. Sorry." Bliss grabbed her bag and headed out of the room. She bumped into a few girls walking in. "Do they still have good stuff, or is it all picked over?" one of them asked.

"Uh . . . I don't know," Bliss muttered, pushing through. She knew they would think her incredibly rude, but it was as if her head were going to crack open.

Bliss raised her hand to hail a cab. It was five in the afternoon, and all the taxis had their "Off Duty" signs on—a shift switch—and worse, it was starting to rain. New York weather. For a moment she missed BobiAnne's Silver Shadow Rolls and the driver who always took her around. Finally Bliss caught a town car that had just dropped off some executive at the corner. "How much to 168th Street?"

"Twenty."

She got inside the car, which felt warm and cozy after standing in the suddenly freezing rain.

She could still feel the Visitor's excitement and agitation. Why did he care? What did he care about some stupid woman in a hospital?

Show some respect, the Visitor said coldly. *Do not speak of your mother that way.*

So it's true. I am her daughter. I am Allegra's daughter, she thought. Her heart was pounding so loudly it hurt her chest a little bit.

Of course you are, the Visitor said in a reasonable voice that made Bliss feel even more nervous. *We made you together. Now, I think it's time we said a proper hello to Allegra.*

FIFTY-TWO

Schuyler

The hospital bed was empty. Allegra Van Alen sat in a chair beside it. Schuyler's mother was the picture of elegance and restraint in a simple black dress and a string of pearls. She looked as if she had just come from the office or a charity board meeting, and not as if she had just spent the last fifteen years immobile in the same bed.

Schuyler shuffled into the room, hesitating. But once Allegra opened her arms, Schuyler hurled herself into them. "Mother." Allegra smelled like roses in the springtime; her skin was as soft as a baby's. Her presence made the room seem brighter, lighter somehow.

Allegra smoothed her daughter's hair. "Schuyler. You came home."

"I'm sorry, I'm so sorry," Schuyler sobbed. "I'm sorry for everything I said to you in Tokyo." She raised her tear-streaked face. "But how?"

"It was time," Allegra said.

Schuyler broke away from the embrace. She couldn't believe what Allegra was saying. "So you're telling me you could have woken at any time?"

"No, darling." Allegra shook her head. She motioned to Schuyler to pull up a chair next to hers. "I felt the stirring deep in the glom. . . . Something has happened to the world. . . . I felt it. It would have been selfish for me to continue to stop taking the blood. To stay rooted in my isolation." Then Schuyler saw what had happened as if she had been there: the comatose woman rising from her bed, tearing into the neck of an orderly who had come to change her sheets. The vampire princess awoken. Sleeping Beauty breaking through the glass.

Schuyler choked back a sob. "Lawrence—"

"Is gone. I know. I spoke to him before he passed to the other side." Allegra nodded.

"He told me about the Van Alen Legacy." Schuyler shrugged. "Do you know what I'm supposed to do?"

In answer, her mother pulled her closer and spoke in a voice only Schuyler could hear. *Listen closely, my daughter. For what I am about to tell you can only be told in the shelter of the glom.*

In the days when we called Paradise our home, the paths between the worlds were open. Angels moved freely between Earth, Heaven, and the underground. But after Lucifer's revolt, when the Dark Prince and his followers were cast out of Heaven, the way to Paradise was shut forever.

But the seven Paths of the Dead remained open. In Rome, we still trusted Caligula then—did not know he was Lucifer behind the mask, did not know he had made it his mission to discover their locations on Earth. As emperor, he ordered a maze of tunnels built under the city of Lutetia. It was here that he discovered the first path.

In his arrogance, he shared his secret with Michael. The Morningstar was never one for hiding his glory, which would cost him. Michael insisted they build a gate upon the path, and forge a key that Michael would hold in his trust. Lucifer agreed.

But of course it was all a lie. Lucifer's transformation into a Croatan was complete by then. His betrayal of the Code of the Vampires created the crisis in Rome. He stole the key at the earliest opportunity, unleashing Abomination upon the world. But we would not know this until it was almost too late.

The Blue Bloods hunted down the demons and their Silver Blood brethren. We turned Lutetia into a safe haven. Michael defeated Lucifer, taking him down the dead's path to the underworld and locking the gate behind him. Michael then ordered the Blue Bloods to find the remaining six paths, and to build gates upon them to keep the divisions between the worlds secure. The gatekeepers were called the Order of the Seven and included the seven original families of the Conclave.

The gatekeepers agreed to scatter far and wide across the earth, hidden from one another. The knowledge of the gates would remain in the guardians' family, passed down through the generations.

The Van Alen Legacy is just the latest name for the work that Lawrence and Cordelia began when they arrived in the New World. When young Blue Bloods were disappearing again, they suspected that what they had feared for centuries was true: that the gates were failing, and that somehow Lucifer and his Silver Bloods had survived the war in Rome and were planning their return to power.

Lawrence made it his life's work to find each gate and guardian, to warn them of the danger. But Charles never believed in the Van Alen Legacy. He resented his father's doubt of the work he had forged centuries before. So Lawrence went into exile. And the Van Alen Legacy was forgotten.

But Lawrence was right, Schuyler sent. They have returned.

Yes, they have returned, and are desperately seeking to unlock the gates—to free the Devil trapped in Hell. This is why we deceived them so long ago. Charles was not the gatekeeper of Lutetia. The gate's earthly anchor had been moved. The true gatekeeper saw to that a long time ago.

How do you know that? Are you the keeper?

No. Of the Van Alens, only Lawrence was a gatekeeper. Remember the Order of the Seven. One gate in each family.

Leviathan and Corcovado. Schuyler understood now.

Yes. Your grandfather was the keeper of the Gate of Vengeance, Leviathan's prison. With Lawrence's murder of an innocent, the gate opened and released Leviathan. But what the Silver Bloods did not know was that the Gate of Vengeance was a solom bicallis. *It can only be used once, and in one direction. Once Leviathan was freed, the path was closed to all.*

The Silver Bloods will not rest. They will seek out the guardians and the gates, until all the Paths of the Dead are free once more.

Schuyler, it is up to you to find the remaining members of the Order, alert them of the danger, and keep the gates secure. As long as the gates hold, Lucifer cannot cross from the underworld to this world. That is the Van Alen Legacy, and now it is yours.

You mean, it is ours.

Alas, that is not to be. I cannot help you in your quest. I have to find Charles. He was lost, somewhere between worlds, when the Silver Bloods let loose that subvertio. *Our destiny is intertwined. He needs me more than ever now. There is something broken in the universe that only we can fix together . . . which is part of your journey as well.*

"Mother, you are leaving me. Again. Now that I need you the most," Schuyler cried, shocked at her mother's news and the enormity of the responsibility that lay before her. Find the gates? Find the guardians? Save the world? How was she supposed to do that alone?

"I am not leaving. I am always with you," Allegra said, holding Schuyler in her arms. "My daughter, I am *in* you. Never forget that."

"So that was really you, then, with the sword? In my dreams?" Schuyler asked.

"Of course." Allegra smiled gently, then stood up. "Now listen closely. Leviathan has shown his hand in Paris. We know he is looking to open the gate formerly located in Lutetia. The Gate of Time. Of this I am sure, for I was there when Michael and I made him keeper. It was guarded by Tiberius Gemellus. Find him. Secure the gate."

FIFTY-THREE

Mimi

When Mimi left school that afternoon, she found Kingsley waiting for her in front of the Duchesne gates, among the usual collection of scruffy-looking boys waiting for their private-school girlfriends. Except Kingsley didn't look scruffy at all. He looked like he'd just stepped out of a magazine: teeth gleaming, dark hair shiny and combed, his cheeks freshly shaven. He was wearing a black leather jacket over a white button-down shirt and battered blue jeans. The rock star look intact.

"What are you doing here?" Mimi demanded, looking around anxiously. "Jack might see you!" Not that she cared all that much. Maybe her twin would even get jealous, seeing them together. If Jack was even capable of any real feeling when it came to her. Who knew what he thought in that thick skull of his anymore?

Kingsley ignored her and pulled her close. He kissed her

soundly in front of a group of titillated freshmen. "Force. Get in the limo." Mimi saw a shiny car the length of a city block idling by the curb. A uniformed chauffeur held the door open.

Mimi had always harbored a secret love for limousines. It was tacky to use one in the city, lest you run the risk of looking like a tourist or like you were off to prom. But this one shone with a wicked gleam. She had to admit it: the guy traveled in style.

She gave Kingsley a look, then slid inside. He stepped in behind her and closed the door. He raised the driver's partition until it closed all the way. The windows were tinted. They were, for all intents and purposes, alone. The car was so wide it was like being in a moving living room. The carpet beneath her feet was lush, and the car seats were as wide as a bed.

"Now, where were we?" Kingsley asked, leaning over so that he was practically on top of her, one hand underneath her shirt and the other tugging the waistband of her skirt.

"Wait. Wait," Mimi gasped, putting a hand against his chest and pushing him away. And she thought *she* was fast. Kingsley was like the world's most talented make-out artist. She had barely gotten in the car and she was practically undressed.

"Sweetheart, I've waited all day," he sighed, burying his face in her neck. But he did as she asked and pulled his hand away from her thigh. He composed himself and leaned back against the seat. "There. Better?"

Mimi tried not to look too flattered. It was nice to be wanted. Kingsley and his voracious appetite. "Where are we going? Or should I say, where are you taking me?" she asked, as the car made a left onto FDR Drive.

In answer, Kingsley held up several plane tickets. "Paris. The Lennox boys are already at JFK. We leave tonight."

"We?"

"You're not deserting the team, are you, Force?" He smiled. "Don't worry, I have everything you need. Got you a new Venator pack. Of course, it doesn't come with those impractical boots of yours, but I'm sure you can find a replacement in the City of Lights."

Mimi buttoned her blouse. "You've got to be joking. Turn this car around right now. I'm not going to Paris."

"Why not?"

He really was a piece of work, this one, she thought. Did she have to say it? "Don't you remember? I'm getting bonded next Sunday. Duh."

"Are you?"

"What are you getting at? Jack is my . . ." *Soul mate* seemed cheesy to say. "He's my twin. We belong together. We always have."

Kingsley nodded as if he were seriously considering her argument. "Right. And that's why you've been sneaking into my hotel room every night for the last week."

Every night! Had it been every night? Surely he was wrong. Surely she had spent *one* night on her own. She had been in denial. This had gone too far. She was cutting it off right here. "You know the Code," she said. "That's just the way it is. I can't deny our bond."

"Bonds are made to be broken," he said. "Just like rules."

"Spoken like a true Silver Blood," she snapped.

Kingsley's face became grave. "You know my secret. You know what we face, the enormity of our task if what Charles suspects is true. The team needs you. Come with us."

Mimi flushed. She had never felt this way in her life. In all of her lives. Loving Abbadon was all she'd ever known. But then Kingsley walked in and turned her every assumption upside down. But did he really want her? Did he really care for her? Did he love her? Or did he just want her around for his amusement?

Kingsley smiled at her, and she knew it was a smile of triumph, the smile of a boy who always got what he wanted. Sure, he wanted her right now, but what happened when he didn't? She knew what the bond was like, the dedication, the commitment to each other and the service they rendered to the community as a whole. The vampires were fading, that much she knew. The Blue Bloods needed them now more than ever. She thought of all the things she and Jack had accomplished together: they had defeated Lucifer in Rome, they had founded the New World. . . .

She was Azrael. She was true to her word. She would not waver from what was asked of her. Who did she think she was—her brother? Inconstant, indecisive, unable to make a choice between foolishness and duty?

"No, Kingsley. I can't." She shook her head. "Let me out of here. Stop the car."

Kingsley looked at her for a long time. Then he cleared his throat and picked up the interior phone and asked the driver to pull to the side. "As you wish."

FIFTY-FOUR

Bliss

*N*ew York Presbyterian visiting hours were over when Bliss arrived, not that it even mattered. Allegra Van Alen had checked out by the time she got there. "But what do you mean she's gone? I just got a call that she was awake. . . . I'm her daughter!" Bliss cried.

"Schuyler was here an hour ago," the nurse said, looking confused. "She walked out with Allegra."

"I mean, I'm her other daughter. Oh, never mind," Bliss said, stomping off and shaking raindrops all over the floor.

She's gone. Allegra was gone. She didn't even stick around long enough to talk to me. She doesn't care about me. She doesn't even know I'm alive. *Do you hear that, Father?* she screamed inside her head. *Where are you, anyway?*

But it was as if the Visitor knew they would not find Allegra at the hospital. Sometime during the traffic-clogged drive uptown, he had retreated again.

Bliss went back home to an empty apartment as usual. She nuked a potato for dinner. Even if she didn't feel really hungry anymore—try *ever*—it was hard to break the habit of having three meals a day.

After taking a few bites she tossed the potato in the trash and went to her room to try on her new dress. Schuyler was right. She shouldn't have bought it. It was too tight in the chest and too short in the hem. And the color wasn't right; the deep purple shade made her look paler than usual, and clashed with her red hair. She'd had sale goggles. She took off the dress and crumpled it into a bag so that she could take it to a consignment shop. Hopefully she would get some of her money back. Ever since the bankruptcy, Forsyth had been stingy with her allowance.

Allegra was her mother. . . . The truth of it hurt—like when you overhear what your friends really think about you. She called Schuyler again, but there was no answer.

Bliss closed her eyes and went to the top of the Cloisters, looking for her friend. She had to tell somebody. But instead of seeing Dylan, she saw someone else.

The man in the white suit. The Visitor. Lucifer. Her father.

"Hello, daughter."

"Where have you been? I went up to the hospital, but she wasn't there anymore."

"Oh, I know," he said. "She was too fast for us. She always was. But no matter. We shall catch up to her soon enough. It's nice up here. What do you call this place?"

"The Cloisters," Bliss said.

"Ah, so this is where you and your young man meet. But don't worry; he won't be bothering us anymore."

Bliss felt her stomach clench. "What do you mean?"

"I know what you have been doing. I know everything you know. You cannot hide from me, Bliss. I hear your every thought. I hear your every word. I know that you have seen what is in my mind, and I am glad. For you must be ready."

"Ready? For what?"

"Hearing about Allegra reminded me we have unfinished business to attend to. Her half-blood mongrel daughter—Schuyler Van Alen. A very good friend of yours, from what I can tell."

"What about Schuyler?" Bliss asked nervously.

"Forsyth has been unable to bring her to me. Leviathan has failed as well. It is amazing how blind I have been to the advantage that is just within my reach. Because you shall not fail me, my daughter. No. You will bring her to me."

Bliss shook her head and stepped away, almost to the edge of the rooftop. "No way! You're crazy if you think I'd ever do such a thing."

Lucifer's face was calm. "Why? Is it because you mistakenly believe Schuyler Van Alen is a friend? What kind of friend leaves you behind? She never called, not even once, did she? Never wanted to know how you were. What kind of friend is that? How could she leave you alone, knowing how much you were suffering?"

Bliss continued to shake her head so vigorously that she thought she would make herself dizzy. "She had no choice . . . she was running . . . Forsyth made her a fugitive!"

"Still, each of us has a choice. Each of us has the freedom to choose how we act, and she chose to leave you alone. Alone with me." Lucifer smiled again, and this time Bliss could see his fangs.

"No. I won't. You'll have to do it yourself if you want it done."

"I have tried, my dear," Lucifer sighed. "Do not forget: we have, as you young people say, 'been there, done that.'" Bliss realized Lucifer meant he had already tried to harm Schuyler during the times he had been in charge, when Bliss was having all those blackouts. "And so far I have not been able to truly harm the girl. Gabrielle's protection is rooted in her blood and must have deflected my presence. But you, my dear, you have your mother's blood in you as well. Same as Schuyler. You will be able to push through where I was unable."

"I'll never do it." Bliss pushed her fists into the pockets of her coat. Her father was insane if he thought she would ever harm her friend.

"Well, now you have a choice: you can do as I ask, or you shall never see your young man again."

"What do I care? He's not real," Bliss insisted.

"He's as real as I am. You think yours is the only world that is true? There are an infinite number of worlds in the universe. The world in your mind is as real as the world outside of it."

Bliss looked down from the roof of the museum. If she jumped, if she fell into the glom, in her mind, could she hurt herself? "What are you going to do? What do you want me to do . . . with Schuyler?" she whispered.

"My dear? Isn't it obvious? You're going to kill her."

FIFTY-FIVE

Mimi

He was right, I look better naked, Mimi thought as she checked out her figure in the spa mirrors. Standing at five-feet-nine, with long shapely legs, broad shoulders, and high, not-so-big, not-so-small breasts that needed neither reduction nor augmentation, she had the kind of body seen on *Sports Illustrated* cover girls—athletic and toned, but still womanly and sexy, with that tiny Barbie-doll waist and graceful, slim hips. The bonding was set for the next day, and she tried not to think of Kingsley anymore. But sometimes he came to mind at unexpected moments. A bad habit she was trying to shake.

"Ready?" her mother asked, closing her locker door and folding a thick white towel around her torso. Trinity looked a bit disapproving to see Mimi so unabashedly nude in the middle of the locker room. Tradition called for the bride to be fully undressed for the ceremony, although it was no longer necessary. But Mimi preferred the old ways and fondly remembered the past baths she'd taken for this purpose—in the Nile River, in a marble tub at Versailles, in a newly installed sauna in Newport.

The female wardens, a handful of Blue Blood girls from Duchesne, and a few cousins were already waiting for them in the fire pool.

"Let's do this." Mimi nodded and led the way to the underground cavern. It had been a week since Kingsley had asked her to leave with him for Paris. Sometimes she wondered what he was doing, if he was thinking about her, but mostly she had spent her time preparing herself for tomorrow's bonding.

The spa was a Blue Bloods–only establishment, patterned after the Roman baths of antiquity. Mimi had booked it for the requisite prebonding ceremony: the bathing of the bride by her womenfolk.

Ritual cleansing was a tradition that the Blue Bloods had passed down through the centuries, manifesting in other cultures under different names: in the Jewish religion it was the *mikva*, in Hinduism, the bath was recommended at four a.m., during the *brahma muhoratham*, or the most auspicious time of day. In the sacred language it was called the *sanctus balineum*.

There were four different pools in the vast underground complex—an ice bath kept at a shocking fifty-seven degrees Fahrenheit; a steamy "vaporous" pool, which was good for the pores; a "harmony" pool, which was the essence of relaxation; and a fire pool, in which the water was kept at a degree of heat that only vampires could tolerate. A human would burn in the fire pool, but for vampires it was a restorative and refreshing treatment.

Mimi walked down the stone slab steps and felt the warm water cover her skin as she joined the group of women and girls arranged in a circle. Shimmering and moving like water nymphs, they began to hum as she came closer.

She stood in the middle of the group and crossed her arms against her chest, bowing to let them know she respected and appreciated their presence at this important stage of her life.

Trinity followed her into the circle, holding aloft a gold chalice. She dipped it into the pool and filled it with the living holy waters. The *sanctus balineum* required water that did not come from a pipe. It was collected spring water, brought in by the truckload from a secret spring in a hidden reservoir.

She poured it slowly over Mimi's head as she said the words:

"This is the daughter of the Heavens," she intoned in a sweet, melodious voice that echoed around the stone chamber. Slowly, the light in the room began to fade, until they were surrounded by total darkness, their vampire bodies glowing in the gloom.

"Amen," the group murmured.

Trinity nodded and continued to chant. "We come today to cleanse her of her earthly sins."

"Amen." The women began to walk slowly around Mimi, singing a soft "Hallelujah."

"We prepare her for the bond that must not be broken. To say the words that must never be unmade."

Each member of the circle came forward and used the gold cup to pour water over Mimi's head, blessing her with their prayers.

When everyone had finished, Trinity placed her hands on Mimi's head.

"This is the daughter of the Heavens. Today she is cleansed of her earthly sins." She led Mimi deeper into the water, and Mimi submerged herself fully into the pool.

Mimi felt the warm water tingle and soothe her skin, felt a light-headed cleansing of the mind as well as the body. She emerged from the waters peaceful and energized.

She felt cleansed of all her doubts, all her confusion. She had no more thoughts of Kingsley, or of what he had asked her to do. She was one with the spirit, she was one with life, with light, with her destiny.

She was ready to be bound.

FIFTY-SIX

Schuyler

*I*t had been a fortnight since Schuyler had met Bliss at the sample sale. After their joyful reunion, Schuyler thought she would be seeing Bliss more often, but the exact opposite had happened. Bliss always had an excuse not to see her. Schuyler tried not to be too upset by her friend's reluctance to hang out. In any case, her mother had set an awesome task before her.

The Repository of History was the first place to look for family records, but since it wasn't safe for Schuyler to go there, Oliver had lugged all the books to her studio apartment. The separation had been good for their relationship. They no longer experienced the daily small irritations with each other brought on by living in the same space twenty-four/seven. Of course, they still saw each other way too often. It didn't even matter that Schuyler was no longer at

Duchesne, she saw Oliver as much as if she were. He had a key to her studio.

"That's a lot of books," Schuyler said, opening the door to let him in.

"Conduits are transferring everything to a computer database, but they're only up to the eighteenth century," Oliver said cheerfully. He placed the dusty stack on the kitchen table. "How are you, by the way?" he asked, giving her a peck on the cheek. The two of them were back in an easy groove. After it had become clear that Schuyler had no intention of reviving her friendship with Jack, Oliver seemed to relax. The threat had passed.

"Okay." She had told him everything that happened with Allegra, had told him how odd it had been to finally speak to her mother—only to have her leave so soon. She hadn't even been able to ask Allegra about her so-called sister. Nope. It was just, *Here's the Van Alen Legacy. Save the world while you're at it, and I'll see you on the other side of somewhere, sometime.*

Well. Schuyler had to get to work, and she was glad she had Oliver with her. With his help, they'd already made a lot of progress, considering they were looking for a family tree that went back to antiquity. It helped that the Blue Bloods kept meticulous expression and expulsion records.

Schuyler put the teakettle on to boil and took a seat across from where Oliver had laid all the books open in front of him.

"Here's what we know," Oliver said. "Tiberius Gemellus was supposed to be emperor, because he was Caesar Tiberius's real grandson and heir—while Caligula, who actually *became* emperor, was adopted. But Tiberius preferred Caligula over Gemellus, and so named Caligula to succeed him to the throne. You would think Gemellus would have been upset, but the records show he was very close to Caligula, and loved him as a brother. The Red Bloods' history books say there is nothing known about Gemellus, which is logical, since most of the real history is hidden from them. I mean us—you know what I mean."

Schuyler nodded.

"But there's really nothing about Gemellus or his family in any of the Blue Bloods records either. It's like he never existed. Or wasn't important enough to keep track of," Oliver said, getting up when the teakettle began to whistle. He poured hot water into two cups and threw in the tea bags.

"But he *was* important," Schuyler said, accepting her cup and blowing on the surface before taking a sip. "He was a keeper. He was important enough that Michael and Gabrielle named him to the Order of the Seven. But where is he now? What happened to him? Who did he become?" Schuyler asked. "How do we find a person who's not in the books?"

Oliver and Schuyler looked at each other. They were both thinking of a rather unusual diary they had found two years ago. Oliver said excitedly, "Usually when something's not in the books, it means . . ."

"It's deliberately been hidden," Schuyler said.

"Exactly." Oliver put down his cup. "So wherever he is, we're not going to find him here," he said, pushing the books away.

"He was brother to Caligula. Beloved by the emperor. His closest advisor. Ollie, I've got an idea. Call me crazy, but do you think that maybe Gemellus . . . was a Silver Blood?"

FIFTY-SEVEN

Bliss

When Mimi had first asked Bliss to be a bonds-maid at her wedding, Bliss had been taken aback. The two girls had not seen each other in over a year, and were hardly friends anymore. But Mimi had seemed a bit desperate, and Bliss took pity on her and said yes. So on the bright October morning that Jack and Mimi were to be bonded, Bliss arrived early at the salon to get her hair and makeup done, as Mimi had directed.

Trinity Force and several other daughters of high-ranking Committee members were already swaddled in robes, reading magazines and drinking champagne. Mimi herself was seated in the middle of the action. The bond-to-be was wearing a fluffy white robe, but otherwise she looked picture-perfect. Her face was made up as exquisitely as a doll's, with ruby red lips and the barest hint of blush. Her lustrous platinum hair was pulled back into a chignon woven with white flowers. She looked gorgeous.

"Bliss! I'm so happy to see you!" she said.

"Oh my god! I know! Are you excited?" Bliss asked, matching Mimi's ditzy-girl tones. "You're getting bonded today!"

"It's about time, don't you think?" Mimi practically screamed. Bliss could smell the alcohol on her breath, but something about Mimi's excitement seemed . . . *forced*. Mimi was smiling so hard her face looked like it was going to crack.

"You're over here. Danilo will take care of you. Remember, Danilo, make my friend pretty but not prettier than me!" Mimi giggled.

"Hey, by the way, I'm sorry I missed that um . . . bathing thing," Bliss said, trying not to feel awkward.

"No worries. You're here now and that's what matters," Mimi said with a brilliant smile. She was exactly the same old Mimi Force, Bliss thought. Totally vain, preening, and self-centered, or maybe she was just getting the bonding jitters.

Bliss was anxious about the event. She hoped the bonding would go quickly so she could get away from everyone. After her encounter with the Visitor the other day, she felt shaken and unsteady and not quite safe to be around. Not that she would ever, ever, ever, in her right mind, ever do such a thing as murder her best friend. She had to convince Schuyler to leave New York as soon as possible. The longer Schuyler stayed in the city, the more dangerous it was for her. Bliss had to keep her friend safe . . . and away from her. But she had yet to figure out how to do it, how to talk to Schuyler without the Visitor finding out.

At least she knew Schuyler wouldn't be at Mimi's bonding, so Bliss wouldn't have to worry about it today. It was a small but welcome reprieve, but she was still nervous.

The stylist straightened Bliss's hair and spackled on the makeup so thick, when she looked in the mirror she hardly recognized herself. Her hair was almost to her elbows, it was so much longer straightened, and her face was a mask of perfection, although that spray-tan made her look a bit orange. She took a cab home so she could change into her dress, a black strapless gown. Pretty basic bondsmaid attire—nothing that would take away from the vision that Mimi was sure to be.

Back at the penthouse, Bliss checked her makeup one last time in the mirror, attempting to tone down the bronzer on her cheeks. Where was Dylan? The Visitor was keeping him from her, she knew, and she hated him bitterly for it. Was he being held somewhere? Hurt? Was it all her fault? How had this happened to her? What could she do? Sometimes she felt as if she were truly going crazy.

As she gazed at herself in the mirror, she noticed she was still wearing the emerald Forsyth had given her two years ago. Lucifer's Bane. She touched the cold stone, and with great difficulty, removed the necklace from her body. She didn't want anything near her associated with her father. She tossed it onto the dressing room table. She felt as if it had marked her skin, but of course that was just her imagination.

There was no one to talk to anymore. Not Dylan. Not Schuyler. She really was alone. She left her room and found the bouquet that Mimi's florist had delivered that morning. An enormous arrangement of white lilies. She picked it up and found a small envelope slipped inside the flowers, with her name on it.

She opened the envelope. Inside was a thin piece of glass. When she touched it, it suddenly transformed into a sword.

"What the . . . ?" Bliss said, holding both bouquet and sword awkwardly. She put down the flowers and took a closer look at the sword. It looked familiar. It was Michael's sword. The same sword that Jordan had used to stab her. What was it doing here?

When she put it down, it turned into a thin piece of glass again. She couldn't just leave it here. She tucked it back into the bouquet and left for the ceremony.

FIFTY-EIGHT

Schuyler

What am I doing here? Schuyler wondered. She was supposed to be home, going through some new books and documents Oliver had dug up in the Repository. He had wanted her to look over the files he'd found, and to call him as soon as she had read them. But somehow her feet had taken her uptown instead. She had walked the eighty blocks to Cathedral Parkway and Amsterdam Avenue.

I have to see it for myself. I have to see him for the last time before he is bound to Mimi. Once he is hers, I'll go.

When she had lived on Riverside Drive, Schuyler used to attend the Sunday services at St. John the Divine. Cordelia preferred her chapel on Fifth Avenue, but Schuyler had a soft spot for the gothic revival church that had been built in 1892 but was still incomplete. For as long as Schuyler could remember, the south tower had been covered in scaffolding, and part of the facade was still missing its sculptural stone carving.

Every year, to celebrate the feast of Saint Francis, the church organized a formal Blessing of the Animals. Schuyler had remembered feeling joy at seeing all the animals, including an elephant from the circus, a Norwegian reindeer, a camel, and a golden eagle among the assorted menagerie. She had taken Beauty several times for the blessing. She hoped her bloodhound was faring well, comfortably at home with Hattie and Julius.

Schuyler walked toward the church, watching as a procession of black town cars and yellow cabs let out a crowd of elegantly dressed guests, who called gaily to each other as they arrived. There was a festive mood in the air as the Blue Bloods came to celebrate one of their most sacred rites of passage.

The sun was low on the horizon. The ceremony would begin just after sunset. Schuyler lingered across the street. She should go. She had no right to be here. She wasn't even invited. This was such a bad idea. The place would be crawling with Blue Bloods, and she was supposed to be in hiding. But Schuyler couldn't help it. Against her better judgment, she found herself walking toward the church. She needed to see it for herself. Because maybe if she did, she would stop feeling this way. If she saw Jack bonded to Mimi, and how happy they were, maybe then her heart would begin to heal.

Schuyler slipped through a side door to a pew in the back behind a column. The orchestra was playing Strauss, and there was a smell of incense in the air. The assembled guests whispered to each other while they waited.

Jack was already standing at the altar, looking so very dashing in his tuxedo. He looked up when she arrived, and she could feel his stare all the way down the length of the vestibule. His eyes flashed with hope. Schuyler shrank in her seat. *He can't have . . . I should go. . . .* But it was too late. Jack had seen her.

Schuyler? Is that you? What are you doing here?

Oh, crap. She shut her mind to him. She had to get out—this was wrong. What was she thinking? But as she tried to slip away, she realized she would be walking right into the wedding party, which was already marching in. She spotted Bliss among the attendants. She was trapped. She had to stay. At least until the bride made her entrance, then she would be able to slip away unnoticed.

But someone else had seen her too. Someone who had been invited to the wedding. Oliver and his family had been walking in the opposite door when she had entered, but he had not acknowledged her presence. He'd just kept walking to his seat.

FIFTY-NINE

Mimi

"You look beautiful, my dear. If only your father were here to see you," Trinity Force said as she adjusted Mimi's veil in the car.

"He's not really my father. You know that, right?" Mimi asked. "Like you're not really my mother and Jack's not my brother. Otherwise, why would I be bonded to him?"

"Family is family," Trinity said. "Maybe we are of a different sort, but we are still a family. We can learn from the humans too."

"Whatever," Mimi said, rolling her eyes.

So. It was finally here. Bonding day. She was wearing the gown of her dreams. A custom-made creation: a real Balthazar Verdugo. Made from fifty yards of the finest Parisian silk jacquard, woven with dozens of tiny silk rosebuds, tinsel paillettes, antique lace, and ostrich feathers, the dress had taken two thousand hours to make, not counting the one thousand hours the Belgian nuns spent on the embroidery. She carried a rosary in her purse: the same one she had carried at the last bonding, in Newport. Diamond-and-pearl earrings from Buccellati were her only jewelry.

Mimi checked her reflection in the rearview mirror, liking how her lips were red and juicy underneath the veil. She *looked* absolutely perfect; if only she *felt* the same way. Instead, Mimi wondered if she was making the biggest mistake of her life.

Bonds are made to be broken. Like rules.

The car pulled up to the church. Inside would be her whole Coven. The vampires would celebrate tonight. There would be dancing and fireworks and many toasts to the happy couple. Everything was perfectly orchestrated. All she had to do was slip into the role. She could do that, if she could just stop listening to Kingsley's voice in her head.

She stepped out of the car, and a sudden gust of wind lifted the veil from her face. Her mother walked her just into the anteroom, where Mimi would wait until it was her turn to enter.

Inside the church, the bondsmaids were walking slowly down the aisle, with the little petal girls. Trinity turned to give Mimi her last words of motherly advice: "Walk straight. Don't slouch. And for heavens's sake, smile! It's your bonding!" Then she too walked through the door and down the aisle. The door shut behind her, leaving Mimi alone.

Finally, Mimi heard the orchestra play the first strains

of the "Wedding March." Wagner. Then the ushers opened the doors and Mimi moved to the threshold. There was an appreciative gasp from the crowd as they took in the sight of Mimi in her fantastic dress. But instead of acknowledging her triumph as New York's most beautiful bride, Mimi looked straight ahead, at Jack, who was standing so tall and straight at the altar. He met her eyes and did not smile.

Let's just get this over with.

His words were like an ice pick to the heart. He doesn't love me. He has never loved me. Not the way he loves Schuyler. Not the way he loved Allegra. He has come to every bonding with this darkness. With this regret and hesitation, doubt and despair. She couldn't deny it. She knew her twin, and she knew what he was feeling, and it wasn't joy or even relief.

What am I doing?

"Ready?" Forsyth Llewellyn suddenly appeared by her side. Oh, right, she remembered, she had said yes when Forsyth had offered to walk her down the aisle.

Here goes nothing. As if in a daze, Mimi took his arm, Jack's words still echoing in her head. She walked, zombie-like, down the aisle, not even noticing the flashing cameras or the murmurs of approval from the hard-to-impress crowd.

Almost halfway down the aisle, she saw someone she wasn't expecting, and she almost stumbled on her satin heels.

Kingsley Martin stood at the end of a pew, his arms

crossed. He was wearing a tuxedo as well. Just like any other guest. What was he doing here? He was supposed to be in Paris! He was supposed to be gone!

He looked directly at Mimi.

She heard his voice loud and clear in her head. *Leave him.*

Why should I? What do you promise me?

Nothing. And everything. A life of danger and adventure. A chance to be yourself. Leave him. Come with me.

He really had some nerve. She had already made her decision! She couldn't leave her twin in the middle of the bonding—in front of the entire Coven! They would laugh about it for centuries, she knew. Who did he think she was? Was he smirking? He totally was. He knew he was making her squirm. Well, she would show him. She would throw this in his face—make him wish that . . . he had never . . .

What was she thinking? Kingsley was *here*. No matter what he said, his actions spoke louder than his glibness. He was supposed to be in Paris, but instead he was here, in the church, at the bonding, because maybe, just maybe, he felt something for her, something real and true and wonderful and something he could not deny, no matter how many jokes he made about it.

Maybe he was here because he loved her.

Let's get this over with, Jack had sent. Jack would love her once they were bonded. But only as his duty. Only because the bond would force him.

Mimi held Kingsley's gaze. *I can't . . .*

SIXTY

Bliss

hat was Mimi doing? Why had she stopped in the middle of the aisle? Who was she looking at? Kingsley Martin? Bliss hadn't seen Kingsley since the trial. . . . How strange that he was here for the bonding. Wasn't he a Venator of some sort?

Martin!

An image appeared. A thin boy, sickly and frail, following on the heels of his older, stronger, smarter cousin. A boy who admired and adored his childhood hero, his Gaius, his protector and his best friend.

Gemullus.

Bliss saw it: The lord Emperor Caligula taking the throne, his younger, frailer cousin by his side. Tiberius Gemellus. The true heir. But there was no envy in Gemellus's heart. Only adoration. He loved him so. He would do anything his emperor commanded him to do. Even agree to the Corruption.

She saw them: Caligula taking the blood of Gemellus, and Gemellus transforming from a sickly boy to a strong one. Stronger than he had ever dreamed; faster, and more powerful, the entire being transformed. And then the despair . . . the agony of the soul unbound . . . the cries of the many in the undead blood, and then penance before Michael . . . and forgiveness . . . and a mission.

And suddenly everything fell into place. The Visitor's voice spoke so fast, Bliss didn't understand what he was saying.

Ofcourse.Gemellus.Ofcourse!Michaelwasacraftyone. Trustinhim-totrustatraitor. Wemuststrikenow.Now.Now.Now.

The unfinished church. In the sacred laws, a church must be completed to be fully consecrated. Of course. Where best to hide the gate than in a sacred spot that was not at all sacred? A church that even a Silver Blood could enter?

Without knowing what she was doing, Bliss cried in a voice darker than the deepest echelons of hell.

Croatan! To me! This is our destiny! The Gate of Time is here! Arise, dark demons of the deep! Arise and awake, your time has come!

And suddenly all was mist as the Silver Bloods entered the church—the only church they could enter in the known universe—and they surrounded Kingsley, enveloping him in the silver mist, thick and impenetrable. They blanketed the church in darkness, their laughter crazed and agonized.

"The girl! Don't forget the girl!" rasped a voice.

Bliss looked. Schuyler was running down the length of

the aisle, running to help Kingsley while the Coven stood in shock. It was as if Schuyler were moving in slow motion through a still crowd.

"No! Schuyler! Stay back!" Bliss yelled, running to save her friend from the demon's reach.

But Leviathan got there first.

SIXTY-ONE

Schuyler

*S*he was in the glom and she was falling, falling, falling. The demon held her in his grasp and he was taking her down to the deep. Down to the deepest dark center of the twilight world. When Schuyler could finally open her eyes, she saw that she was chained to some sort of gate, and there were two men standing on either side of it. On one side was a beautiful man in a white suit.

She recognized him immediately. Lucifer, the former Prince of Heaven, the Morningstar. She never thought a man could be so handsome; his beauty was so dazzling it was almost too painful to see. Like a knife that cut deep beneath the skin, his beauty exacted a price from the beholder. She understood the difference between him and the false image on Corcovado. The true Morningstar glowed with a pure inescapable light.

He stood upon a path of molten lava, the rocks hissing

with steam, and Schuyler knew: this was a Path of the Dead. They were standing before the Gate of Time, and Lucifer was held behind it.

On her side of the gate stood Leviathan, her grandfather's murderer. A cloaked demon, hooded, so that Schuyler could only catch a glimpse of his charred skin and glowing ember coals for eyes. She should be afraid, but instead of fear she only felt murderous rage. She didn't know how, but she was going to get out of this and she was going to make them pay. It sounded absurd and weak, but Schuyler knew that as long as she was alive, as long as she had breath in her body, she would do everything she could to fight the white shining presence that stood before her, as beautiful as the sun on the surface, but as ugly as a pile of festering maggots inside his immortal soul.

Then Schuyler saw that there was someone else whom they had brought with them to this dark shadowy place: a third man who lay sprawled underneath Leviathan's foot.

Kingsley Martin groaned.

"Gemellus. Of course. I should have known," Lucifer said. His voice rumbled gently, hypnotic and commanding. He sounded like a movie star.

Kingsley blinked his eyes open and coughed. "But you didn't. Not for a long time. Good to see you again, cousin. Do you mind asking your dimwit brother to get off of me? It's rather uncomfortable down here." In answer, Leviathan kicked him viciously in the ribs. Kingsley gasped and choked, and Schuyler winced.

"Tell me, Gemellus. Do the Uncorrupted still have you on that choke chain? Still answering to Michael's bidding, are we? Even when it was I who made you what you are today. I who showed you how much more we could be when we took the undying blood for our own." Lucifer leaned against the gate, looking through the bars. An animal in a cage.

"I had no idea . . . I didn't know what you were offering," Kingsley whispered. "I was only a boy. The others I took—they're still in me. I hear them. I live with their suffering. It is . . . unbearable."

"You were the weakest of us! A disgrace to the vampires. You were nothing!" hissed Lucifer.

"And now I am worse than nothing," Kingsley replied.

"A pity you think so. You never did understand the scale of my ambitions," Lucifer sighed. "Although I will grant that moving the gate from Lutetia was a wise move. Leaving only the intersection as a trap."

"Nice, right? That was my idea." Kingsley smirked.

"I thought so." Lucifer nodded, as if satisfied. "Michael needed a liar of his own to come up with the right deception. A devil to think like the devil."

Kingsley chuckled. "You always did have a way with words."

Lucifer acknowledged the compliment with a bow. "As you are well aware, I have been waiting quite a long time for this. And here is a gate at last. Shall we open it?"

Schuyler realized just what was happening. As Allegra had said, the gate was imbued with celestial power. The power of the angels. It kept Lucifer and his malice away from the earth. With it, the Morningstar was imprisoned underground. But once it was opened . . .

Kingsley laughed. "You know each gate demands an innocent life. And I am far from innocent."

"Ah. Of course. And we have brought one," Lucifer said, and Schuyler saw Kingsley look up and notice her chained to the gate. His face dropped, and all the fight went out of him.

Then Schuyler understood why she was here.

She was a sacrifice.

SIXTY-TWO

Mimi

Mimi stood stock-still in the middle of the aisle, while all around her was panic and chaos. She could hear someone screaming from somewhere far away. What happened? Where was Kingsley?

Then Jack was at her side, a hand on her elbow. "Croatan! Into the glom! Now! Follow me!"

Thank God she wasn't wearing her stupid bonding dress in the glom. It made it so much easier to run. Her twin brother was streaking through the darkness like a missile, and Mimi ran to follow him. "Where are they?" she asked.

"They've taken Schuyler down to the borderlands, to the gate," he said as they ran farther and faster down to the deep, down to the dark, down to the place where memory and time are no longer, and there is only the path of fire.

Schuyler had been at her bonding! What had she been doing there! This whole thing was probably her fault! Wait—

"You know about the gates?" she asked. "About the Order?"

"Yes," Jack said. "Charles told me. He suspected that after Leviathan was freed, the Silver Bloods would go after the one in Lutetia."

"And he led them to the intersection instead," Mimi said, putting everything Kingsley had told her together with what Jack was telling her now.

"Right."

"But that didn't work too well, did it?" asked Mimi. No one had gotten what they wanted in Paris.

"Not for them and not for us," replied Jack, looking grim. The Silver Bloods had been unable to open the gate, and Charles had been unable to trap the Silver Bloods, and now he was most likely trapped in the intersection himself.

They reached the gate. It was just as Kingsley described: twelve feet tall, welded deep into the crust of the earth. Mimi knew this was just its physical manifestation in the glom, something only they could see. The true barrier was Michael's spirit and protection that kept the Silver Bloods from crossing. But where was Kingsley? Mimi couldn't see him—there was only Lucifer standing behind the iron bars. That stupid Van Alen girl was chained next to him.

When he saw them arrive, their former commandant smiled. "Azrael, Abbadon. How good of you to join us."

Mimi had to fight the urge to kneel.

This was the Morningstar before her. Their one true prince. How magnificent he looked, how lovely. Mimi remembered how she had followed his every command, how together the three of them had conquered Heaven and Earth for the Almighty.

How glorious their triumphs had been! How beautiful they all were, resplendent and soaring to the sun. How could anyone fault them for basking in their own beauty and glory? How could anyone fault them for thinking the glory was their own?

But no—it was his fault they were stuck here; his fault they were cursed to live out their lives on Earth. Paradise was just a dim memory, almost a myth—even to them—shut out from warmth and love of the Almighty forever. If only . . .

They had tried. . . . They had switched sides at the last moment, choosing that clodhorse Michael over their general. But it had been too late. . . . It had been too late, even then, back in the early dawn of the world, when she was still young. . . .

"Release her!" Jack cried. "Now, serpent."

Mimi looked at her brother, at her twin. She had never seen him so angry, so hell-bent on destruction. They had fought side by side in Lucifer's army once, and had fought against him ever since.

Jack leaped over the gate, his sword aflame. To vanquish his foe and rescue his love.

Without hesitation, Mimi followed him into battle.

SIXTY-THREE

Schuyler

When Schuyler saw the Force twins, she didn't recognize them at first. They were shining as brightly as Lucifer, and they looked like him too. For a moment it was as if three celestial angels stood before her, gorgeous, unknowable, and remote as gods. Schuyler wasn't sure if they were about to fight Lucifer or bow to him. Mimi certainly looked rapt. Then Jack had crashed over the gate, to the other side, and she knew it would be a fight to the death.

In the blink of an eye, Lucifer took the form of a silver dragon, breathing crimson fire. And Jack had transformed as well, taking the form of Abbadon, raising his crude hammer.

The silver dragon and the dark lumbering beast flew toward each other, locked in a furious battle of claw against claw, fire against fire, and they rolled and battered and spit venom and hate. The dragon was thrown against the gate, but in a moment had the beast between its claws. But the beast fought its way out of the dragon's hold, and struck a blow with its weapon against the dragon's hide.

Then they were human again: white prince against dark knight, their swords showering the dark with sparks, and Jack matched Lucifer blow for blow, until with a sudden frenzied rush, he cornered Lucifer against the gate.

"Let her go!" Jack ordered, his voice a murderous growl.

"Why? Playmate of yours? Looks a lot like her mother, doesn't she? You always did have that silly infatuation with Allegra." Lucifer smiled. "Abbadon, will you ever learn? The Daughters of the White are not for the likes of you."

"Do it!"

"No." As he spoke, Lucifer disappeared into a fine silver mist.

Before Jack could move, Leviathan reappeared, the hooded, silent demon with his glowing black spear. The same spear that had killed Lawrence in Corcovado. The same spear that he sank, swiftly and silently, into Jack's back.

Schuyler screamed as she watched Jack fall, choking, to the ground. Then Lucifer stood before her once again, and this time his fangs glittered in the dark, like knives. He was coming for her. He would take her into his own conscious-ness, to live a million lifetimes trapped in the darkness that was his corroded soul.

Then suddenly, something came between them—something that screamed like a banshee—that came with a mighty rustling of wings—and the devil released his hold.

Schuyler was free.

SIXTY-FOUR

Mimi

*I*n the darkness of the glom, Mimi unleashed the full powers of her Transformation. She could feel her wings sprout, could feel her horns grow, curling above her forehead. This was her true form as the dark and terrible Azrael, the Angel of Death. These were the wings of the Apocalypse, the harbinger of Hades, of sorrow and ruin. All this she encompassed in her soul and her being.

With all of her strength, she threw herself against the Morningstar, pinning him against the black rock, but her claws found no leverage, and soon she was simply holding a pile of dust. Lucifer would not be taken so easily. But Schuyler was free. *I owed you one, Schuyler Van Alen.* Now we are even, Mimi thought.

"Not bad, Force."

She turned.

Behind the gate, Kingsley and Leviathan were caught

in a stalemate. The demon had his spear at Kingsley's neck, and Kingsley had his sword poised at the demon's heart. Neither would give an inch, Mimi saw. But maybe if . . .

"Stay right where you are, Force," Kingsley said slowly. His handsome face turned to her behind the iron bars. "Don't come any closer."

"Why? What are you going to do?" Mimi cried, although she already knew. She could see the white aura that began to surround him. He was calling up a *subvertio*, fashioning a white hole of death.

"I am going to destroy the path," Kingsley said. "It's the only way."

"Don't." Mimi shook her head, her eyes glistening.

Kingsley looked at her with the utmost gentleness. "Do not cry for me, Azrael. Do not waste your tears. You made your decision. And this is mine. Sacrifice seems to be my destiny. A funny thing for a selfish man, isn't it? They always called me weak back then . . . but maybe weakness is a strength of a kind."

Mimi pressed her face against the bars, as close as she could get to him.

She couldn't bear for him to go without knowing what she had been about to do—she had been planning to leave Jack to be with him. She had meant to forsake her bond and throw her destiny to the wind. *I can't*, she was going to say. *I can't do this. I'm coming with you.*

"Kingsley, I . . ."

Kingsley smiled his Cheshire smile. And without another word, he called up the white darkness—the *subvertio*—a spell that unlocked what could not be unlocked, that destroyed what could not be destroyed.

There was a deep rumbling, a shaking, like the strongest earthquake, and the iron gate crumbled, and the path began to melt. The demon shrieked, but Kingsley just looked at Mimi the entire time.

Azrael . . .

In a flash, they disappeared. The path, the gate, the demon, and the Silver Blood.

Kingsley was gone. Trapped in Hell for eternity.

Mimi collapsed to the ground, as if her heart had imploded in her chest.

SIXTY-FIVE

Schuyler

She had done it. She had brought herself and Jack back from the glom. They were back in the church, lying a few feet away from each other. She coughed, spitting out toxic black dust. She was covered in soot, like a chimney sweep. She wondered if this was a consequence of what had happened in the glom or if it was part of the Silver Blood mist that had blanketed the church during the attack.

"Jack . . . Jack . . ." she whispered, crawling to his side. He was bleeding from the hole in his back. . . . The demon's spear was corrupted. It carried the black fire within it. Jack was dying. *This* was the nightmare that had plagued her for months . . . the same despair that washed over her now. She was losing him.

She turned him over so she could cradle him in her arms. Her tears fell on his cheeks. He could not hear her.

"He needs the *Caeremonia*. Red Blood," said a voice from

the other side of the church. "It is poison to the Croatan and will deflect the fire. We need to find a human." Mimi Force was still wearing her bonding dress, but like Schuyler, she was covered in black soot, her face was bruised, and her eyes were red. She walked slowly toward Schuyler. "I know it will work. Kingsley told me," Mimi said, leaving the church to find a human who could possibly save her brother.

But there was no time. There was no time even to use the Call. Then Schuyler realized . . .

"I'm human," she said. "I'm a half-blood." Half of her was vampire, but the other half was mortal and weak but filled with vibrant life—the life that vampires needed so badly for their own. It was this half, this side of her that would save her love.

"Jack, listen to me," she whispered, leaning down. "Listen, you need to drink. . . . You need to drink from me."

Jack opened his eyes slowly and stared into hers. "Are you sure?" he whispered.

"Yes, you must. It's the only way." Schuyler knew that Mimi did not lie. And it made sense, somehow, that something so weak could also bring so much life—because that was exactly what blood did. It brought life.

Jack gasped. "But I could hurt you. . . . The risk is too great. The Corruption . . . I might be tempted to . . ."

Taking the blood of a fellow vampire was against the Code. It was what the Silver Bloods did to their victims. If Jack lost control, both of them were doomed.

"I trust you," Schuyler said, leaning down to him, while he pushed himself up and put an arm around her neck.

"I don't want to hurt you," he whispered, his fangs sharp and white, the edges as thin and dangerous as a razor.

"Please, Jack," Schuyler said. She closed her eyes. "Do it now!"

In answer, Jack sunk his fangs into the base of her neck, and Schuyler bit her lip at the sudden intrusion. She had not expected it to hurt so much—was this what the humans experienced? This dizzying sense of otherness, of sweet relief and exquisite pain, as a vampire sucked the life force out of them? She had never felt closer to Jack in her life. It was as if he were touching every part of her—as if their very souls were merging in the blood exchange—as if he were opening every secret she'd ever had—as if he knew every last bit of her . . . tasting and reveling in it. . . .

She swooned. . . .

Dark and lovely and precious . . . so sweet . . . so sweet . . . so sweet . . .

SIXTY-SIX

Bliss

he Visitor had returned. He sounded manic, hysterical, barking orders that she did not understand. Bliss was groggy. The demon had knocked her out when she'd tried to help Schuyler, and now her head was throbbing.

WAKE UP, CHILD! GO! THIS IS YOUR CHANCE!

What . . . what did he want? What was happening? She looked around. In the middle of the aisle, Schuyler was holding Jack in her arms, like a Pieta.

She stumbled forward, still holding her bouquet. What was Schuyler doing with Jack Force? Jack was supposed to be bonded. But no, Schuyler had never followed any of the rules. The Code of the Vampires had never applied to her. What had the Visitor called her? Selfish. Unremarkable. A false friend.

Bliss felt so lost and alone. Maybe the Visitor was right.

Maybe he was the only person she could really trust. Her mother had not even bothered to wait for her, to see her, to speak to the daughter who needed her so badly. As for Dylan, well, maybe he was false too—had he really disappeared? Was he really being held? He had been able to break through before—what was stopping him now?

There was nothing to stop *her*.

Maybe the Visitor was right. She couldn't think anymore; she couldn't see straight. All she knew was that she was so tired of listening to the voice in her head. She was so very tired of fighting.

Do it!

DO IT!

KILL HER!

So very, very tired of resisting and being good . . . And maybe if she did what he wanted, he would stop torturing her. Maybe if she did what he wanted, she would finally have peace. . . .

Bliss walked over to where Schuyler was sitting and removed the shard of glass from her bouquet.

SIXTY-SEVEN

Schuyler

"**Y**ou're going to be all right," Schuyler murmured. Jack lay asleep in her arms. She knew he would live. She could *feel* it. Her blood would save him. It was the only thing that would save him. It would bring life back to his body and fight the black fire from Leviathan's blade.

She looked around the empty church. Mimi had not yet returned. Her former nemesis had looked broken and lost. Something had happened back there, down in the glom.

Schuyler hugged Jack tighter, but then heard footsteps. Someone was headed her way. Someone was standing— looming—in front of her.

"Bliss, what are you doing?" Schuyler cried. Her friend looked like a witch, with her wild red hair and her torn black dress, holding something shiny and ominous in her hand.

"I'm so sorry, Schuyler. I'm so sorry," Bliss sobbed.

Schuyler moved Jack so that he would be safe. She stood up and covered him protectively. "Bliss, put down the knife."

"I can't . . . I have to," Bliss whimpered. "I'm sorry but I have to."

"What do you mean? What's going on? What's happened to you?"

"My father . . . he's in my head. He tells me things. He says I have to do this or I'll never see Dylan again."

"Your father?" Schuyler asked. But she already knew the answer to her question. What had Cordelia once told her? *We fear one of our oldest families is harboring the Dark Prince himself. We don't know how and we don't know who, but we suspect the betrayal is at the highest level of the Conclave.* Bliss Llewellyn was the Silver Blood all along. Bliss carried Lucifer in her. Then Schuyler remembered something Lawrence had told her as well: *Your sister will be our death.* Bliss was her hidden sister. Bliss was born to kill her.

"No, Bliss, you don't have to . . . I can help you. We can do something about it. You don't have to do what he tells you."

Bliss did not respond. Instead she lunged at Schuyler, who ducked just in time. But Bliss caught the hem of Schuyler's skirt and dragged her down. Schuyler could feel the blade start to inch its way toward her chest. This was it . . . Jack had risked his life for her and she for him . . . but it was all for nothing. How could she have not known?

"Bliss! Please!" Schuyler sobbed. "Don't!"

Bliss held the blade above Schuyler's heart, an inch from her chest, but at the last moment, she hesitated.

"I'm so sorry. I'm so sorry!" Bliss cried as she released her friend, the tears streaming down her face.

"Bliss—stop—what are you doing?" Schuyler screamed. "No!"

With a mighty thrust, Bliss plunged the archangel's blade deep into her own heart, breaking the glass into a million pieces, and ending her life.

SIXTY-EIGHT

Mimi

he Coven was up in arms. Forsyth Llewellyn had disappeared. Kidnapped by the Croatan? Or was he Croatan himself? Who knew who they could trust anymore? Mimi wondered why he had been so keen on their bonding. Had it truly been for the sake of the Coven, or was it something else? Had he known what was hidden under the church? Meanwhile, the Conclave was in shambles. This was the end of everything—Silver Bloods in the church! At a bonding! It was madness, inexcusable. There would have to be meetings to discuss what must be done. More and more meetings, and proper investigations, and no decisions made. Mimi understood that the Coven needed her and Jack now more than ever. More even than yesterday.

The church had survived the attack intact, except for a fine black dust that covered every surface. As Mimi walked through its doors the next morning at dawn, she was glad, in a way, that she and Jack would be alone for the ceremony this time. Because their bonding was not just about the two of them, but the survival of their people. It was their duty.

She was wearing a simple T-shirt and jeans. There would be no society photographers this time, no honored guests. It would be just as it had been in the early days of Rome. There would be no witnesses to their bonding, but they needed none. All they needed was to say the words to each other.

This was their fate and this was their way.

She walked to the front of the altar and lit a candle. Jack wouldn't be long. They had shared a cab to the church, but he had asked her to wait for him inside while he took a call.

But as the minutes ticked by and Jack did not walk through the church door, Mimi understood. He would *never* walk through the door. He had lied to her yet again, because he was not worthy of her. He would never be worthy.

Not like . . . but she could not say his name aloud. *Kingsley*. All that could have been flashed in Mimi's mind: the two of them hunting Silver Bloods together . . . a life of danger and adventure . . . a chance for her to be herself again. . . .

Her phone vibrated. It was a text from her brother. It said two words:

I'M SORRY.

Mimi blew out the flame. There was no need for it now.

So. She was right. Jack had forsaken her to be with the half-blood. He would not honor their celestial bond. He would not do his duty. She had sacrificed her love, but he would not sacrifice his. He had cast his lot to the winds—tempting fate, death, rebelling against the laws of Heaven and the laws of their blood bond.

She would never forgive him for that. She could have left for Paris when Kingsley had asked. She could have chosen happiness as well. But she had not. She had made her decision too late.

And now she was alone.

The Code of the Vampires decreed that anyone who violated the Sacred Law was condemned to death, the blood burning. Charles had refused to subject Allegra to the sentence. But Mimi was a different matter.

Mimi walked out of the church, knowing that if she ever saw Jack again, she would have to kill him.

SIXTY-NINE

Bliss

hen Bliss woke up the day after Mimi's bonding, she was lying in a comfortable bed under a patchwork quilt. Across from her sat an ordinary woman with ruddy cheeks and a quizzical expression, wearing a worn cashmere sweater and a wool argyle skirt.

"Miss Murray?" Bliss asked. What was her history teacher doing sitting across from her?

"You've had a hard time of it, love. Take it easy; don't exert yourself."

The room was small and cozy, and Bliss realized this was the entire apartment. She had never been in a space quite so small. It was the size of a closet, practically. There was room for a bed and a stove and nothing more. If Bliss wanted to exert herself, she could cook dinner while lying in bed at the same time. But even though it was small, it was warm and comfortable.

"What am I . . . ? What happened? Where's . . . ?"

"Shhh," Miss Murray said, putting a finger to her lips. "You should rest. She'll be here soon. She wants to talk to you."

"Who . . . ?"

A woman appeared out of the air. She was fair-haired and green-eyed, clad in white raiment that glowed softly with a pure white light. As soon as Bliss saw her, she knew. "Allegra," she breathed. "It is you, isn't it? Where am I? Am I dead?"

Allegra Van Alen smiled serenely. She looked a lot older than Bliss remembered from the hospital. The woman in the bed had seemed frozen in time, but this Allegra, standing in front of her, had lines on her face, and her hands were wrinkled. There was gray in her blond hair. But she was still very beautiful. Seeing her made Bliss want to weep.

"Come," Allegra said, holding out her arms. "Come here, my daughter."

"So it's true," Bliss whispered. "I am yours."

"I am sorry I have not been here for you, but your existence was hidden from me," she said, and the sadness in her voice was unmistakable.

"Then how? Why?"

"You came to visit me not too long ago."

"Yes." Bliss nodded. She remembered that surreptitious visit to the hospital, while Allegra remained immobile in her bed.

"When you came to see me, I felt a presence I had not felt in a very long time. I was very afraid and I was very angry. I screamed. I think the whole hospital heard me. But now I understand that Charles and Lawrence did what they felt they had to. They did it for love, and sometimes love makes us do the irrational . . . even the inexcusable. But I don't know if I will ever forgive them for what they tried to do to you," Allegra said quietly.

Bliss curled her fists up in the quilt. She had a mother, but she had also been robbed of one. "So Lucifer did not lie to me," she said stonily. She felt conflicted and agonized.

"No, he did not. You are ours."

"But how—how—you were bound to Michael."

Allegra nodded. "Yes. It is a long and painful story. But know that we made you together. In love."

"Where are you? Are you here? Are you actually here?"

"I am in you. I did not find the link until now. As I told your sister, I will always be with you."

"Okay." Bliss blinked back her tears.

"Do you notice anything different about yourself?" Allegra asked.

"Like what?" She had no idea what Allegra was talking about—until she stopped to think about it. There was silence. She was alone in her body. The voices were gone. The heaviness—those many souls that had lived in her— they were gone. Most important, the Visitor was gone.

"Michael's sword killed your blood link to Lucifer. Your

father was using you as a way to reach through the boundary that was keeping him in the underworld."

"So I'm not dead. But my father is dead in me." Bliss was overwhelmed with relief. She had her life back. She'd done it—she had successfully killed herself, just as she and Dylan had known would be her task. She'd done it. . . .

And then, as if she had conjured him from the air, Dylan appeared next to Allegra. "I'm proud of you, Bliss," he said. "Michael's sword released the souls that were trapped in your blood. You freed them. You freed me."

"But now I'm never going to see you again, am I?" she asked.

Dylan smiled. "It's unlikely. But I never say never."

"I wish you wouldn't go. I'll miss you so much," Bliss said.

"I'll miss you too."

Dylan put his hand up, and so did Bliss. But this time, instead of touching air, she felt his warm hand grasping her cold one. She looked at Allegra. Somehow, she knew her mother was making this happen. Dylan leaned down, and she could feel his lips, soft and inviting, gently kissing hers.

Then Dylan was gone. But Bliss did not feel anguished. She felt at peace. Dylan was not broken and incomplete anymore. He was whole.

"You are healed." Allegra nodded. "You are no longer a Silver Blood." She paused. "But you are no longer a vampire either."

Bliss started. No longer a vampire—but what did that mean? Did it mean she was just human?

Now, listen closely. Bliss heard Allegra's voice in her head—in the glom—as if she were speaking directly into Bliss's mind. *A long time ago when the world was young and the paths between Heaven and Hell were still open, Lucifer brought the beasts out of the ground, the hounds of Hell. But their alliance with the Silver Bloods was short-lived. The wolves are demon fighters. They stood with the Blue Bloods during the crisis. But over the centuries we have become estranged. You must find them. The Blue Bloods will need them in the final battle with the Silver Bloods. Find the wolves. Tame them. Bring them back into the fold.*

But where do I start?

I have not left you alone. You will have someone to help you with your task. Someone who loves you and will take care of you since I cannot.

Bliss understood. Miss Murray was standing next to Allegra, and she did not look like an apple-cheeked history teacher. Instead, her eyes were gray and serious . . . and Bliss gasped.

Jordan?

You knew me by that name once. Her teacher nodded. *But my true name is . . .*

Sophia.

Quite right. Good girl. Miss Murray beamed.

Is that what I should call you?

I think Miss Murray will do for now. Although, if you like, you can call me Aunt Jane.

Michael's sword. You were the one who slipped it into my bouquet. I'm right, aren't I? Bliss asked.

Her teacher did not deny it. *I knew you would use it the right way. I had faith in you.*

But if I'm not a vampire anymore . . . how can I do anything? The thought of being human scared her. To live without the incredible abilities given by the undying blood . . . to be so frail and weak . . . and absolutely powerless.

Do your best. That is all I ask of you, her mother told her.

"Where are you going?" Bliss asked, using her voice now.

"Somewhere no one can follow. But do not despair. We will meet again, Bliss Llewellyn."

"Allegra, before you leave . . . can you tell me . . . what is my name? I mean to say, Mimi is Azrael and Jack is Abbadon. But I don't know my real name. I never have. Do I even have one?" Bliss asked.

"Names are forged in Heaven. Your father named you Azazel, the Darkling. But I shall name you Lupus Theliel, Angel of Love, and my Wolfsbane."

SEVENTY

Schuyler

uring the ride to JFK, Schuyler kept to herself. She was still exhausted from yesterday's events, but there was no time to rest. The documents Oliver had found, which he had been so excited about, were a small package of notebooks that he had discovered in files kept by Christopher Anderson, Lawrence's Conduit.

Fifty-five notebooks detailing everything her grandfather had found concerning the Van Alen Legacy, and every possible lead. The keepers of the third gate, the Gate of Promise, were most likely still in the city of Florence, which was where they were headed now.

Last night, when she finally came home, Oliver was waiting for her in her apartment. When she walked in, it took him a while to accept the fact that she was truly alive and standing in front of him. He had been convinced he had lost her forever. They hugged each other close, but Schuyler was still too distraught and confused about everything that had happened with Jack, to give Oliver much of her attention.

She listened as he filled her in on what had happened to everyone else during the attack and the aftermath; most of the Blue Bloods had gone to hide in the Force Tower, as they had been instructed by the Conclave. They had all come out safe.

But for how long?

The cab pulled up to the terminal, and Oliver unloaded their bags. He had been quiet too, during the trip. And he looked at Schuyler so intensely now, as if he were trying to memorize her face.

"What?" Schuyler asked. "Do I have something in my teeth or something? Why are you looking at me like that?"

"I'm not going to Florence," Oliver said as the cab pulled away.

"What do you mean you're not going to Florence . . ." Schuyler said, just as Jack Force walked up to the terminal.

Yesterday, Mimi had finally come back to the church, and had taken her brother away. Jack had been too weak to speak when Schuyler saw the two of them off in a cab. From the possessive way Mimi had held on to Jack, Schuyler knew they wouldn't get a chance to say the things they wanted to say to each other anyway.

There were no traces of the lost, broken girl that Mimi had been when she'd returned. And Schuyler understood that the struggle for Jack's heart was far from over. Maybe she and Jack just weren't meant to be, and the two of them would just have to accept it. It was enough to know they had risked everything for each other. Maybe the memory of their love was all that they were allowed. She didn't know. She only knew that she had so much to do. And if she had to leave Jack as part of it, then there was nothing she could do about it anymore. She had to fulfill her legacy.

But when she saw him, and they looked at each other, she knew she would never be able to leave his side. He had recovered well; he looked tired, but then so did she. They had been through a lot in the last twenty-four hours.

You're here, she sent. *My love.*

I wouldn't be anywhere else.

"I came as soon as I got your message," Jack said to Oliver.

Oliver handed him his own backpack. "Your flight is leaving soon. I suggest you guys get in there—security's a pain these days. Especially for international."

"You called him? Oliver, what's going on?" Schuyler asked.

"I asked Jack to meet us here. I told him you were going to Florence. I asked him to go with you."

"Oliver!"

"Sky . . . stop," Oliver said. "And don't interrupt me, because I have to say this. I know you would never leave me. I know that. I know you would never be able to make a decision, so I decided for you. You have to go with him."

Schuyler found her eyes filling with tears. "Ollie . . ."

"You cannot choose between us. So I chose for you. Jack can protect you in ways I cannot. Yesterday, when Leviathan took you, I'd never felt so helpless in my life . . . and I knew . . . I knew I couldn't be there for you, not in the way that he can." Oliver gulped. "I would rather have you safe, whole, and alive . . . than with me."

"Oliver . . ."

"Now go. Before I change my mind. But you know I'm right. I'm always right, Schuyler." He never called her Schuyler, only when he was serious. Or angry. Or maybe a little of both. This couldn't be easy for him. It wasn't easy for her to listen to.

"But what about you?" she asked. "I marked you. . . ." The Sacred Kiss would mean he would pine for her forever. She couldn't let him live the rest of his life that way.

"I'll be all right. You'll see. I don't believe in fatalism. And you'll call me, won't you? Once in a while? I can still help you . . . from over here. I think I can, anyway. But I know this is what was meant to happen. I can feel it . . . the rightness of it . . . and, like I said, I'm never wrong." Oliver shoved the tickets into Jack's hands.

Schuyler pulled Oliver close and hugged him tightly. "Thank you," she whispered. *Thank you for loving me enough to let me go.*

"You're welcome," Oliver said. He smiled, and she knew she had heard what she'd left unsaid. The connection between them—vampire and Conduit—sparking at last.

"Good-bye, Ollie," Schuyler whispered.

"Take care of her," Oliver said, shaking Jack's hand. "For me."

Jack nodded and shook Oliver's hand vigorously. "Always."

Oliver saluted them both, then he walked quickly away, jumping into the nearest cab he could find. Schuyler watched him go, finding that her heart ached in the deepest way . . . but it did not break. They would be friends. They would always remain friends. She loved him still.

Next to her, Jack put out his hand.

Schuyler grasped it tightly. She would never let go. Not in this lifetime. She knew what this meant. They were going to risk it. They were going to go against the bond, the Code, everything that stood in their way, so that they could be together. They would risk everything for their love. Just like her mother. Just like Allegra.

No one would choose your life, she had told her mother.

She had been wrong.

Together, hand in hand, the two of them walked into the terminal.

Saint-Tropez

*I*sabelle of Orleans, at home, looked just as intimidating as she had at the party. The countess received them at her villa in Saint-Tropez, on the sun-splashed terrace that looked over the bright blue Mediterranean. It was their first stop on the way to Florence, and it had been Jack's idea to try to achieve what Schuyler had failed to secure months before.

"So, you are refugees from Michael's tribe," Isabelle said, her voice low and gravelly. "What makes you think I shall give you what you ask? Why should the European Coven even care about two wayward children?"

"Your Grace, we understand your skepticism . . . but we are desperate. Without the protection of the vampires, we will not be able to carry out Lawrence Van Alen's great work," Jack said.

The countess raised her eyebrows. "So you are here

in Europe to try to fulfill his legacy?"

"Yes, Your Grace." Schuyler nodded.

"Then why did you not mention it sooner?" the countess demanded, causing her two lap dogs to yelp.

Jack and Schuyler exchanged a glance. "Our apologies," Jack said.

"I shall grant you access to the European Coven, and give you my blessing. While you are within our borders, the New York Coven will be unable to touch you."

"Thank you, Countess. You don't know how much this means to us," Schuyler said, relief and gratitude evident in her voice.

The countess ruminated. "This war has taken the life of my most trusted friend."

Schuyler nodded. She had heard the body of the real Baron de Coubertin had been found floating in the Seine, a few weeks after the attack. "We are so sorry to hear that," she said. She knew what it meant to lose a Conduit.

The countess shrugged sadly. "You know, I was always a friend to Lawrence and Cordelia. It was Charles I could never stand," the countess sighed. "I know he had to punish my brother, but I thought the punishment was unnecessarily draconian. Surely there must have been a way to live in peace together without resorting to such stringent measures. Well. There's not much we can do about that now, is there?"

"Your brother, Your Grace?" Jack asked.

"Why, Valerius, have you forgotten me so soon?" The countess smiled, looking suddenly coy and flirtatious. "Oh, how much we three sisters fought over you when you came of age! Handsome Valerius! But of course Agrippina won you, as always. Well, perhaps not anymore." She winked and looked at Schuyler. "You're a lucky girl, my dear."

"I'm sorry?" Jack asked.

"Back in Rome, you knew me as Drusilla," the countess told them as she got up from her chair. "Come, children. I believe lunch is being served. And my chef makes an excellent tomato salad. You will join me, won't you?"

The
Van Alen
Family Tree

Cordelia Van Alen ——— (m) ———
Seraphiel
The Angel of Song
(b)

z Catherine Carver

Steven Chase ——— (m) ———**Allegra Van Alen**—————
(Red Blood) *Gabrielle, the Uncorrupted*

z Rose Standish

Schuyler Van Alen
Dimidium Cognatus
(Half-blood)

—— **Lawrence Van Alen**
Metraton
Heavenly Scribe

z John Carver

—————————— **Charles (Van Alen) Force** ——(m)—— **Trinity Burden Force**
Michael, Pure of Heart

z Myles Standish

Benjamin (Jack) Force—— (b) ——**Madeleine (Mimi) Force**
Abbadon   *Azrael*
The Angel of Destruction   *The Angel of Death*

z Valerius   z Agrippina
z Louis D'Orleans   z Elisabeth Lorraine-Lillebonne
z William White   z Susannah Fuller

Acknowledgments

The Blue Bloods books are the most fun and rewarding books to write, and I wouldn't be able to write them without the help, love, support, patience, and devotion of many people. First off, thank you to my husband, Mike Johnston, for reading all the same books I did as a teen. My name is on the front cover, but these books are ours together, in every possible way. Thank you to Mattie for being the light of our lives. None of this would mean anything without the two of you, but you guys already know that.

Thank you to my lovely editor, Jennifer Besser, for being such a champion of the books and for gasping on the phone about the Bliss chapters. Yay! And thank you to everyone at Hyperion: Go, team! Thank you to Jennifer Corcoran for the fabulous publicity, Nellie Kurtzman and Ann Dye for the awesome marketing plans, Elizabeth Clark for the gorgeous covers, and Jonathan Yaged for the faith, Simon Tasker and Dave Epstein from the sales force (a true force to behold!). Thank you to my agent, Richard Abate, for keeping me focused and for the above-and-beyond hand-holding. Thank you to Elizabeth Yates, Melissa Myers, and Richie Kern at Endeavor, and Kate Lee and Larissa Silva at ICM.

Thank you to my mom, to whom this book is dedicated, especially for saying, "The books are so exciting. I forget that you had written them!" Now THAT's a compliment from your mom! Thank you also to the rest of my wonderful, fabulous, and infinitely supportive family: Pop, Aina, Steve, Nicholas, Joseph, Chit, Christina (most of whom run the promotion/Web/fan mail side of the business with a lot of good humor and ideas). Also thanks to Mom J, Dad J, and all the Johnstons. A big thank-you to Tita Odette, Isabelle and Christina Gaisano. (There, you can show it to all your friends now, Tina!)

Thank you to my BFF, Jennie Kim, who always likes to be mentioned in these things. (Jennie, you can show this off too. Heh-heh.) And thanks to my NY and LA main girls and main gays Katie Davis,

Tina Hay, Tom Dolby and Drew Frist, Gabe Sandoval, Tristan Ashby and Jeff Chu, Tyler Rollins and Jason Lundy, Andy Goffe and Jeff Levin, Peter Edmonston and Mark Hidgen, Kate and Harold Hope, and the ever-cool Kim DeMarco.

I would also like to thank the late Miss Jean Murphy, who taught history and art history at the Convent of the Sacred Heart, and who brought the world of ancient Rome to life in a dusty classroom. Miss Murphy always said it was like history's greatest soap opera. I know she's up there with the greats.

Most of all I would like to thank the Blue Blood faithful, just the most amazing, enthusiastic, intelligent, and gorgeous bunch of kids I have ever met. (I mean it: I am always so blown away by how smart AND good-looking you all are!) Thank you for bringing my story of the reincarnated vampires into your lives. Thanks for following the journey, and hope to see you at the next stop!